Ghos

Treblinka:

A Novel

By: Hubert L. Mullins

This is a work of fiction. Names, events, and some places are purely the work of the author's imagination and real places listed here within are done so with heavy doses of elaboration to suit the story. Any resemblance to anyone living or dead, is purely coincidental.

For my son, who lets his dad peck away at a keyboard all day . . .

And for my wife, who understands her husband can't hear a thing when he does it, and loves him just the same . . .

Author's Note

Many of the events referenced in this story are true. Treblinka was an awful place where a great many awful things happened. My story, while aiming to be frightful, could never come close to the level of real-life atrocities that occurred there between 1941 and 1944. It is estimated that 925,000 people perished within its forested border, with only 67 survivors to escape. And as of 2016, none are left alive.

But this is a novel, a story of fiction, and as such, liberties are taken. I mean zero disrespect to any of the victims, or by extension, any surviving relatives. It is not my intention to take away anything from what happened in those sixteen months of terror, but to use the period and the location as a backdrop to serve a story that is set in another time. If anything, I would hope that you take away from this novel that, despite being fantastical, the most horrific parts of it *did* happen, and I sincerely hope you never forget that.

Hubert L. Mullins

7/19/2019

Treblinka

January 3rd, 1943

When the Entity hovered above the ground, some two-hundred feet in the air, the northern part of the night sky was completely obliterated by a thick, greasy cloud of black. They'd started burning the bodies on giant, open pyres, and the billowing smoke looked like a demon rising from the earth. The Entity hadn't been awake for long, but the old ways returned to him rather quickly. In all of the world's history, death was the one thing most common—the one thing that united something as vile and wicked as he, with those common men and women who drew breath.

And the Entity thought this was quite good.

In half a heartbeat he was standing on the ground, but no one could see him unless he so chose it. The hour was late, no more than a few past midnight. Most of the killing took place in the day, and that was the time he normally lingered about, but as the bodies charred and turned black, like long slivers of rot, he smiled. Death fed him.

His hands, metaphorically speaking, didn't need to get dirty. Not once did he pull a trigger, stab a heart, push someone from a cliff. But he was always there in the aftermath, savoring the aroma as the soul parted from the flesh, tasting it, feeling it warm his insides. He didn't know what he was, but he did know that as long as there was death, he'd survive.

It had been that way for years—he was there a decade ago when the Chinese floods killed millions, sweeping clean the shanty villages and valleys with mud. He was there during the Spanish Flu, in India and Japan where people coughed bloody phlegm in the streets. He was even there for the Black Plague, and what a wonderful time that had been! People died in taverns and churches and lodge houses as regularly as the wind blew. He could still taste that meal, a third of Europe falling to ash, enough that it engorged his spirit and left him satiated for years.

Now, it seemed that war was what kept him fed.

The current squabble felt across the globe was ending more lives than any of the conflicts to come before, but they simply weren't enough. Not many on this earth could put to death as efficiently as biology. But still, he rather admired the Germans and their ovens and gas chambers. No one had perfected killing as much as the Führer and his legion of like-minded monsters.

Like a ghost and shadow, the Entity strolled the camp, feeding on the fear and the freshly killed. The extermination chambers were empty, the diesel tank engines which supplied the suffocating exhaust cold, and a team of Trawniki guards used hoses to wash out the filth from inside. Anyone sleeping within the camp were either Germans, conscripted Soviets, or Jewish slave-laborers. No one came to Treblinka for an extended stay. This place was designed for killing in mind, and that's what happened moments after they stepped off the trains.

Most of the commanding SS were asleep at such an early hour, warm by their stove fires, but the Entity could always count on seeing Franz Stangl, White Death they called him, walking the grounds, a tiny cigarette hanging from the corner of his mouth. He'd been out a long time, as evidenced by the dusting of snow on his shoulders. The SS respected him, the Trawniki and Jews feared him. His gaze fell through everyone he encountered, as if he didn't see them, as if he were thinking of new and exciting ways to improve the already lethal Treblinka. A man after my own heart, the Entity thought, had he actually had a heart.

The Entity rarely interfered with the schemes of man. Although he could offer suggestions, he found that nature, as always, did better when it was allowed to work unprovoked. And so the Entity remained in the shadows, watching men do awful things to one another, and tasting the death that came in its wake.

Of all the camps he'd explored, Treblinka was his favorite. Perhaps it was in his weakened state, perhaps it was the nostalgia for such large-scale, efficient killing, but he was growing worried that the hunger would soon be upon him. He was omnipotent, and by such he knew the Russians were pushing from the east and, if the weather worked in their favor, would be here within a year. The Nazis would abandon the camps, most likely hide all the evidence, then turn to whatever front they thought they could win and push back. Either way, the killings would stop. The mass deportation of human cattle . . . would stop.

Nature needed to take back the reins.

Toward the end of his stroll, just before he retired to his lair, the Entity moved up the rail line, toward the Malkinia junction. Treblinka was the northernmost of the three death camps built in the last couple of years, and it was also the most expertly hidden. Legitimate Polish trains used the route all the time, never once noticing the spur line, never once realizing that just beyond the trees there was a camp. And in that camp, death found almost fifteen thousand souls per day. A train came each morning, sometimes two. Franz Stangl ordered the gassing at breakfast and by the time he had his poached egg and blood sausage brought to his quarters for lunch, the killing was done for the day. But the burning, so late into the Nazi's desire to hide their crimes, never ceased.

A train was coming along the track as the Entity moved northward. Even the humans would have known it had they walked along the metal, balancing foot over foot with arms held out like a bird, just the way the entity had seen children do ever since train tracks first threw down across the land. The vibration was evident that a long trainset of cars would soon present itself. As he met up with it, some four miles up the path past the faux train station at Treblinka, he found it was a steam engine—as they all were—and it was pulling a total of forty-nine cars. The engine looked like a giant, rolling coffin—a sleek testament to men's ingenuity. These passengers were lucky—they were in third-class passenger wagons complete with commodities not often seen in train cars bound for Treblinka—window slats and seats. Still, they were crammed inside so tightly that people were stacked like chairs. Most of the trains to enter the camp were made up of freight or cattle cars. In the warmer months it wasn't uncommon for the majority of the prisoners to already be dead upon arrival.

The conductor slowed the train, and a puff of steam hovered in the air above it. As the Entity stepped aside, he could see the men operating the engine—two of them—simply sit back, breathe tired sighs, and then begin chatting quietly. This was normal—the camp trains had to sometimes stop to let legitimate trains pass first. After all, *Operation Reinhard* was Hitler's big, elaborate secret.

As the Entity surveyed the train he tasted the fear and uncertainty grip each and every one of those aboard. There were over four thousand sweaty, but cold Poles, ranging from young children to the elderly. In his omnipotent mind he could delve into the heads of them all, pulling out memories, thoughts, wishes, and hopes. If he cared enough to be sadistic he would replace those with horrid images and premonitions of what was to come. But tonight he didn't. Tonight he was tired, and weak, and wanted to be off to his lair. Later, he would return and feed from those before him—how he loved the taste of their deaths as their souls seeped away, how their bodies, sometimes upright in the crammed gas chambers, would release a final puff of breath as the Trawniki pulled them to the pyres.

Scared voices spoke silently. Though it was dark, a starless sky even if half of it was blotted out by the oily billow of smoke, the whites of eyes and sheen of teeth could be seen. Glass was not a luxury of this train, and cold lips chattered while expelling little puffs of steam. None of them could see the Entity, but he was entranced in their fear—it was almost as delicious as their deaths would be at sunup. He found himself slowly wafting down the line, taking in their faces so that it might satiate him for a few hours until a proper meal could be had.

They were all wondering why the train had stopped. None were in good spirits, but then again, how could they be? Some of them had already died—the train probably left the Warsaw Ghettos a couple of days ago with the promise they'd be heading to work camps across the Bailystok line. Never were they given food or water and this particular train was open to the elements. The Entity tasted the scant few inside the cars who'd perished, but it wasn't as delectable as he'd hoped. They'd been dead for hours and the freshness had dissipated.

As he made it to the twelfth car past the engine he found himself face-to-face with a child. The adults crowding around turned dull eyes out to the blank, dark countryside but the child—a little girl no more than five who'd never known life outside a ghetto—was looking right at him. Sure, he'd been put to sleep many times, but he'd been around since the beginning of time, and now, in the heart of Poland during the second great war, a human was seeing him without his consent.

He didn't know if he could speak. That wasn't an ability he possessed. Whenever he influenced the mind of a human, it came to him as an internal monologue, but the humans always heard and they always obeyed. Now, he was feeling something he hadn't known in his lifetime. In his mind he willed the girl to look away, to forget what she saw, but somehow, miraculously, she refused.

This anomaly stunned the Entity for a moment, and just before he'd made the decision to retire to his lair, the little girl's arm shot through the opened portal and took hold of him. He had no arms, no legs, nor head, nor body at all. What he had was a consuming, flowing darkness that men could only feel, not see. He was as substantial as the smoke coming from the pyres burning Jews just miles down the road. And still, somehow, this child had grabbed him.

That was the moment the Entity understood the feeling that had washed over him like some kind of holy reckoning. He'd been all-powerful, omnipotent. The alpha and the omega. The beginning and the end. But now . . .now he understood.

He was *afraid.*

Berlin

January 7th, 2019

If anything had surprised him at all in his two-week jaunt across Europe it was that the nightlife operated in a much different way than his Salisbury, North Carolina back home. After dark, his town all but shut down, businesses pushing forward the curtain as if they were hiding some deep, dark secret. In truth, it was just the opposite, and, as one might suspect, his hometown was as boring by the day as it was at night.

Not like here at all.

Edmund Riley sat at a small bistro table outside a coffeehouse, undeterred by the cold weather. He was bundled tightly, having planned this trip months in advance and knew the winter could be harsh in many of the stops. But he hardly noticed the chill in the air as he watched the bustling nightlife of Germany's capital city. True, he'd only been here for one night—having arrived by train from Hamburg just that morning—but he was certain the city never slept.

Within the narrow gap of buildings he spied no fewer than three stores, a restaurant, a nightclub, and a park. On down the street was a dimly lit cemetery, the massive headstones leaning to and fro like drunken golems. There were people everywhere—hundreds of young, vibrant men and women like himself who just wanted to live life and have fun on a cold, winter night. He could get used to this kind of place but alas, he'd be leaving on another train in the morning. As luck would have it, he wouldn't be traveling alone.

A girl had just brought him a steaming cup of coffee—it smelled wonderful but he wasn't much of a coffee drinker. He wanted something with a little more kick but that would have to wait until his friends came along. For now, he was content to people-watch, sipping his bitter drink, and playing with the little device he'd pulled from his backpack beneath the table.

It was a camera, but such a word hardly described the piece of expensive technology he held across his lap. It looked more like the P.K.E. meter on the *Ghostbusters* movie, minus the moving wings on the sides. This camera had a handle and a large viewscreen but it didn't take normal photos; this one took infrared shots that made a person look less like a body and more like a Picasso painting of reds and yellows and oranges. Impractical as it was for most things, Edmund was still glad he brought it along.

He surveyed the area and pointed the viewfinder across the street and up toward the second story of a stark, white building. Although the device couldn't see heat through the walls (something Edmund wasn't sure even existed but something he was *absolutely* sure he couldn't afford), it could still pick up through the windows.

No sooner had he moved the wand up to the third floor did the viewscreen change from a dark array of blues to a bright, pulsing red and orange. It took a moment of fine-tuning but once he had the image in focus he almost fell out of his chair. Edmund worked hard to keep his hand steady and not laugh at the same time.

There on his viewscreen were two hot shapes, red pulses that moved in concert with one another. The top shape moved forward as the bottom shape moved back, but even though they weren't clearly-outlined people, it was easy to see what they were doing. Edmund could almost hear the couple's moans as the one on top gyrated back and forth, his head moving from orange to red in such a pattern that it had to be the beating of his heart. Despite the chilly wind, Edmund could feel the flustered heat rising to his face.

His thumb moved up to hit the record button, for surely his friends would want to see this later, but just before he could tap it, the couple having sex completely disappeared from the screen, only to be replaced by a much larger mass of orange and red. Edmund moved his chair back when he realized someone was standing just in front of him, looking at him with an icy stare that didn't understand, but knew it couldn't be good.

The first thing Edmund noticed after the questioning eyes was the large, white letters on the man's vest that read POLIZEI. His arms were thick, but it was hard to tell if the officer was muscular or just beefy since he had on a coat. His hat was white with a dark blue bill that made him look like a navy officer. Edmund's eyes, as they always did when he saw a cop, drifted down to the man's sidearm.

"Sorry," said Edmund, immediately shutting down the device and placing it on his lap. "It's new. I mean, I paid almost five-hundred dollars for it and I just . . . wait, can you even understand me?"

Throughout Edmund's whole spiel, the officer simply stood in an imposing manner, arms crossed over, listening to the American explain himself. At the end, Edmund wondered if he'd just broken some sort of Peeping Tom law, one that would be far more severe than those back home. Flashes of a harsh, German prison flooded his thoughts and his fingers shook as the real world—not the one his family had painted for him with money and privilege—threatened to swallow him up.

"Officer! Officer?" a voice from inside the café said. Edmund turned to see the doors pushing open, the smell of coffee and his friends—Bill and Sophie—come storming out. The policeman turned interested, yet stoic eyes toward them. Bill was clutching his cellphone.

"He is an American and is taking pictures for his school newspaper," Bill lied, speaking directly into his phone. He held it up for the officer to hear, which had now been translated into German by way of a handy app that Edmund wished he'd known about when he'd traveled through Paris and was flirting with a beautiful Japanese girl at a bar.

The lie held and the policeman, after glancing skeptically at Edmund, simply nodded and walked off, slowly meandering down the street toward the cemetery.

"Why in the world did you come to Berlin to spy?" asked Bill. Edmund was on his feet, hugging his friend across the distance of the tiny bistro table. Sophie just looked on with a smile, her hands stuffed into her jacket pockets.

"Damn, it's good to see you, buddy!" said Edmund, taking a seat again. "How long has it been?"

"Eleventh grade," Bill said, certainty in his voice. He turned to his girlfriend and said, "You remember Sophie, right?"

"Sure," said Edmund, shaking her gloved hand. It was weird and strangely grown-up for twenty-year-olds to be shaking hands, but here they were.

"How was your flight?" Edmund asked, taking his seat again.

"Not to be rude, but could we go somewhere for food?" asked Bill, to the point. "We've not even been to the BnB yet and we're starved."

It was the first time Edmund realized they were dragging their suitcases behind them—a total of two bags on wheels and two across their shoulders. Edmund stood, gave the coffeehouse a last look.

The name was Spitzenröster, something he found remarkably funny, but it only served coffee. Now that he thought about it, he hadn't had a single bite to eat since he'd been on the train, and that was at least ten hours ago. Now, sitting here with his friends on the cusp of nostalgia, a grumble awoke in the pit of his stomach.

"C'mon. I saw a place. It's on the way to the hostel." Edmund took the rolling suitcase from Sophie and said, "Please, let me. You guys must be exhausted."

She nodded. "We are. I don't travel nearly as well as I did when my parents dragged us across the country."

Edmund left a crisp euro under his mug and led his friends down the street, toward the cemetery. Even though this part of town was rather upscale, he was surprised by the amount of graffiti found alongside the buildings. The neighborhood felt safe, but he remained oddly alert, never feeling truly at ease in an unfamiliar city.

They passed through the cemetery, the sign reading Dorotheenstadt. From here the street opened up into a large park that ran parallel with a four-lane highway. Still, there were more people about than Edmund had ever seen. Salisbury was minuscule in comparison to Berlin.

"Have you seen a lot of Europe?" asked Sophie, snatching Bill's hand as they trundled through the crosswalk.

Edmund nodded. "I landed in Paris. From there I went to Antwerp, then on to Amsterdam. Last night I was in Hamburg and now here we are."

"I'm sorry we got such a late start," said Bill, adjusting his carryon.

"That's my fault," Sophie chimed in, voice rising with irritation. "My dad . . . he just wouldn't hear of me traveling at Christmas. My sis came in, then my grandma and then . . ."

"Guys, it's fine," said Edmund, stopping dead in the street and turning around. Sophie's cheeks were flushed red. "You're here now, and we're going to see Addey tomorrow, right?"

"Have you heard from him?" asked Bill.

Edmund just shook his head. “No. We’d talked about meeting at the train station in Warsaw tomorrow, but I’m yet to get him to confirm it.”

“Isn’t this cutting it a little close?” asked Sophie.

“Either way we’re going to Poland,” said Bill.

Edmund nodded, pausing for a minute to get his bearings. He used the uncommonly tall university building, the Charité, to help lead him toward their lodgings for the night, and with it, a place to eat.

“I haven’t been able to get Addey at all,” Edmund said. “He hasn’t returned texts, calls, or emails. Not even video chat, and he used to love doing that.”

“How long has it been since you actually talked to him?” Bill asked.

Edmund thought for a moment. The last time had been weird—a text message that said he was glad Edmund was visiting, but wished they could do something else besides heading to the eastern part of Poland and . . . snooping.

“It’s been over a month,” he said.

“Oh, wow,” Bill said. “I hope the guy is okay.”

Edmund nodded, his chin to his sternum. “Yeah. Me too.”

They stopped in at a quaint little restaurant called the Hirschhaus that was full of mounted deer heads. It was dimly lit, and the food, although not to Edmund’s taste, was rather good. At this point in their hunger, anything put in front of them would have probably been rated five stars. Sophie and Bill shared a large bowl of goulash, complete with beef and vegetables and heavily seasoned with paprika. Edmund had what looked like from the menu a heavily garnished hotdog but when it was brought out, tasted nothing like any hotdog he’d ever had. He simply stripped the mess off the bratwurst and ate it plain, then ordered a bottle of red wine for their table.

“Gotta love Germany,” he said, toasting his friends.

“Yep,” said Bill. “Drinking age is eighteen.”

As they started walking again, Edmund assured them it wouldn’t be much longer, and that their hostel was just over the next hill. By now it was getting late, almost midnight, but Berlin hardly slowed because of the hour. If anything, there were more people out and about now than there had been when he’d ordered his first cup of coffee.

"So why did you bring your expensive IR camera to Europe with you, Ed?" asked Bill. He was loosened up a little now, the wine warming his spirit, and he exaggerated swinging his arm as he held Sophie's hand.

"Addey thought . . . well, I thought, it would be neat to do the ghost thing again. You know, since you're here too. Get the *Nun Hunters* back into active duty." This last part he took on a serious tone, almost militaristic.

"What's a *Nun Hunter*?" asked Sophie.

Edmund turned around, switched hands on the rolling suitcase. "You haven't told her? Aw, c'mon, Bill. Are you embarrassed?"

"What? Tell me," insisted Sophie.

"We had a little group back in high school," said Bill. "Me, Ed, Adlai—Addey I mean, and a few other guys. We fancied ourselves paranormal investigators."

"Like those TV shows?" Sophie asked.

Edmund snorted. "That stuff is fake. We were going to be better than that."

"What's with the name?"

Bill said, “Because a lot of the places we investigated were old Catholic churches. We were sure we’d see a dead, creepy nun floating around.”

“Oh,” said Sophie, giggling. “I just assumed it was because you didn’t see anything. Get it? *None* Hunters?”

“Very funny,” said Bill.

“So you want to go chasing ghosts?” Sophie asked. “That’s it?”

Edmund nodded. He could see the hostel now, nestled along a copse of squat little shops. Smoke puffed from the chimney and he was looking forward to being inside now that the wine was starting to wear off.

“Could be fun,” Bill said. “I’m sure Europe has no end to ghosts.”

Very true, Edmund thought. But he had one specific in mind. He’d mentioned it to Addey, as well, but it wasn’t received with as much enthusiasm as Edmund would have liked. Still, if they were to see Addey tomorrow, he hoped he could convince his friend to go on one last hunt. After all, Edmund had been interested in this particular haunting since the day he’d read about it.

The German name of the hostel was so long with so many dotted letters that Edmund didn't even try to understand it. A lot of German people, at least those under thirty years old, spoke English, and as such, a trend started where most every sign would be accompanied by the English translation just below it. The name of their hostel was simply, "The Gold Raven."

Edmund Riley's first rule of travel: Sleep cheap. The big money on any trip should be spent doing things that were fun or interesting. Who cares how fancy the room looks in which you're sleeping? This hostel was clean, but smelled musty. The beds weren't even beds at all, but wooden pallets on the floor covered by a thin pad, a sheet, and a blanket. Edmund had his own room and Sophie and Bill shared the one across the hall. As far as he could tell, there weren't any other occupants here which was good. He didn't like the idea of the communal bathroom down the hall.

Edmund said his goodnights and was sure Bill and Sophie were both sound asleep by the time he'd brushed his teeth and changed into his pajamas. For a little while he sat looking out the window, nursing a bottle of water he'd brought all the way from the train station in Amsterdam.

He pulled out his phone, the soft, white glow illuminating his face in the darkness of the room.

He was horrible at returning phone calls and texts. His mom and dad had both sent messages to wish him a Merry Christmas. He'd also gotten one from his eleven-year-old sister, Megan. He had replied to them all a day after New Year's Eve. Even his quote-unquote girlfriend Samantha had sent him daily texts yet he only responded to the ones that were direct questions.

Bored, unable to fall asleep right away, he lay on the pallet and scrolled through his messages. He'd sent so many to Addey in the last month. The first ones, simply greetings and niceties that read, "Hey", "What's up?", "You okay?" were all received, as noted on the delivery timestamp in his messaging app. The later ones, the more desperate ones such as, "Adlai, where are you?" and "We're still meeting you on the 8th, right?" were never delivered, as if his phone had been shut off. However, Addey had managed to leave one, final text that made Edmund both sad and worried at the same time.

True, he may have lost or damaged his phone, and if that were the case, Edmund had no other way to contact him. When Addey left in the middle of their tenth-grade school year, Edmund had failed to get another number.

Around the same time Addey stopped returning texts he also stopped updating his social media. Even though he wasn't as avid about keeping an online presence as most Americans, Adlai did check his messages regularly and post the odd photo of the night sky. He'd not logged into his account in over a month.

It all troubled Edmund but hopefully the mystery would unravel tomorrow. Addey knew of the meetup. Even if his phone was damaged and he'd lost all contact information from his friends in America, he still knew they'd planned to meet in Warsaw tomorrow afternoon.

As Edmund rolled over and shut off his phone, he fell asleep hoping his friend would be there, and that he didn't have to carry such worry across the rest of Europe.

Berlin to Warsaw

January 8th, 2019

Edmund Riley's second rule of travel: Travel cheap.

As he looked out the large, slightly tinted economy class window of the train, he couldn't help but think the view was probably the same in first-class. Sure, they saw those gorgeous vistas two-seconds before the cattle in economy class, and they had slightly more leg room, but the price Edmund and his friends paid to take them from Berlin to Warsaw was but a fraction of what those stooges in the suits had proffered for a little extra space.

It was a long trip, only a couple of hours less than it took to fly from Pittsburgh to Paris. His travel rule may very well change after seven hours in a steel box, zipping east through open fields and sudden, dense forests. Most of what he saw out the window was uneventful, reminding him of farm country back home, with less emphasis on commerce. It was a beautiful countryside, with gently falling snow along sloping hills, but Edmund cared more about the card game in front of him than the cows wearing blankets.

Whenever a group of friends played cards, it was unspoken that they played to the least-common denominator. Edmund didn't know how to play Rummy. Sophie nor Bill knew how to play Poker. But all three had mastered Go Fish at an early age. And why not play a child's card game? Here they were, three children, barely twenty, racing across the European countryside without a care in the world.

"I feel like the attendant keeps staring at us," said Sophie, drawing up her cards.

Edmund cast a glance over his shoulder and caught her a few rows up, pouring steaming tea for a gentleman by the bathroom door.

He shrugged dismissively. "I think she's trying to figure out what we're playing. I wouldn't imagine many people between Germany and Poland play Go Fish."

"Who you talking to?" Bill asked, and then took a long swig from his water bottle. "You haven't stopped checking that phone."

"Samantha," said Edmund, drumming fingers across its screen.

They all knew about his girlfriend back home, but he hardly acknowledged her at all these days. Edmund was caught somewhere between growing up and staying a child, and the transition was weighing heavily on him. It destroyed most every relationship he tried to have. Besides, it wasn't Samantha at all he was trying to text.

"She's a bit of a night owl, huh?" Sophie said.

"What?" Edmund asked.

Sophie's eyes glanced up to the centrally-mounted television showing the train route, and in the corner of the screen read the time—it was early, just twenty minutes to nine o'clock.

"Isn't it about three in the morning back home?" asked Bill.

"Right," he said. "She just worries, is all." They seemed to accept that answer and he was glad because he didn't feel like piling on more lie, nor did he want to admit he was checking up on Addey.

By now Edmund probably seemed like a crazy person with the number of texts and calls he'd attempted to make to his old friend. Bill, while also being a good friend, had only tried recently to contact him, to lay down a more concrete plan for meeting in Warsaw later today. As of now, it wasn't feeling so promising.

Bill was looking at Edmund, and in that moment, he was sure his high-school buddy knew the secret for what it was—Edmund was truly worried about his friend.

"So how did the two of you end up together?" Edmund asked, feeling the sudden need for a change of subject. He turned to Sophie and said, "I remember you from school, but I never . . . I dunno, I never figured the two of you would date."

"I fell in love with his pictures first," she said, looking up at Bill admiringly. He just grinned as he reshuffled the deck.

Bill had been the school newspaper photographer when Edmund attended West King's Cross High. Sophie was the yearbook editor. It was simple math that their paths would converge and, being the likable fellow that was Bill, and the hopeless romantic that was Sophie, the two started dating in their senior year. By this point Edmund had already moved to Salisbury, but he kept in contact with Bill.

He remembered Sophie, vaguely, and the night Bill had texted and told him that the two were dating, he quickly pulled out his yearbook and found her—a plain, short-haired freshman in a black and white photo who wouldn't catch the eye of chess club nerds. But now, Sophie was quite the bombshell and if Edmund was being sincere, actually out of Bill's league. Still, he was happy to see them together, in a relationship that Edmund didn't think himself capable of cultivating and maintaining.

Sophie drew from the deck and that's when Edmund noticed the tiny, yet pretty diamond on her ring finger.

"So you guys are engaged?" he said, feeling a tiny twang of jealousy that he couldn't explain. Was it because he wanted Sophie? Of course it wasn't. What he wanted was to be mature enough to handle an engagement and subsequent marriage of his own.

"We are," she said, smiling proudly and holding up her hand and wiggling her fingers so that it caught the overhead lights.

"Congratulations," Edmund said flatly, but didn't mean for his voice to come out so stilted. The smile quickly returned to his face.

Around noon, lunch was served. Unlike the planes he'd been on, Edmund found it unique that the train employed a chef who, upon order, made whatever the passengers wanted from the menu. The European trip was Edmund's first long-haul, as his dad had called it. Until now, he'd only been as far as Florida. And as such, Edmund was not what the fine folks on this train would call 'cultured.'

So for lunch, Bill had a beautiful cut of smoked beef, Sophie had a lemon fennel chicken dish with a Kaiser gouda roll, and Edmund had a large bowl of macaroni and cheese. To be fair, it had an odd, flaky cheese topping that he was certain he'd never seen in America, so his meal had a smidge of cultural cuisine to it.

After the dining attendant had taken away their dishes and refilled their drinks, Sophie excused herself to the bathroom. No sooner had she left their little group did Bill whip a box out of his jacket pocket and place it on the table.

Before Edmund could raise a question, Bill said, "So the ring Sophie's wearing is a SuperMart special I got on sale for twenty dollars. But this . . ." His voice trailed off as he flipped back the lid.

Inside was a ring, and even with Edmund's limited knowledge of such things, he knew this was no twenty-dollar ring. The band was gold and the stones were diamonds, carefully arranged in a figure-eight. Bill didn't work—he was still living at home, just like Edmund and Sophie, so it was a wonder that Bill's uptight dad had sprung for such a rock.

"I'm going to make a real proposal at Dracula's castle," said Bill. It took Edmund a moment to catch his meaning, but then remembered that after meeting up with Adlai in Poland, they were going to shoot straight down to Romania and tour the fabled Vlad the Impaler's supposed home.

"That must have cost a fortune, dude," said Edmund, admiring the array of sparkles.

Bill made a derisive little snort, as if it didn't matter. "We both agreed to save money for this trip and she insisted I not worry about another ring but I can't have her going around wearing that cheap thing for the rest of our days. So I picked this up last week at Vanderbilt Jewelers."

"How's your dad doing with all this?" Edmund asked.

If he remembered correctly Charles Sanders was a 'douchebag pain in the ass' as far as Bill was concerned. Bill came from money (unlike Edmund whose dad didn't start making a decent salary until the Salisbury move) and his dad lorded that over Bill's head all the time.

"He was fine when we were in high school. When I put off going to college for a year, he blamed her. And when we got engaged it made things even worse. But we made a deal: When I get back, we're going to get married first, and then it's straight off to school."

"She's a great girl, really," said Edmund. "I'm really happy for y—shit, here she comes! Put it away."

Bill scrambled to get the box closed and the ring back into his pocket before Sophie sat back down. Edmund, to stifle his grin, for he knew if he looked Bill in the eye he'd burst into a fit of laughter, began shuffling the deck of cards.

"Has anyone been able to reach Addey?" asked Sophie.

She called him by the nickname Edmund had given him long ago, although she never knew him well enough to say it. Addey had been an exchange student since his freshman year and Edmund had been his best friend. But halfway through tenth grade, Addey left unexpectedly. Something had happened to his grandparents but Edmund never got the full story, nor did Addey ever talk about it. Their relationship grew even closer through the magic of social media. It had been two years since Edmund had seen Bill, but four years since he'd seen Addey.

"Same as yesterday," said Edmund, holding up his phone. "I have a feeling he's going to be a no-show. Then what?"

Bill shrugged. "I guess we check out Warsaw for a day or two, then head down to Romania." He offered a sly wink to Edmund.

Although they had a European itinerary, it was loose at best. Edmund had around three-thousand dollars in his bank account and he guessed Bill had about the same, if his dad hadn't gone completely apeshit after the engagement. They had places they each wanted to see, with no real order in which to visit them. The only thing that dictated their travel would be the rail system.

It was starting to rain outside as they crossed into Poland. The landscape was very similar to Germany, although Edmund saw, for the first time, windfarms in the distance. The air outside looked frigid, although there was no way of telling that from within the comfortable cabin. A cloudy sky hung oppressively overhead and Edmund was awash with a sense of foreboding that he couldn't quite explain. Perhaps it was the lost contact with his friend, perhaps it was *History Channel* binge he'd put himself through prior to coming to Poland.

Or perhaps it was something else entirely.

Warsaw

January 8th, 2019

Sometime after lunch, Edmund settled back into his seat, watched the cows and farmers zip by and somehow, lulled himself to sleep. It wasn't restful—none of it ever was when he wasn't sleeping in his queen-sized bed back in Salisbury but there on the train he'd been so deep in slumber that he barely registered Sophie nudging his arm.

Edmund woke, noticed that Bill was still asleep and the passengers of the train were rising from their seats to grab their overhead belongings. It was the first time in seven hours he didn't feel the vibration of the train moving them along. Out the window were walls of multicolored glass, a waning sun beyond. People hurried back and forth, towing suitcases on wheels. Everyone was dressed so differently, all walks of life converged in one place, and then off to all corners of the world.

Sophie was rousing Bill when Edmund rose and started to pull down their things. He checked his bags, nodded a sleepy smile to Bill, then followed his friends up the aisle and out of the train.

A large, copper placard read Warszawa Centralina above them. Rain pelted the outside of the train station and the cold air rushed through the opened ends. People were bundled tightly, all of Europe similarly gripped in the coldest month of the year. Edmund didn't fit in here, but that had been the case in nearly every city he'd visited. It seemed the further east he traveled, the more removed he became from normalcy. He thought, *sweet Jesus, how would I feel inside China?*

"Where are we supposed to meet Addey?" asked Sophie, looking the massive train station over. Most of it disappeared underground onto island platforms. There was a restaurant, a coffeeshop, and a little information kiosk. Bill looked to Edmund.

"When we last talked he said he'd look for the first incoming train from Berlin and he'd be there." Edmund held up his arms. "That's right here."

They stood around, watching the train continue to pour travelers like some giant vein that had been cut open. It was easy to lose anyone in this shuffle but surely they stood out. Sophie with her goth curls and boots, Bill with his close-cut hair, denim jeans and sports coat, and

Edmund, perhaps the simplest of all, with his duster jacket and frilly hair.

As the station cleared, more trains seemed to go than come. They'd hit a lull in the day, and with the thinning crowd it became ever more poignant that Addey wasn't going to show. A few families here and there also waited, but the next train wasn't scheduled to arrive for another forty minutes. If Addey were here, they'd see him.

"Eight more trains come from Berlin today," said Edmund, looking up to the large monitor above the information kiosk.

"The last one isn't for another twelve hours," said Bill. "Do you really want to wait around here all day?"

He didn't have an answer. It seemed silly to put his friends through that after they'd only just arrived in Europe less than a day ago. There was the option of *him* staying behind and letting them go sightseeing—he'd much rather wait for Addey to show up than see whatever it was Warsaw had to offer, but that sounded equally silly, not to mention downright selfish. Bill and Sophie hadn't just come to see Europe. They'd come to be with Edmund.

Sophie could tell he was searching for the answer, could probably see the hurt in his eyes that his friend had either stood him up or far worse, was unable to come at all.

"Do you have his home address?" she asked.

Edmund shook his head. Addey didn't talk about his parents a lot, and when he did, it was never in a polite way. As far as he could tell, Addey had been raised by his grandparents until he came to America.

"What's Adlai's last name?" she asked him, bringing up her phone.

"Chobot. Rhymes with robot. Why?"

She had brought up the phone directory for Warsaw and was typing it in.

"Wow, there's a lot of those here," she said, looking up at Bill who'd decided to stand and stretch his legs after sitting for seven hours. "There's over three-hundred Chobots in Warsaw. We won't likely find him that way."

"So that's it then," said Bill. "He isn't here, and we've no way to track him down."

That seemed to be the case, Edmund thought glumly. This trip had been about rekindling the friendship they'd had before fate split them up, sent them in two different directions. He'd wanted to chase some ghosts, talk about Polish life, talk about anything because Addey was one of the few people out there who truly understood him. And now, the reunion just wasn't in the cards. Edmund stood up, shuffled his bag to the other shoulder and then came up with an idea.

"The Żubrówka!" he said, fishing in his jacket pocket for his cell.

Sophie and Bill just looked at him curiously, waiting for an explanation.

Edmund shook his head, as if they should've been able to follow his train of thought. "For graduation, Addey sent me a gift. A bottle of Żubrówka. It's this famous Polish vodka that has a blade of grass in it. Stuff was nasty! But it came in this sweet bottle."

"I vaguely remember hearing about this," said Bill, brow furrowed. He looked at his girlfriend and shrugged.

"Yeah, you did!" said Edmund. He'd pulled up his Facebook app and was searching through years' worth of posts, past silly quotes, love and relationship tags from Samantha, and through the endless chain letters and prayer requests. Finally, he came upon the slew of graduation congrats—family and friends who always seemed to be so surprised when a kid finishes high school. He was looking for a very specific post he'd made after receiving that small, yellow box from Poland.

"Found it," he said, walking a small circle while he read. "From my boy, all the way back in Poland. Thank U Addey!" He turned the phone around to show his friends.

The picture Edmund had posted along with the caption showed a frosted glass bottle with bright gold letters that read 'Żubrówka' above a bison on a yellow field. Serving as a platform for the bottle was the box it had been shipped in, bright yellow with enough postage stamps to make it look like a military hero. But as Edmund stretched the photo and zoomed in, the return address, in big black letters, could easily be seen.

"Hold on, I'm looking it up," said Sophie, putting a hand on Edmund's phone to steady him. She typed in the address written on the box, the glow of her phone lighting up her studying eyes. "This is about seven miles from here."

"Let's go," said Edmund walking off. He was certain they could rent a car, or at the very least take a cab.

It wasn't practical but he'd even read about the Veturilo service that would rent them bicycles. That was bound to be pleasant in January, but whatever it took to see Addey and—

—neither of his friends had moved. He trundled his suitcase back to the stalled couple, a solemn look in their eyes.

"What?" he asked, confused.

"What's wrong, Ed?" asked Bill. It was serious when he shortened his name.

"What do you mean? I'm just worried about Addey, is all."

"You act . . . I dunno. *Scared.*"

"I am. I just want to make sure he's alright." Edmund was feeling his face grow flustered, angry at having to explain something that should have simply been accepted by his friends.

"There's a dozen reasons why you've lost contact. Did something else happen?" Sophie asked. "You're . . . a little manic. No offense."

Edmund couldn't meet her gaze. He shook his head, but Bill was smart enough to tell when his friend was dodging.

"What did he say?" asked Bill. "Addey said something before he disappeared, didn't he?"

Edmund looked up, just nodded. He thumbed to his photo app because he'd taken a screenshot of the final message Addey had sent because he didn't want to lose it. It had haunted him from the moment he'd read it—Addey had sent it the day before Edmund asked if they were still going to meet in this very spot. Edmund just handed his phone to Bill with the picture pulled up, then turned around. The message, he had memorized.

I think it's great that you're coming to Europe, but I'm not so sure meeting is a good idea. Something's happening here. Something that people won't talk about. I know what happened to my grandparents but mama and papa won't talk about that either. I'm scared to go on the ghost hunt with you, Ed. If you do come to Warsaw, please, please. I'm begging you. Stay away from Treblinka.

"What's Treblinka?" asked Sophie.

Bill answered. "It was a Nazi death camp to the east of here. No one ever talks about it. Anytime you turn on the History Channel it's always about Auschwitz. But a lot of bad stuff happened in Treblinka, too."

"Why would Addey think you would go there?" asked Sophie.

Edmund said, "That's where I'd pitched the idea of ghost hunting. There's a legend around there."

"He just sounds spooked," Bill said dismissively. "I wouldn't worry about him too much."

Edmund shook his head. "He was all for the ghost hunt a year ago. I don't understand what he could've found out since then. Or what he thinks is happening around there. But I want to know."

"He said he wants you to stay away from Treblinka," Sophie said.

"We're not going to Treblinka," said Edmund, "we're going to . . ." He pulled up his phone and switched back to Facebook, "Sienna Street."

"Look, let's take it down a notch, okay, Ed?" said Bill. "I get that you're upset. I get that you're worried. But let's get settled and we'll check out his address first thing in the morning."

He looked at his watch. Twelve minutes past five. It would be getting dark soon and he didn't know how Addey's parents would take to the sudden appearance of three Americans afterhours. His heart was thudding in his chest, as excited to follow the lead to Addey's house as to the ghost hunt. But a small part of him, the logical part, said that he should side with his friends. They should eat, find a place to stay for the night, deal with travel arrangements, and then with a clear head, look for Addey.

"Okay," he conceded, nodding and putting his phone away. "First thing tomorrow?"

"First thing," said Sophie.

"After breakfast," Bill said, winking to his friend and giving him a good-natured slap across the back. "C'mon."

***

Warsaw was more spread out than Edmund would have guessed. Unlike Germany with the tight, nondescript buildings, Poland seemed to rely heavier on the embellishments. True, that was probably not the case for either of those places but the short jaunts from point A to point B that Edmund took showed very little in the way of diversity.

But Warsaw was pretty. The streets were wide, giving as much room to pedestrians as to vehicles. In some places the area seemed to fade away so that the flair of some monument could sprout from the ground. Buildings were of varied color with tapering, rounded roofs. Edmund didn't pay much attention to any of this because Bill took the lead in getting them where they needed to go. Edmund was lost to his thoughts.

The streets weren't as crowded as he would have guessed, either. True, the cold seeped into his bones worse here than seven hours west in Germany, but he wondered if Warsaw's vibrant nightlife was located elsewhere. It was getting dark, something that seemed to happen in Europe earlier than back home. He was tired, a little dejected, and wanted somewhere warm so he could think.

Because they waited for twenty minutes on a cab, Sophie had enough time to pull up a bed and breakfast on her map. The cab and driver both smelled like some sort of spicy meat and Edmund didn't think his nose would ever come to accept the strange food of this land. Sophie showed the driver her cellphone's screen and without a word, he pulled away, taking a roundabout back in the direction of the train station.

"How did people ever travel without technology?" asked Bill, watching as Sophie pulled up the BnB to double-check that it had a vacancy.

"Slowly," said Edmund.

The rest of the night was uneventful. An old man ran the BnB, his face lighting up at the three Americans as they came into his home and paid cash at a small lectern he'd placed in his foyer. A tiny, eager Corgi did circles around the newcomers' legs as Bill pulled out his wallet. The man looked at them as if they were his grandkids, then tried to take their bags away to which the boys of the group graciously stopped. Instead, the old man said something in Polish, threw his hand up to wave, then went back to his cozy chair by the fire.

They ate in a little restaurant within walking distance, each having Pierogi and bottled water. Edmund's system couldn't take much more of the strange food and he vowed, sometime soon, that he would find the European version of a 7-Eleven and buy all the junk food he could afford.

The next day when Sophie checked the map, she announced they were now four miles from Adlai's house. Rather than take a cab, Bill suggested they try to rent a car. There was a rental place called Nomad that offered surprisingly cheap rates. At first, the man running the place didn't want to rent to them—they were just kids, after all, and the minimum rental age in Poland was twenty-one. But when Edmund slid the guy a few extra zlotys, the deal went through. The extra cost wasn't much of a burden—with Poland's exchange rates they were only paying twenty bucks a day for a car, and that was even after the rental dealership's bonus.

So as Edmund sat in the driver's seat of the 2013 Fiat 500, he made a discovery—the car was a manual shifter, and he hadn't the slightest idea of how to drive one. It was also disconcerting having the steering wheel on the right side of the car, although he'd been told Poland, unlike the United Kingdom, drove on the same side as they did back home in the good ole U.S. of A.

"Bill?" he asked to his friend who sat across in what should've been the driver's seat in a normal world.

"Shit, I have no idea, Ed." He looked at the gearshift as if it were the most alien thing he'd ever seen.

“Are you boys kidding me?” asked Sophie from the back. “Ed, get up.” She pushed his seat forward as soon as he was out, then traded him spots.

“Where did you learn to drive a stick?” asked Bill.

“Candace taught me,” she said, adjusting her seat. Edmund was pretty sure that was her sister who lived out west. Nevada or maybe New Mexico.

“Full of surprises,” said Bill, kissing her hand before she took it back to man the gearshift. She placed the cellphone on the dash and let the GPS take them to Adlai’s house.

The route cut through the Old City, and now Edmund could see that most of Warsaw’s activity was away from the rail line. Sienna Street was dead in the center of a colorful district with wide roads and wrought-iron fences covered in dead vinery. Their GPS delivered them to a tall, two-story apartment building but the three of them had to get out of the car and search for the address. Lofty apartment buildings were all over the place, moving off to the south until they ended at a synagogue with a domed roof.

Edmund took the lead, finding the correct apartment building just four doors past the little graveled turnabout where Sophie had pulled the car. He wasted no time pounding on the frame, a little too forceful which made him back up and check the street for anyone who may have come out to investigate the noise.

Then the door swung in and, not surprising to Edmund this late into the journey, the smell of some smoked meat wafted out. Standing in the darkly lit doorway was a woman, perhaps elderly, perhaps not, but entirely too difficult to tell for sure by the way a shawl wrapped around her head. She was smoking a little yellow cigarette and her skin tone matched the filter. Her bug eyes glared up at Edmund, questioning him without even saying a word.

“Hi, we’re looking for Addey. I mean . . . Adlai.”

At this, her eyes lit up, but they quickly narrowed again. Edmund wasn’t sure if she understood what he’d said or if she’d simply recognized her son’s name. He pulled out his phone, quickly found an old school photo that depicted Edmund, Bill, and Addey, all sitting on the bleachers, waiting on a local acting troupe to perform *Beauty and the Beast*. He showed the old woman.

She started speaking a string of Polish—at least that's what Edmund assumed—but she turned around, as if talking to someone in the apartment. Edmund looked at Sophie who had just brought up her cellphone app to translate, but before she could, a man appeared in the doorway, nearly knocking over the old woman. She disappeared in a cloud of smoke, wandering back into the dim apartment.

"Adlai," the man said. He was taller than Edmund, but lanky and wore his pants so comically high that it made him look like a grasshopper. "Adlai. No here."

"What?" Edmund asked. "Then where?"

The old man, likely Addey's father, launched into a barrage of Polish that was so animated by the way he held his hands up that Edmund assumed he probably didn't even realize he wasn't talking English anymore.

"Slow down," said Edmund.

He relaxed a little, bit his bottom lip as he struggled to come up with the words he needed. Something in his eyes looked sad and distant, but they gleamed when he finally managed the word, "Sick."

"Sick?" said Bill. "So Adlai is sick."

"Yah," said the man. "Adlai sick."

"Did he . . ." Edmund's voice trailed off, unsure if he even wanted to know.

"He no here," said the man. "He get sick. He chase . . ." Again, his voice trailed off, searching for the right word. "Sonderzüge. He get sick."

"So if he's not here, where is he?" This question came from Sophie who'd stepped up to talk. "Warsaw? Is he in Warsaw?"

The man nodded. "War. Saw."

Sophie pulled up the map on her phone and zoomed out. She held it for him to see and said, "Show us."

The old man, who looked as far removed from such technology as possible, pulled out a pair of bifocals from his shirt pocket, then looked at the map with his nose high in the air. He pointed to a spot far to the east of where they were standing and said, "Bed. Bed here. Sleeping."

When he touched the screen, the app placed a bookmark on the spot. Edmund watched as Sophie zoomed in and found the building, nestled right by the Vistula

River. The large cross icon indicated this was some sort of hospital or clinic.

"Thank you," said Edmund.

They started to walk away, but the old man turned and said, "Adlai friend."

Edmund stopped, faced the old man who looked like he'd just aged twenty years. The woman, Addey's mom, was peeking out into the street behind her husband.

"Yes. I'm Adlai's friend."

"Adlai sick."

"Right," said Edmund. "That's what you said."

He shook his head, as if his meaning was escaping this American kid. "Adlai . . ." His eyes searched the sky, the language barrier becoming frustrating. "no wake again."

Edmund didn't know what that meant, but made his blood turn cold, either way. There was no answer he could give the old man, so he simply smiled politely and followed his friends back to the car.

"What did that mean?" asked Bill.

“I have no idea,” said Edmund. “I hope it’s not a roundabout way of saying he’s dead. But let’s go see him, shall we? Sophie?”

“Hold on,” she said, scrolling through something on her phone. “Either of you catch that word? He said Adlai was chasing something.”

Bill said, “Solder, Sonder?”

“Sonderzüge,” Edmund said.

Sophie took a moment to search it. From the backseat Edmund could see the image pop up on her phone, an old black and white photo crowded with people, and for the second time in only a few minutes, his blood turned cold.

“It means Special Trains,” said Sophie, confusion in her voice. “I don’t understand.”

Edmund said, “Special Trains were what the Nazis called the trains that carried the Jews to the concentration camps.”

“Oh,” said Sophie, starting the car. “But Addey, he was . . . *chasing* one?”

“Yeah,” said Edmund, a bitter taste in his mouth because this was part of the reason why he wanted to come to Europe. “He was chasing the Ghost Train of Treblinka.”

***

What they saved in car rental they spent in gasoline. By Edmund’s estimates and his rudimentary understanding of gallon to liter conversion, they were paying over double what he’d paid to fill up his Ford Escort back home. While Bill pumped the gas, Edmund stocked up on snacks—things that looked like potato chips or candy—but he knew better than to accept them at face-value. Europeans loved to take something simple and change it a little, to make it something horrible. Peanut butter, chocolate and applesauce for one. Or a cinnamon roll filled with cream corn.

It was another eight miles across the city, past the train station, and far to the east where the Vistula River cut a swath across Warsaw’s north-south border. In warmer months beachgoers actually came to the river’s edge and spread blankets and volleyball nets. Right now, with the bone-chilling wind, Edmund couldn’t even visualize such a thing.

The GPS brought them to a small, two-story building that looked very out of place with the riverfront properties lining the street to the left and right. A large, fenced-in area filled with picnic tables was attached to the side but there was no one out there, certainly not in this kind of cold. Edmund didn't bother trying to read signs in this place, but the large, neon placard didn't show a hospital cross like he'd expected, but a female's hands held together, as if in prayer.

"This isn't a hospital," said Edmund. He turned to his unsure companions and added, "Is it?" Poland, and most of Europe was so strange and alien at times that he walked around in a constant state of uncertainty.

"Maybe it's a clinic," said Bill. "C'mon."

He led them through the double doors and into a warm lobby that smelled of urine. In the time it took Bill to approach the man sitting at the receptionist's desk, Edmund had given the place a once-over, and had instantly deduced that it wasn't a hospital.

The odor, the soft music coming from down the hall, the three men sitting in heavy robes in a commissary watching television—it all made sense now. Edmund had spent many hours of his childhood coming to a place like this, when his grandmother had fallen and broken her hip and could never live alone again.

"It's a nursing home," Edmund whispered to Sophie. She blankly nodded.

"Adlai Chobot," said Bill to the man who simply nodded and motioned for the group to follow. Sophie raised an eyebrow to Edmund and he to her—back in the United States there'd be at least a few questions before someone off the street could venture into the halls of an assisted living facility.

The receptionist ushered them past a pair of reaching old men who, despite their words in Polish, were just as sad. Edmund hated places like this—hated the smell, the food, the way the hired help smiled while scraping shit off bed-sore ridden asses. It broke his heart to think of his friend interred here. What could possibly have happened to land Addey in such a state?

At the end of a long, depressing hall, the receptionist stopped, held up a hand and said, "Chobot," before quietly nodding and walking back to his post. The door was cracked open, and as Edmund paused to enter, he realized his friends were waiting on him to go first.

Edmund eased the door wider, unsure what waited, but quite certain it wouldn't be his friend, sitting up, smiling and enjoying a cup of Jell-O. Inside, the room was dark, so he flipped on the light, his eyes burning.

Adlai was slightly elevated in bed, eyes closed, his stoic face giving no hint of pain or discomfort. His hair had been cut back neatly, his dark skin shaven. Someone had been taking care of him, Edmund thought with a bit of comfort. There was an array of machines—heart monitor, IV drip, ventilator. A tube ran from beneath the single, pale sheet that must have led to a cath.

"Addey?" Edmund said, reaching out and taking his friend's cold hand in his own. It was foolish to even think he'd be heard, but what else was there to say? To do? Edmund looked the room over, not seeing a single personal item. The television remote lay upon a table that was so neat that it probably hadn't been used in years. No flowers, no cards. No trace of a meal eaten here. Did his parents come visit him? Did they come and say his name, just as Edmund had?

Bill and Sophie said nothing, simply hung by the door to the bathroom, letting Edmund have a moment with his friend. He just sat on the edge of the bed, looking at his friend, wondering what could have happened.

"This explains why his dad said he wouldn't wake up," said Edmund. "It's a coma, right?"

"It's weird," said Sophie. "My best friend in elementary school was in a car wreck and she had so many machines keeping her alive, but she also had wounds. I don't see any of those."

Edmund pulled up the blanket and found a dingy hospital gown atop hairy legs, the cath tube running down the edge. He pulled down Addey's robe from the collar but saw nothing more than heart monitors and a tube bandaged to his stomach. There wasn't a single thing to suggest trauma. So how did he end up this way?

They sat for a moment longer, and as Edmund was about to say something to Bill, a woman entered the room, almost stopping dead from a sprint. She looked at the three kids sitting around Addey and her eyes beamed.

"He's never had a visitor," she said excitedly. This nurse, a younger lady who couldn't have been many years older than Edmund, spoke in such good English that it made him long for his own country.

"His parents?" Bill asked.

She just shook her head. "No. They came once to fill out the paperwork to get him here but that's it. They've not been back."

Edmund's anger flared, wondering just how a parent could so easily turn a blind eye to a sick child. He was lucky he came from a family that would never have done such a thing.

"What's wrong with him?' Sophie asked.

The nurse entered the room and fixed his collar. That's when Edmund knew she was the one who'd been taking care of him, the angel who'd made sure he didn't develop sores and who kept his hair neatly trimmed. She said, "We honestly don't know. He doesn't have much brain function. Heart is fine. The prevailing theory is a stroke, but he's not been properly tested for that. When they found him, they took him to the hospital for examination, kept him three days, then it was his parents' prerogative to send him here."

"So they just abandoned him," Edmund said, voice rising.

“I wouldn’t be so tough on them,” she said. “They both work, they’re both, what’s the word? Elderly? You see the machinery needed to keep him alive. This could not be done at home. As awful as it sounds, this is where he needs to be.”

“Still, they could at least come visit,” said Edmund.

She nodded, conceding the point. She moved past Edmund and opened up the drawer under the television and pulled out a green storage tote. Inside was a pair of jeans, a sweatshirt, shoes, and a clear plastic bag holding a wallet and a few other odds and ends.

“This was all of his belongings,” she said. “His phone was found about twenty meters away, and it was a miracle someone saw it out there in the snow. My guess is that it’s broken. We forgot to give all of this to his parents and they haven’t returned any of our calls. I suppose you can have it.”

“Thank you,” Edmund said, taking the baggie and opening it.

“I’m just starting my shift. I’ll be at the desk should you need me. It was good of you to come visit him.” With that, she turned and left.

Inside the bag was Addey's wallet which held a few banknotes, a credit card, driver's license, a voter ID card, and a little metal cross on a green background. Edmund held it up for his friends to see, nearly fighting back tears. Bill and Sophie just grinned.

This was a pin from their high school, West King's Cross. During the fall, the yearbook committee held a fundraiser where they sold the pins which the students dubbed Impurity Crosses. The idea was that a boy gave one to the girl he fancied and if she accepted it, they went to the spring formal together. It was bad luck for a boy to graduate with an Impurity Cross still on his person. Addey never got the chance. He never dated, never had a girlfriend while at WKC. He'd kept his cross in his wallet and dragged it all the way back to Poland, where it would stay forevermore.

Tucked in the jeans of his pocket was a small key with a blue, diamond-shaped tag. It read: Krakus House – 1. Edmund remembered the name coming up on several occasions when he talked about visiting Poland.

The only other item Edmund cared about was Addey's bright green cellphone, a sleek newer model than the one he'd had back in high school. Edmund tried to power it on but naturally the battery was dead. He was left there holding the device, staring into the black void of the screen and wondering what it could tell him. Without much thought, Edmund slid the phone into his back pocket.

He didn't care to take any of the other belongings with him. The only logical thing to do with them was deliver them to the Chobots, but Edmund wasn't about to go back there, not after what the nurse had told him. Carefully he folded the pants and the shirt and placed them back neatly in the tote, then returned the tote to the drawer.

He looked at his friend one last time, put a hand up to his cool brow, then followed his companions out into the sad, dim hallway. The pair of robed gentlemen had moved on, replaced by a single lady with braided hair who watched them from a wheelchair as they passed by. Edmund just smiled and tipped his head.

At the desk, Edmund turned to his friends and said, "Go on, I'll be out there in a moment."

Sophie and Bill nodded, joined hands, then marched out toward the car.

The nurse was putting checkmarks in a ledger when Edmund approached the counter. Again, her eyes lit up, happy to see one of those who'd been nice enough to visit her curious patient. He took a business card from a little deck on the counter, flipped it over, then scribbled his cellphone number and name on it.

"If there's any change, could you possibly give me a call?"

She took his number, glanced at it, then nodded sincerely.

Edmund started to walk off, but turned back just as she had started to busy herself once more with paperwork.

"You said he was found."

"Excuse me?"

"Adlai. You said they found him. Where?"

Her face darkened. "In the woods. About half a mile from the Treblinka Memorial."

Warsaw

January 8th, 2019

Edmund stayed quiet for most of the evening and Sophie nor Bill pressed him to talk. Seeing Addey in such a state was a much bigger deal for him and they understood that. He was torn between feeling bad for his friend and feeling like an embarrassing drag on this trip.

The evening was uneventful. They ate, they did a little sightseeing around the city by foot, then settled in at the BnB just as the sun was going down. Edmund stooped down to pet the Corgi in the old man's foyer, said his goodnight, then went up to his room.

"Where to in the morning?" said Bill, leaning against his doorway in the hall. Sophie was gathering her bathroom bag to go take a shower.

Edmund shrugged. "Doesn't matter. I know you want to get down to Romania. That would be fine."

"We can hang around another few days if you want," said Bill. Sophie walked by, kissed him on the cheek and then headed to the bathroom, wordlessly letting them talk.

"Maybe," he said, distant. "I'm sorry I'm not much fun right now."

"Let's do some ghost hunting." This comment was made from down the hall, just as Sophie was about to go into the communal bathroom.

"Seriously?" asked Bill, laughing a little.

"Why not? Ed brought his cool little infrared camera, after all. It's what he and Addey wanted to do. So let's go do it. Addey will be there in spirit."

Bill turned to look at Edmund and raised an eyebrow. "Whatcha think, buddy?"

Stay away from Treblinka, Addey had said.

Edmund shrugged, but couldn't hide the tiny smile that had surfaced. "Could be fun. Let's talk about it in the morning."

"Okay," Bill said. The bathroom door behind them shut as Sophie went in. "Well sleep well."

Unfortunately Edmund could not sleep well at all. At two different times throughout the night he'd heard some sort of siren. It wasn't the warble of an American ambulance or cop car either, but a strange, high chirrup that was so off-putting that he woke from a dead sleep.

It was nearly two in the morning when he sat up in bed and decided to take a shower, rather than wait until after he slept. While undressing, he found Addey's phone in his jeans pocket and the events of the day came back to his tired, troubled mind.

He turned it over, immediately clueless as to the type of charger he would need. Perhaps he could find one of those universal, knock-off brands. Those were abundant in America and online, but he wasn't so sure around here. It had been a struggle just to track down a can of shaving cream early this week.

Still, if he could only charge the phone and see what was on it . . .

Half an hour later he was bathed, dressed, and standing by Sophie and Bill's bedroom door, listening for any sort of movement on the other side. They were asleep, surely, but if he'd heard even the slightest noise, he'd planned to knock and ask if they wanted to go for a late-night walk.

Downstairs, the old man, which they learned earlier was named Eliasz, was sleeping soundly in his chair, the recliner tilted back. The Corgi, named Boczek, was curled across his lap. Edmund had a key to the door, but it was unlocked. He held up his hand and grabbed the bell, then did his best to walk himself out while keeping it from ringing.

It was chilly out, doubly so with Edmund's wet hair. The street in which the BnB operated was residential, so this late at night there weren't people milling about. He followed the sounds of the highway, remembering that foot traffic crossed a median bridge, and on the other side of that was a conglomerate of shops—which may not even be open at such an hour.

Warsaw was lit up at night. In the distance a plane was coming in, its flashing light growing closer to the ground as it cut across the sky. Most every building and monument had floodlights to keep them bright, and neither were in short supply after he crossed the bridge.

He passed two synagogues on his way there. So far he'd lost count of them while in Warsaw, at least the ones that were easily identifiable by their domed roofs. Edmund thought, eighty years ago, those kinds of places would be bulldozed just for existing. Had the Germans decimated this city instead of *almost* decimating it, Warsaw would look a lot different today.

When more people started to appear, tightly bundled in their skinny coats and scarves, he knew he was headed in the right direction. The sounds of music drew him toward the apparently late-night shopping district. For the first time since leaving Paris he was in his element, as Edmund had been a heavy drinker in high school and the year following it.

The street was lined with clubs and pubs, ritzy to questionable. A barrage of neon lights and smoke-filled entryways drew his attention to several places at once. He ignored all of this after spotting what looked like a gas station at the end of the club street.

Inside, he found one attendant, a middle-aged woman who didn't even see him enter but instead remained glued to a black-and-white television program behind the counter. He was about to formulate a way to ask for a charger, but decided against it for the moment and went to shop for snacks since his supply from earlier was almost gone.

Edmund took anything that looked crispy—chips, dried apples and peaches, even some kind of Japanese import that had a cartoon girl on the bag with jalapeno peppers for eyes. He walked past the book and magazine rack, mostly averting his gaze because the wall of strange, scribbled polish gave him a headache, but he quickly backtracked, his eye catching something on the center rack.

It was today's newspaper.

There were two photos dominating the center—one was a man, probably mid-twenties, and the other was an older woman, possibly late-fifties. Both looked like snapshots provided by family members, like those that turn up on the news when a tragedy strikes. What caught Edmund's attention was the photo on the other side of the text accompanying the story.

It was old photograph of a holocaust train.

In it, hundreds of dark shapes were being herded through the large, opened door on the side of the car, like some giant creature eating Jews. A couple of SS guards faced the camera. One was smoking a cigarette, his hand resting on a rather vicious looking machine gun. His eyes seemed to scoff at a disapproving photographer, as if he was asking, "So what?"

The train photo was connected to the two people pictured above, and the three paragraphs of Polish in between. He had no idea what the words said, but he could translate it—slowly, with assistance from the app Sophie had helped him download.

Edmund took the paper from the rack, then moved to the rear of the store where he could rest it on a standing table by the window. Cigarette butts littered the surface so he used the paper to sweep them away, then placed his phone next to it.

Slowly, he translated the article, but the app wasn't very precise. It didn't account for how certain words were conjugated, nor did it take into consideration a singular or plural word, to which Polish could be wildly different. Each time he grew frustrated and told himself that he'd take the paper back to the BnB for Sophie's help, he honed in on a juicy word that made him continue.

When he translated the word 'ghost' his heart fluttered.

He could already see that the word Treblinka was tied to the article. Now, the story of Addey, the hesitation to go ghost hunting, it was all starting to fall into place, although he didn't have nearly enough pieces yet to understand.

"Ghost Train strikes again?" said the translated headline. "God, what's it mean? What's it *mean*?" he muttered to himself.

He continued his translation, paying no mind to the occasional shopper floating by him, to the muted vibration of the clubs' music against the windows, to the large SUV, as uncommon as could be in Europe, that had rolled up to the first gas pump.

His fingers tapped, entering in all the strange words he could, typing full sentences that the translator app managed, but mangled with just enough clarity that he still caught the general gist of what was being said.

From what he gathered, these two people, a Rebekah Mazur and Jozef Wozniak, both of a place called Wyszków, had been missing for two weeks. Lots of people, a surprising amount of people, disappeared in Poland, as if they flitted away into the fog. What made these particular cases strange is that both, shortly before going missing, witnesses had mentioned seeing an ominous, 'antiquated' train heading along an empty span of track on the Bialystok line.

Rebekah's car was found stalled in the middle of the road, her door open with no sign of her anywhere. Jozef worked at the post office, and he'd left his portal unlocked. Someone had even witnessed him leave—saw him exit the building, turn to the east and head through the woods.

Finally, the last part of the article which garnered the most attention from Edmund was the mention of the ghost train, and how it had been linked to several disappearances over the years. As the article read, "The Ghost Train of Treblinka rides every winter, and each time she does, a few souls decide to ride along with her . . ."

"So those are the latest, eh?" came a deep, British voice from behind Edmund. The store was so quiet and the voice so out of place that he started, then whipped around embarrassingly fast to see a pair of men standing by the soda coolers.

"What?" asked Edmund, unsure what the first one, a tall, gaunt man dressed all in black, had meant.

He pulled a green bottled soda from the cooler and nodded toward the newspaper Edmund had on the table. "Them. Guess those are the newest to go missing? I see the train there." He rolled his eyes at the mention of train.

Edmund wasn't sure what to say, so he only glanced back at his paper and agreed. "Yeah. Says the Ghost Train claimed them."

The men laughed—the second one, dressed equally dark but wearing a driving hat, said, "Rubbish. They've more superstition in this bloody country than the whole of our island."

"Maybe they just . . . ran off?" said Edmund. "Happens all the time. People just leave without telling anyone."

"Or we have a serial killer on the loose," said the taller one. "There's no Ghost Train."

Edmund wasn't feeling combative enough to argue. Sure, he always believed in ghosts, but as he grew older the notion started to feel very childlike, so he only spoke of it to friends. But perhaps it was the strangers' tone, or perhaps it was their flippant dismissal of the idea that brought him all the way here to see Addey, but Edmund found himself at least willing to defend it.

"I'm going to see for myself tomorrow," he said, then proudly added, "I'm a bit of a ghost chaser."

The men looked at each other, and although they didn't fall over laughing, Edmund knew they were working to keep it out of their faces. Instead, the first one turned to him and said, "Then I suppose we shall be seeing you again, friend."

"How so?"

The taller one sat his soda on the table and extended his hand. "I'm Brian Harrick. This here is my colleague, Marcus Davies. We've come all the way from Surrey to locate information on a missing person, although you won't find her in any of the newspapers now."

"She's a bit of old news," said Marcus.

"Right. In a couple of days she'll have been missing for a year."

"Who is she?" asked Edmund.

"Can I have your name first, good sir?" asked Brian, attempting to put as much levity into the odd conversation as possible.

"Edmund. From Salisbury."

"I've no clue where that is. But anyway, we are looking for information on a Katherine Walker." He reached into his jacket and pulled out a folded piece of paper, a flyer that had probably been in circulation ever since the girl had gone missing. "She was twenty-two at the time of her disappearance. Backpacking with some friends a little north of Poniatowo. She said she was going walking one night and never returned. Her parents have been looking for answers ever since."

"And that's why we're here," said Marcus.

"Indeed. Flew in from Kraków last night and are headed that way now, so perhaps we'll see you while you're . . . hunting ghosts." Edmund assumed 'that way' meant toward Treblinka, because those who went missing seemed to be relatively close, at least in the eastern part of Poland.

"If not for the train, what do you think happened?" Edmund asked. "Three people have gone missing around there, right?"

Marcus said, "Actually about sixty people have gone missing around there. All the way back to 1948."

"It's a serial killer, nothing more," said Brian. "There's so much wilderness out there. Untamed forest, caves, mines. He's been lucky, but I guarantee there's a fellow somewhere out there with a sick and twisted room, probably full of the rotting heads of his victims and—"

"And you think someone's been at this since the *forties*?" Edmund said. "I think the Ghost Train is more plausible."

Marcus shook his head. "You Yanks love your killers, right? Surely you've heard of copycats? That's the most logical answer, eh?"

Edmund shrugged and started to gather up his things, tired and unwilling to steer the conversation any further.

"Keep that," said Brian, giving him the picture of Katherine. "God knows her mum printed enough of 'em." The girl in the photo was quite beautiful. Although it was black and white, he was fairly certain she had blond hair. She had what his dad called a hawk nose, but it didn't detract from her face—she had the cheekbones and chin to support it. Edmund folded it and put it in his pocket.

"Well boys, it was nice meeting you. Perhaps we'll see each other again."

"Perhaps we will," said Brian. "My mobile number is listed in the contact information beneath the ole girl's photo. If your . . . ghosting nets any real findings, do give me a ring?"

Edmund smiled and nodded, then left the gentlemen who made a straight line to the counter to buy their sodas. He lingered by a stack of cookbooks, wondering why on earth such a place that sold so many random items even existed, and watched them leave. They got into the large SUV and headed north, taillights disappearing into the hazy night.

When Edmund got to the counter, he pulled out Addey's phone, held it up for the woman to see, then tapped the charging slot along its bottom. She considered him for a moment, then turned to the pegboard behind her to survey the universal adapters. She was friendly enough to open two packages in order to help him find the right fit, but was rude enough to charge for all those that she tried. Edmund didn't care. He slid his bank card and took his purchases back to the BnB.

He was exhausted by the time he stumbled into bed. Edmund hooked up Addey's phone but nothing happened. For ten minutes he waited, hoping the battery had only been in the dregs, but would soon power on. No such luck. After staring at the black screen for thirty minutes,

Edmund's body was losing the battle to stay awake. Whether the mystery of Addey's phone would soon be revealed or not, he physically couldn't make himself wait. A week of weird sleeping arrangements, jetlag, and inconsistent food had finally caught up to him.

He'd been asleep for fifteen minutes when Addey's phone powered on, filling the room with soft, blue light.

Treblinka

January 3rd, 1943

Anger beget fear.

Had the child not loosened her grip, he may very well have dissipated into the ether, into that unknown void between life and death, Heaven and Hell. His essence was unraveling as her fingers graced what was noncorporeal. But he was spared that cold morning, for when the child reached through the slats to touch him, an older woman, possibly a mother, possibly a stranger who'd been equally and randomly slated to die at Treblinka, put a comforting hand on the child's arm and pulled her away from the cold. It was the Entity's only saving grace.

He staggered, his form becoming more tangible as his energy waned. As he traveled up the length of the stalled train and into the engine, he put a thought into the mind of the main conductor, a horrible man named Klaus Wagner. And lucky for the Entity it didn't take much convincing because he didn't think he had the mental capacity to influence a more steadfast heart. Klaus, without possibly knowing that the thought had been implanted, turned to the second conductor, a man named Otto—a man with secrets, a man running—and explained the plan just as the Entity had whispered it into his ear.

The engine came alive and slowly the train started to back down the line.

***

His lair was a culmination of many different peoples. The Poles found it, mined silver from it until it was nothing more than useless, black rock. The Germans laid the track, hollowed it out, and just as quickly forgot about it. And finally the Entity made his way there—just a stone's throw from Treblinka where he could linger in the darkness and taste the death floating on the air, like warm apple pies on a windowsill.

The tunnel was massive—had to be if all forty-nine cars and the engine were to fit. It was wonderfully dark, especially at the far end that may as well have been reaching right into Hell. With the engine off, it was deathly silent, despite so many shivering bodies crowded in the cars.

Humans were more unpredictable than not. At least in the last few centuries. He was certain the cars would be screaming, that the Jews would be crawling over each other to escape the train, but they weren't. They'd been crammed together in the ghetto and were crammed together now. Their spirit had been broken, and for that, the Entity was glad. Broken spirited people rarely caused trouble.

But the little girl . . .

Some people were good—to the point of it giving them power. True goodness in the world was rare, and often those who possessed it didn't even know it. The Entity was afraid, more so than he'd been in thousands of years. Why, the last time he'd encountered such goodness in the world was when they were nailing the Son of God to a cross.

Thankfully he'd been full when fate put him on that hill, his metaphorical belly bulbous with fresh death. After all, he'd dined well during the Siege of Jerusalem. But now, after being asleep for so long and needing to feed impossibly frequent to keep himself satiated, he knew his power was on the decline. He needed half the world to die right now to feel restored.

It angered him to be at the mercy of a child who'd only known of the world for a fraction of his own years. He made sure to stay away from that particular train car, so he simply lingered nearby in the darkness. If she got out, if she grew curious again and wanted to touch him, he didn't know if he'd have the power to escape. Why did he even bring her here?

The Entity was forevermore curious of the humans.

Perhaps a small part of him wanted to study the girl, to understand the power she held over him. But alas, that wasn't possible. He'd misjudged her potency. Those long years past, after Christ, after the scant others who were powers of good, had dulled his memory of why he should have been afraid. It bothered him that he couldn't probe her thoughts as he could any of the two-million Jews he'd lingered near in just this past week. He didn't know her name, where she lived, what she feared and loved. It was difficult not having that sort of leverage against a human.

No matter, he would be rid of her soon.

The Entity stared Klaus in the face—at such close proximity the German engineer would never be able to resist such influence.

There's a girl in the fourth car. No more than five years old. Kill her.

"Kill her?" asked Klaus.

"What?" Otto said. Both men were coming out of the stupor the Entity put over them in order to make them more complacent.

Do it. Go now.

Klaus nodded in the darkness but no one other than the Entity could see it. He slid the door back, hopped down to the floor of the tunnel (which had been covered in gravel years earlier thanks to the German) then put his hand up to the cars as he walked, partly to count, partly to keep his balance.

Halfway there, he pulled out his sidearm, a sleek little Beretta M1934. It was new to him—had been sent from his brother in Italy only a week ago and the Entity could feel his excitement to finally get to fire it.

A chorus of wonderful cries rang out as Klaus stepped up to the door, unlocked it, and slid it open. The Entity hovered nearby, not seeing the inside, fearful that if he even turned eyes upon the child she would somehow weaken him further.

"Back! Get back!" Klaus said to the chaotic train car. His voice rippled down the line, and more frantic cries answered the call. When he fired his gun, the windows lighting up in a brilliant flash of white, the whole train clamored to a frenzy. It had only been a warning shot into the air, the bullet sparking against the train's roof and filling it with the smell of cordite.

"Which one? Which one? There's *four* little girls in here!" said Klaus to the darkness, because no one ever heard the Entity's voice, only his suggestion.

The Entity whispered into his mind. *Then kill them all.*

Without hesitation, the gun went off—three successions—*pop-pop-pop!* The trains came alive with a ruckus that the Entity had to fight to drown out. Being so omnipotent was a curse more often than not. The Jews were screaming in half a dozen languages, focusing on thoughts of their children, their homes before the stark walls of the ghetto, and what they'd do differently in their lives if only God would deliver them from this cold, dark nightmare. But in his weakened effort to silence the prisoners, he failed to realize that there'd only been three shots. Not four.

"I can't kill her. I *won't* kill her," said Klaus.

You will *kill her. Now.*

The Entity used as much essence as he could spare, tightening a vice around Klaus's mind. The man was evil, but he was weak. All he cared about was his family—his wife and two girls. Perhaps he saw something in the child that he saw in his own daughters. But that didn't make sense because he'd just splattered the brains of three others before stopping at this special, nuisance of a girl.

The Entity dared to float closer.

Inside the car, the adults had scrambled to the far end, looking more like a bag of beans than a group of people. They were so pressed together, so afraid of this big, stocky German man and his outstretched gun. Could they even see by now? He was certain even humans could grow accustomed to the dark after they'd been in it for so long. At least three bloody shapes lay face-down on the cold, metal floor.

The little girl huddled in the corner, covering her face. She was truly afraid and the Entity loved it, even though she tasted like poison. Those three deaths were but an *hors d'oeuvre*, as the French called them, barely enough to make his nonexistent mouth water. Klaus's Beretta was trained on the child, his arm shaking so bad that he had to steady it with his other. This hesitation infuriated the Entity.

"I can't do this!" he said. Klaus had tears streaming down his face, arms growing heavy. How the Entity wished to be corporeal, so that he could simply pull the trigger himself.

Your superiors want this. You know they do. Why, if you fail, they will leave at once for Cologne and do far worse to Ingrida, Gisela, and Gertrude.

Traveling so far was beyond his current abilities but the Entity thought for sure that threatening Klaus's wife and girls would usher him to act. How could a man, as evil-hearted as Klaus, hesitate after so easily killing three others? The Germans, after the last ten years, had been taught from birth that these people weren't really people at all, that they were nothing more than diseased cattle.

"He's lying to you," said the little girl, her sobs stopping only long enough to utter those four words. Klaus couldn't understand her—he'd only learned a handful of useful words in Polish, mainly directional because that's the only interaction he ever had with them. But somehow this child had heard, and was understanding, what the

Entity was saying. After all, it wasn't really a language, it was a projection. Yet this mere girl had intercepted it.

Klaus was crying profusely now and that's when the Entity understood. He wasn't fighting the influence. The Entity simply didn't have the power to make him kill this girl. She was some sort of light for the world, and no matter how much power he possessed, no matter if the bombs decimated all of Europe, would he be any more able to convince Klaus to pull the trigger.

In the end, he did pull it.

Klaus turned the gun up, placed the barrel under his chin and showered the ninety-one people huddling in the back with his brains. As the body dropped to the floor the Entity floated back, feeling his rage build like never before. He peeked into the minds of several others, willing them, bargaining with them, and finally begging them, to simply reach a hand out and snap the little girl's neck. None would touch her.

And somehow, within that power, was the ability to undo him. This was the weakest he'd been in six-thousand years. If he fell back asleep, so be it. He always woke, leapfrogging through the years until a calamity fell upon mankind with such fervor that he couldn't slumber through the deaths.

He traveled to the engine and found Otto, and whispered a suggestion into his ear.

A moment later, the man cried out, "God, Klaus, no!" upon entering the train and finding a bloody mess. He was starting to get his wits about him, which was bad. The Entity wanted to keep the train here, hidden, with a group of people already dying who would steadily feed him, bolster his strength enough to leave the lair. How that child had weakened him . . .

The longer the child stayed so close, the more his energy would leave. Perhaps he couldn't kill her. Perhaps he couldn't coax anyone else to do it, but that didn't mean he couldn't still orchestrate her death. As he always said, nature was a far better killer than man.

Otto moved Klaus aside, then took the girl by the hand. It was no small wonder that the man could even touch the child's flesh. The Entity was sure that if Otto tried to harm her, he would stall, magically unable to do so. The conductor pulled the screaming girl so that she stood in the darkness of the cave.

It was almost dusk by the time the Entity launched the plan of taking her off the train. From this end, only five cars total from the mouth of the tunnel, the sun cast enough guiding light to the outside.

This was the first time the Entity was able to look upon her, despite how it hurt his eyes, like that dreaded creature from the Stoker novel. She was small, even for her age. Her face was dirty and sunken like all those who were currently competing for scraps. Somehow, after all this time, she still held a doll which was nothing more than a wad of straw surrounded by a polka-dotted dress. Eyes rimmed red looked out toward the light, and she blinked back tears.

"Go!" said Otto. When the girl just stared up at him with a frown, he repeated it again. "Go!" This time he gave her a heavy shove in the direction of the light. The child couldn't understand his words, but she understood his meaning, so she tightened her hold on the doll and started following the tracks out of the tunnel. It was the first time the Entity noticed she didn't have on shoes.

Every so often she would slow, turn back around, then start walking again. Most likely she was leaving family aboard the train. Such was the case of all these Jews.

Watching her become nothing more than a silhouette against the circle of light did his proverbial heart good. Already he was feeling more powerful, but he wished he could follow the child out into the coming night to witness her death.

And how death would come for her on swift wheels.

She was a Polish child in German-occupied Poland. It was January. She was hungry, thirsty, tired, barefoot and without a coat. This part of the world was untamed, and on any given night the countryside of Poland was plagued with roving packs of wild dogs. The odds were stacked against her. *Some*thing would kill that little girl before the sun came up tomorrow.

The Entity had to eat. He turned, nearly staggered, and brought the full brunt of his malice to Otto, flooding the man with suggestions.

You have sixty rounds to go along with the Mauser on your hip. Klaus's Beretta is by his corpse, and another forty rounds are on his *hip. You know what needs to be done.*

"I shouldn't do this. I am supposed to take them to the camp. Oh, God . . . *Klaus*."

They would die in the camp either way. Look at them. They are cattle, they are an affront to everything you stand for.

"I don't have enough bullets," said Otto, probably feeling as if he'd lost his mind because after all, this whole battle was being fought there.

No. You don't.

Otto had started to walk off, to actually do the awful, awful thing the voice in his head had ordered. But the magnitude of logic outweighed the otherworldly suggestion.

"But . . . we loaded over four-thousand of them." He just gazed down the dark tunnel, to where forty-nine cars sat quietly.

A moment passed as the silence had returned to the cave, and it was the last time it would be silent until the awfulness was done.

There is that big, metal alligator wrench under the seat in the engine .

Warsaw

January 9th, 2019

Edmund woke to the sound of fists beating on the door. When he finally stirred enough to find his wits, he knew he'd overslept—that much was apparent by the light pouring in through the window that he'd failed to shade last night. He was wearing only his boxers and the t-shirt he'd worn all day yesterday when he flipped back the quilts and bounded across the room to crack open the door.

"You want breakfast?" asked Bill. "Eliasz told Sophie there's a little place around the corner that serves American food. Can you imagine?" She was standing behind Bill, rocking back and forth on her heels. Both were fully dressed.

"Yeah, sure," said Edmund. "Um, let me get dressed. The Pierogi didn't sit well last night." He made an exaggerated, sickly face by blowing out his cheeks.

"We'll be downstairs," said Bill, then led his girlfriend down the hall.

Edmund threw on his clothes and stuffed his wallet and money into his pocket. While he was fastening his wristwatch, he took notice of Addey's phone. The screen was off, but that was as normal for a powered-up battery as a dead one if it was left inactive for too long.

He pressed the button on the side, overjoyed when Addey's lock screen, a large, gnarled tree with an autumn backdrop, flared to life. Edmund had been so worried that getting it charged would be the first obstacle, and that next he'd have to contend with figuring out a passcode. But when he slid his thumb, revealing the sea of Addey's little square apps, he knew the phone was his to peruse.

Wasting no time to navigate to pictures, Edmund noticed that his friend cared little for memories. Comparatively, Edmund had at least six-thousand photos on his own phone, whereas Addey only had thirty-six. Looking at their timestamps, either Addey only decided to start taking pictures two months ago or that's when he bought the phone.

A few photos were simply scenery and sunsets. One was a close-up of an old man pulling a handcart with a pair of goats following behind him. Edmund thumbed past most of these, feeling they were uninteresting, and of absolutely no use in helping to understand why Addey was comatose.

The last six photos, and one video, were taken on the same night. Edmund paused at each one, trying to study for hints that probably weren't there. Most were too dark to make out, but he'd snapped a shot at the mountainside, a thicket of brush and dead, skeletal trees. The problem with taking pictures outside in the dark was that there was nothing for the flash to bounce from, so there were very few details.

Another picture showed an old, overgrown train track, the metal so rusted that it blended in with the gravel floor. Was it a tunnel? A few of the pictures were of green buildings, painted to match the trees and forest floor. Men were walking around, and although Edmund couldn't be sure, he thought he saw one brandishing a rifle. Poland was home to many animals—roe deer, wild boar—and hunters probably weren't so rare.

The last photo was the oddest of the bunch, and was taken with a blurry table in the foreground, as if he'd been crouching behind it when he snapped the picture. Edmund pinched the screen to zoom in on various parts, noticing strange things like a row of microscopes, a man wearing a hazmat suit, and a bank of computer monitors. This reminded him of the biology department back at King's Cross.

Edmund didn't understand any of it, and he didn't care once he swiped over to the video. It intrigued him before it even began because the info along the bottom claimed that it ran for a staggering two hours and twelve minutes.

He watched it. The first six minutes, anyway, because after that there wasn't much to see. And when Bill and Sophie knocked on his door an hour later, then worriedly let themselves in, he was still sitting there watching it, pulling the timeline back to the beginning and letting it play until there was no more. And when Sophie and Bill sat down beside him, the three watched together, and had more questions than ever before.

***

It started with Addey running through the woods in the dark.

The three Americans huddling around the tiny screen could tell that it had been frigid that night, and that a storm was settled directly over Addey. He held the camera up, and it made Edmund dizzy to watch the choppy footage as his friend panted, running at a full gait toward a hill covered in skeletal, frosted brush.

"What's that noise?" asked Sophie.

"Shhh," Edmund said. "Watch."

Addey was yelling something in Polish, his voice heartbreakingly rough. He sounded sick, sad, hurt, all of the things that made Edmund's worry surge. Still, Addey ran, the camera so shaky that just about anything could be in front of the lens.

"Dziadek babcia! Dziadek babcia!" he kept repeating. He was near the top of the hill, and as the trees began to thin, the three watching could see it . . .

As fast as a bullet, as silent as a whisper, through the mesh of trees, hurtled the train. It seemed normal, albeit old fashioned, like those trains back in America that took kids on the *Polar Express* tours through the Appalachian Mountains, but something about this one didn't look right. When it moved, it left smoky contrails in its wake, as if it were a giant loaf of bread straight from the oven. The video was too grainy, too shaky to make out details, but it was undeniably a train.

As Addey made it to the top of the hill, the train's whistle screamed, a thick blanket of steam heading skyward, and he stopped in his tracks—because the train was doing the same thing. For a split second, the camera swept across it, revealing so many cars that it would be impossible to count, but then settled on the engine. That's when the three Americans watching the video—and Addey—saw a man hop down into the dusting of snow and turn his eyes toward the one filming.

Edmund could sense Addey's hand start to shake, could feel his own shaking knowing that this was the very phone that had captured the sight of the conductor stepping off. For a moment the man stood there, a span of fifty feet away, eyes that couldn't be seen yet boring down on Addey just the same. He was holding something in his hand, but it was hard to see so far off with so much shaking.

Then, the figure was rushing to Addey.

Sophie made a gasp and put hands over her mouth. Addey screamed something in Polish, then turned to run. The camera was shaking as he headed past the train—he ran alongside it for just a moment, long enough to film a few outstretched hands, and then he was veering off to the right, back into the forest. Addey ran for another thirty seconds and then the phone clattered to the ground. The camera was still facing up, filming the snow. If not for the heavy wind, it would've covered the lens. Addey screamed out once, but it was far off, meaning he didn't collapse alongside his phone, just as the nurse had said.

"Is that all of it?" asked Bill.

"I've watched an hour of it, but it just films the sky," said Edmund. "I guess until either the memory was full or the battery died."

They let it play, saying nothing, just listening to the sounds of the woods. There was some sort of chatter in the distance, but that could be anything. None of them knew specifically where this was filmed. For all Edmund knew, an entire city could be just behind the mountain. More than once it sounded like someone stepped in the grass close to the phone, lingered a moment, then started walking off.

"I want to go here, guys," said Edmund, watching as the snowflakes continued to fall around the camera. He didn't see Sophie or Bill look at each other, but knew they wanted to go, as well.

"We can call the car rental place, pay for an extension, then head on over today," said Bill.

"I'd like that," Edmund said. He was about to mention the men he'd met at the gas station last night when a figure suddenly appeared onscreen, looking very much like a giant from the camera's position on the ground. He lingered only for a moment, but it was enough to startle the three sitting there, and Edmund quickly scrubbed the video back.

"Who is he?" asked Bill.

It was a large man, his face in the shadows. By the shape of the hat, Edmund was sure it was the conductor, the man who'd stepped off the train and started to chase Addey. He didn't see the camera, probably wouldn't even know what such a device was because Edmund was fairly certain Addey's cell had just captured a ghost.

"He's SS," said Bill. "Look at his collar and his armband." He scrubbed the video back a third time and hit pause, just as the brute came into frame, and sure enough saw the SS pin on his collar and the Swastika on his arm.

"What's he holding?" asked Sophie. Now it was her turn to move the video back. They'd watched this man's three-second step-in and step-out of frame at least ten times.

"A club," said Edmund. "Blackjack, rather. They carried them and beat the prisoners who got out of line."

"It doesn't look like a club," said Sophie. "The bottom is . . . weird."

Bill managed to pause it just right so that when the man was about to walk out of frame, he lifted the weapon at an angle that let them study it a little better.

"I know what that is," said Edmund. "When dad worked at Trans Continental Railways back in Lynchburg, he'd help uncouple the cars. You know, the really old coal and gravel cars that were falling apart. Anyway, dad used one of those things to break the rust before grabbing hold of the lugs."

"What's it called?" asked Sophie.

"He always called it an alligator wrench."

***

Later that afternoon, they paid Eliasz for an additional day because of his hospitality, and he thanked them by preparing a lunch that looked like beans but smelled like bacon. He was a very gracious host while they'd been staying, and Edmund hoped that the rest of

Poland was as accommodating, especially since they'd need another bed and breakfast later tonight.

As the temperature dropped and the sun started to weaken, they put Warsaw to their taillights and headed east. Most of Poland's countryside existed in fits and starts—rolling fields and windmill farms in one moment and traffic jams the next. If not for their GPS, Sophie probably would've gotten them lost because all of the names on the signs looked the same. Many were written so small that Edmund could barely see them because so many letters—ungodly long words—were scribbled on the metal.

"So I had a little convo with Eliasz while you boys were loading up," said Sophie. "I asked him about the Ghost Train."

"Oh yeah?" said Edmund, eating his to-go bag of weird bacon-smelling beans.

"Said his sister's neighbor's son went missing in the eighties. They blame it on the train."

Edmund said, "Seems a lot of people have gone missing over the years. The superstitious ones always blame the train."

"Then the naysayers should watch Addey's video," said Bill.

Sophie shook her head. "People would still disbelieve it. I mean, how do we know that's what it was? It looked like a normal train, didn't it? Aren't ghosts supposed to be, I dunno, white and see-through?"

"You've seen too many cartoons," said Edmund, although he didn't really have a counter argument. How did that old rule go? The one used to explain away strange occurrences? The most logical, simplest reason was usually the correct one. Maybe it was a real train. Maybe there were no ghosts. Maybe the man with the alligator wrench was just a lunatic who terrorized the Polish countryside.

But that didn't account for how the train could come and go. It was many cars long, as evidenced in Addey's video, so where could such a long, snaking, physical thing like that hide? There were so many questions at the moment, and Edmund didn't feel like confronting any of them until he could see the spot where Addey had fallen.

"How did Addey's dad know that he was chasing the . . . what did they call it? The Special Train?" asked Bill.

"Sonderzüge," Edmund said. "He must have told them before he left. Addey probably planned to be gone for a few days." Then, Edmund's mind changed gears and he thought of the video. "He was so frantic when he was chasing the train. Why? If any of us saw a ghost, we wouldn't be screaming at it, running headlong toward it. At best, we'd observe it quietly, and film, hoping we weren't noticed."

"Maybe he was excited," said Sophie. "Ghost hunters live for that sort of thing, right?"

Edmund nodded. "We do. But he wasn't excited. He sounded . . . I don't know. Almost sad. Pleading, like he saw something else, someone—"

"Like someone he knew," said Bill. "Shit, Ed, what was he saying in the video. Pull it up?"

Addey wasn't good at making smart passwords, and although Edmund knew he was violating his friend's personal data, it was justified because it might net clues as to why Addey was currently in a clinic.

On screen, Addey was running through the woods again. Sophie turned the radio off so the whole car would be filled with the nonsensical man as he chased after the train. Dziadek babcia! Dziadek babcia! he said as he neared the top of the hill. Sophie slid Bill her phone so that he could translate while she kept her eyes on the road.

Edmund kept repeating the video so that Bill could more accurately type. It was an odd word, and probably didn't sound anything that resembled its spelling. Bill found a spot in the recording where Addey's words weren't drowned out by the rushing wind, his breath, or the train, and held Sophie's phone up so that the microphone could directly hear.

"Ah, it starts with a D," said Bill, seeing Sophie's phone magically type the text onto the screen.

"What's it mean?' asked Sophie.

"It means grandpa, grandma. He's calling out for his grandparents over and over."

"Addey went back to Poland during high school because of his grandparents," said Edmund. "I never got the full story. But something had happened to them."

Sophie and Bill looked at each other, then he stared back at Edmund and said, "Could it be that they went missing?"

Edmund just dropped his head to his lap and shook it, not knowing. “It’s possible.”

Edmund had just finished telling them about his odd run-in with the British private investigators when their Fiat pulled into a city called Wyszków—the very home of the two missing people as told by the current polish newspapers.

Wyszków was a large city, from what they saw on the EarthTrotter app, but they were skirting the southern edge of it as they headed east. They had a late lunch in a small diner filled with working-class people—farmers and the like—and watched out the window as two men swept the steps leading up to a synagogue.

“I read a story about this place,” said Edmund, meaning Wyszków. “Did you know that when the Germans rolled through here during the war, they bulldozed all the Jewish graveyards, and then used the headstones to pave some of the paths in the death camps?”

“What?” asked Sophie, turning her nose up at the idea. “No way that happened. Where did you hear that?”

“From Addey. What the Germans did here is quite engrained in all the people.”

Bill looked at his girlfriend with thoughtful eyes. "You live in such a bubble, babe. The world has always been a cold, cold place."

"Yeah," she said, conceding the point. "I suppose it has."

"The key, Edmund," said Bill. "That's where Addey stayed, right?"

Edmund nodded. "It's where we're going to stay tonight, too, as long as they're still offering rooms."

The beauty—and curse—of running a bed and breakfast was that days of operation could be lucrative, so a BnB that was open one day, might decide to close down for a week, with no warning or reasons given. One of the last things Addey had mentioned when the ghost hunting was still on their to-do list was stay at a BnB that was close to Treblinka.

As the sun began to set behind them, a chill ran through their cramped car as it headed toward the eastern edge of Poland. They followed the rail line, both new and old, the highway set up close to mimic the same pathways. Unlike the rest of the world, this place hadn't grown up much since the fledgling days of the railway. Much of

Poland was encompassed by wide, open fields and thick clusters of forest, with the occasional road cutting a swath across the countryside.

The Bug River snaked sloppily out their left-side windows, the steam coming off the water making Edmund shiver. They passed through several, unremarkable and nearly indistinguishable towns on their trip eastward. None of them could make sense of the names, but Edmund had been following his phone's GPS to a town named Ozelki, a tiny hamlet just west of Poniatowo. And from there, less than a mile south to Treblinka.

"I thought the town was to the north of Poniatowo," said Bill, looking at his own phone. "This doesn't make sense."

Edmund shook his head. "The camp was named after the town, which was close by. The actual camp is a few miles south of it. Remember, the Nazis were hiding their crimes. They didn't build the camp in a town. They built it in the woods, away from people."

"How did they get trains into the woods?" asked Sophie.

Edmund said, "They built spur lines off the main track." He pointed out the window, to where the Bug River ran alongside the train tracks cutting a silvery line east to west. "See that? That's part of the original line. That's the very route the trains from Warsaw took when they came to Treblinka. They left heading east just like us, stopped at a station to the north of us, and then headed south.

"Can you imagine it?" Edmund continued, thinking back to a more horrible time. "Loading up in the middle of the night in the ghetto, maybe your family goes into the same car as you and maybe they don't. The ride took about four days. No food, no water. Half of them feverish with typhus."

"How could people do that?" Sophie asked, shaking her head. "I don't mean the Nazis. How could the people willingly get into those trains knowing what awaited them?"

"They *didn't* know," said Bill.

"That's right," Edmund said. "They were promised things. They were told they were being relocated, to better conditions and opportunities, to places where they could work and earn money. Families loaded up with all their belongings because they were fed a lie."

"Why did the trip take four days?" Bill asked. "Trains are fast, right? We made this trip in one evening."

Edmund shook his head. "Because they had to bypass other, legitimate trains. There was a lot of waiting, stalling on the tracks so that real trains could pass. And then, when it was clear, they left the main line and headed right down the spur and into the hidden camp."

"Is the spur still there?" asked Sophie.

"Nope. All train tracks leading to death camps were dismantled. At the Treblinka Memorial there are symbolic rail ties of stone where the spur used to—hey, turn here!" He'd been following the GPS and off a wide, dirt road sat the sleepy town of Ozelki.

The streets were lined with white-roofed cottages and telephone poles tipped with weird glass insulators. Each time they ventured further into the wilds of Poland it was like taking a step back in time. Edmund checked his phone—it barely had service, although he was certain their BnB would offer Wi-Fi, as did every place in the world these days.

A large, Catholic church dominated the western part of the town, sitting slightly elevated on a blanket of dead grass and dandelion stems. The only way the passing car saw it was because of the numerous flickering tealights along the steps and in the windowsills.

"Not many people out," said Sophie, leaning forward to see the road now that most of the streetlights were out.

"Everyone here is in the farming trade," said Bill, coincidentally as they passed a wagon laden with bales of hay. "Early to bed, early to rise, and all that jazz . . ."

He was right about all of that, thought Edmund, but it still didn't alleviate the feeling that they were in a world that felt removed. Edmund was used to cities, even smaller ones like Salisbury and Lynchburg, and the absolute lack of people was foreign and alien to him. This isolation made a slight panic well up inside him, for how easily was it to get emergency services way out here? He didn't like to think of having a heart attack, flipping the car, or anything worse than that, so far from civilization.

"That's it," said Edmund pushing through to the front seat. He pointed to the structure up on a hill overlooking Ozelki. "Krakus House."

The Fiat pulled up to a spacious, yet empty lot. Krakus House looked very much out of place in Poland, although the three young adults didn't realize it. Krakus House was modeled after the stave churches wherever Norsemen built. It was wide, made of thick, indelible wood so sturdy that a bomb wouldn't move the structure one inch. There were three floors, the windows wide enough to drive their car right through. On the top, a sharply pointed roof that looked more show than function.

Edmund was the first out of the car, gazing up at the place with wide, wonderous eyes. Even in a land he'd never been, this BnB was something to behold. Clearly, it had been around for ages, most likely the ancestral home passed on and on, like the businesses back home.

"It doesn't look like anything around here," said Bill, likewise taking in the grandeur. "Ed, how expensive is this place?"

He shook his head, broken from the reverie. "Not too expensive if Addey stayed here. This was going to be our base of operations for the ghost hunt."

Sophie and Bill just looked at each other and Edmund, for the first time, wondered just how long they were going to allow him to hijack their vacation. A part of him still felt bad, but he wanted answers. After all, Sophie was the one who suggested they continue the ghost hunt. Once Edmund had enough answers to clear his head, they'd leave this cold place and do what they could to stay in touch with Addey's nursing home.

As they stepped upon the wide, wrap around porch, the snow began to gently fall. The windshield of the car was already gathering a dusting when Edmund looked above the door and read, what he assumed was *Krakus House*, in Polish. Above that was the wooden relief depicting a rather valiant looking man who reminded Edmund of Lancelot from the Arthurian legends. This knight held a sword above his head, as if ready to strike down a ferocious beast. Sophie and Bill, both chilled to the bone, paid it little mind and entered the foyer.

The floorplan was large and open and reminded Edmund of some medieval mead hall. The tables and chairs were made of thick wood to compliment the structure. Long, rectangular chandeliers hung low enough to light the candles. Two fireplaces raged in opposite corners, although contemporary heating must have kept the place so warm. A massive staircase climbed straight up the middle, tapering off at the sides to become a landing across the whole room.

Above that, a third-floor balcony encircled the foyer. It was eerily quiet, but a shuffling over by the counter drew their attention the moment they entered through the door.

In true mead hall fashion, there was a long bar that ran the length of the common room. And just like the rest of Krakus House, the wood looked as if it had been lifted into place by giants. A thin, pale girl with long blond hair pulled into a braid put her hands on the counter and surveyed the three newcomers with warm, but curious eyes. If Edmund had to guess, he figured she was about their age, but he couldn't be sure. Something about how Europeans dressed and wore their clothes made him very disoriented to such things.

"Hi," said Edmund approaching the girl. "Could you tell us if a guy stayed here about a month ago by the name of Adlai Chobot?"

She just stared at him for a moment, as if not comprehending. But then again, that had been the case all over Poland thus far. Edmund had pulled up the photos app on his phone and was swiping through to find one of his dear friend when the girl spoke.

"I remember him," she said with only the slightest pinch of a Polish accent. The girl subtly looked over her shoulder, and that was the first time they noticed the old woman sitting in a wheelchair, watching a small television on the counter. A thick, wool blanket was wrapped tightly around her shoulders and Edmund couldn't tell if she were sleeping or held the rigidity of a stroke survivor.

The girl continued. "He stayed for two days. Went out the third night, and he didn't come back."

"Did he leave anything?" asked Sophie.

The girl nodded, once again looking back at the oblivious woman. "He had a few changes of clothes, but nothing valuable. It's our policy to give to Caritis Charity after two weeks if it's not claimed. By then, we didn't know that he'd gone missing. That he'd gone up—"

"Lena?" called the coarse voice of the woman in the wheelchair. Edmund looked past the girl at the counter to the old lady to see her turned in the direction of the voices, head looking unstable atop her shoulders.

Lena looked back to the old woman and the two shared a conversation in Polish. Edmund had no idea what they were talking about, but the younger girl seemed somewhat perturbed. As the old woman seemed to give

Lena a zinger to end the conversation, she turned back to the television, eyes heavy.

"Sorry," said Lena. "Do you need a room?"

Bill could tell that Edmund was similarly perturbed by having the questioning take such a turn, so he stepped in and said, "Two rooms, actually." Edmund fixed him with confused, irritated eyes but Bill just shook his head.

"Second floor. You can have rooms two and three," she said, a little more urgently than was probably needed.

"Someone else staying here?" asked Sophie. "I didn't see any cars out front."

Lena said, "No. We've misplaced the key to the first room and just aren't renting it out right now." Edmund didn't know how to tell her that he had the missing room key in his pocket. He'd probably just leave it on the counter when they checked out for good.

As the three were standing back out in the cold, in the moderate snowfall, Edmund asked his friend why he didn't let the conversation continue.

"That old lady didn't like her talking about it," said Bill. "You're going to have to get the girl alone to ask."

Edmund just nodded.

Their rooms were large, most likely used to accommodate families rather than the odd college-aged student who was tramping across Europe. On the second floor, they had bathrooms in both corners, but with only two rooms occupied, that hardly mattered. The darkness and snow afforded little view, but there was life in the town, as evidenced by the scant glow of a light, like demon eyes scattered across the land.

Later, Lena cooked them all dinner—venison with potatoes prepared with olives in a way Edmund had never seen before. They ate wordlessly because the room was so massive, so reverent, that it seemed almost sacrilegious to break the silence with idle chit-chat. When Edmund took his seat, he noticed that the old woman had moved on, but he couldn't tell where.

Lena was about to disappear into the kitchen, but Edmund stood up and approached the bar. The girl looked like a deer caught in headlights, as if she wanted to run off but was too transfixed on the approaching danger instead. Still, she offered a placated smile that was probably rehearsed for potential guests.

"Can I ask a little more about Addey?"

"Addey?"

"Adlai. Chobot. Can you tell me anything else about what happened?"

She thought for a moment and said, "I told the police everything."

"The police were involved? How?"

"Because he was unresponsive and they expected . . . how do you say it? Foul play? They came here and asked questions, but my grandmother dealt with them. I was working in the cellar."

Edmund looked at his friends before he turned to Lena and said, "What can you tell me about the Ghost Train?"

Her face went pale as she surveyed the Americans. Edmund couldn't tell if she wanted to yell at them, cry, or ask them to leave. She was fighting some internal battle as she breathed a deep sigh, and then said, "If you're here to chase the train, please don't."

"What? Why?" Edmund asked.

"Your friend got lucky," she said unexpectedly. "He's alive."

“He’s in a coma,” Edmund clarified.

“But he’s alive. That’s more than can be said about those who went looking for the train.”

“Please, do you know the spot where my friend was found?” Edmund asked, voice pleading.

“Go home, American. Please.” She turned and started to walk off.

“Hey!” he shouted, so loud that Sophie made an audible gasp. Lena quickly whirled back around, green eyes wide. “I have come all the way across the Atlantic to see my friend. He’s in a coma and the only thing I know is that he went looking for his grandparents on that train. His parents were no help and you are most likely the only person left who can keep this from becoming a dead end. So please. If you can help me with any of this, I would be forever grateful. Just tell me where he was found, so I can see the place for myself.”

Lena looked at him with sad eyes for a moment, and just when they thought she was going to open up, to tell them all of how the man called Addey was found in the woods, she simply shook her head. “I can’t.” And then, she slid back a partition leading into the kitchen and shut it behind her.

Edmund banged his fist so hard on the counter that the silverware shook. He was angrier than he'd ever been in his life and the irrational part of him wanted to hop the bar and chase after her. Visions of the old woman brandishing a shotgun kept his feet on the floor, and a more rational notion swept over him. He would wait, try again later. How could he leave Poland without answers? His friends looked stoic behind him, Sophie, spearing potatoes quietly with her fork and Bill giving him the pursed lips look that said, *You should know better than this, buddy*.

"Ed, we'll go to Treblinka in the morning, okay?" said Bill. "Maybe we'll find some answers there."

He just nodded and said goodnight, storming up the steps and into his bedroom without another word. Part of him wanted to punch the walls, but he knew that the sturdy Krakus House would win that fight and he'd be no closer to finding out what happened to Addey. It would be smart to stay in the proprietors' good graces.

Later that night, and slightly unnerved by the silence, Edmund got up and went to the bathroom. The room below was still, but he could hear the faint sound of the small television behind the bar. Their mess had been cleaned up on the table. As Edmund sat on the toilet he thumbed through his list of messages—his girlfriend, his dad and little sister. He sent placating replies to them all, the expected notes that he was having fun, wished they were here, blah, blah, blah.

He was still looking at his phone when he opened the bathroom door to walk out and there in his path stood the old woman, looking positively spectral, almost like a ghost herself. Her hair was as white as the snow piling on the windowsills and one eye matched, turned to the ground and filled with milk. Stroke evidence was clearer upon closer inspection, as the right side of her face hung loose, like a latex Halloween mask trying to fit over too small a head. But the one eye was piercing green, so if Edmund thought she was invalid, that she was unaware of the world and her surroundings, that notion was quickly squashed as she zeroed in on him.

“Towel,” she said in a rough voice. It took him a moment to understand what she meant until he looked down and saw a stack of neatly folded towels in her outstretched arms.

It was also the first time he really noticed that she was standing—that she wasn't wheelchair bound—and that she'd trudged up the steps to make the delivery. Edmund simply took them from her and then, without even a curt nod, she turned on her heels and walked off with far less trouble than he would have ever guessed.

"You speak English?" he called after her, just as she placed a shaky hand upon the railing to go down the steps.

She half-turned, fixed him with her good eye, and said, "perhaps," before disappearing.

***

After breakfast the next morning, their Fiat was navigating east and they quickly entered the town of Poniatowo. From there they headed south, into a lightly wooded area where traffic was stalled by large work trucks. Most of the vehicles on this highway ran straight into Belarus, but the new world and the old crossed paths as farmers, sometimes pulling carts by horse, slowed all lanes to a crawl.

Like most everything they'd seen outside of Warsaw, this part of Poland was equal parts large, open farmland and thick, dense forest. The road grew progressively worse the further south they got, but the scenery improved. Last night's snow was still on the ground, but it was also in the skeletal branches of the chestnut trees that lined the road.

Out in the fields were several small fires where farmers were burning dried potato vines. Occasionally white-thatched cottages broke the monotony, and out here old, Catholic churches outnumbered the synagogues.

Edmund had seen many photos of the modern-day memorial, so when the car passed beneath a stone arch and onto a dirt path that looked like a logging road, he knew they were close. The forest sprouted up again, the same forest that was used to conceal the Nazis' crimes almost eighty years ago. Sophie pulled the car over at a small building at the edge of the memorial grounds.

Despite last night's snow, the air wasn't chilly. Edmund shed his jacket and pulled out his phone to take photos. He didn't think they would find much evidence here to support what happened to Addey, but it was still a once-in-a-lifetime visit. Not every day did you see the place where almost a million people were exterminated.

They walked the path in silence, in awe by the serenity of the forest. This place was probably just as calm and quiet back then because the Nazis worked hard to keep the site hidden, and in order to do that, they had to maintain order.

Past another building and a parking lot was the sign that read Treblinka. Beneath it, carved into the rock, was a map of the camp as it existed in the 40s. The camp was large, spanning around twenty-two acres, and now massive, stone pillars marked the boundaries of the once secretive place.

"Do you see those?" asked Edmund pointing to a series of stone rectangles leading off toward the memorial.

Sophie said, "They look like . . ."

"Railroad ties," finished Bill. "Symbolic."

"Right," said Edmund. "It's part of the spur line. They lead right up to where the train station sat, where the Germans unloaded their prisoners to be rushed straight to the gas chambers."

They followed the symbolic track up to a stone platform, noting the quiet and solitude of the memorial. It reminded Edmund of his trip to Washington D.C., and how despite the Lincoln Memorial being crowded with hundreds of people, a calm hush fell across the building. But here, they were the only ones out—the memorial didn't even seem to be open.

"Imagine it," said Edmund, stepping up to the stone platform. "You're in a train and you've been stuck for three or four days. Finally, you come into the forest and the trees are close enough to grab through the windows. You stop here, at a train station. All is well because it looks like a *real* station. There's a board showing all the stops the train makes after this one!"

"Wait, they made up a fake list of train stops?" asked Sophie, always in such disbelief.

Edmund nodded. "They even had a fake wall clock. It was painted on the wood. Anyway, Jews got off and were greeted by doctors. But the awful thing is that there *were no doctors*. Treblinka didn't have any medical facilities. It was all to keep order."

He turned around, started walking into the woods where Sophie and Bill followed behind.

"They used this path," he said, pointing to a graveled road that was lined with little headstones bearing names. "The SS called this the 'road to heaven' because it led straight to the gas chambers. Men and women were brought here for undressing." He pointed to the right and then the left.

Toward the middle of the camp was the largest memorial structure. It was a stone around twenty-five feet high with a Menorah carved into the top. Along the center was a crack running the entire length which belied the artist's intent and appeared broken. Around the giant stone was a sea of smaller, jagged rocks, each with a name written on it. Edmund had read that there were close to twenty-thousand of them, and each was inscribed with Jewish villages and communities in Poland that were obliterated by the Nazis. One stone stood out, much larger, as if overseeing the rest, like a protective mother. This one belonged to Warsaw, where the Germans nearly wiped the Jewish culture from the map.

"That's where the gas chambers sat," said Edmund, pointing up to the massive stone memorial. Sophie and Bill quietly followed behind, holding hands and listening to the history lesson that Edmund had researched in great detail.

"The Jews would come up the path, naked, and then were told they were getting a shower before moving on. But they were packed into the chambers so tightly that after they were all dead, they still stood upright until the

Germans carried them out. It's even said that some people would release their last breath after being moved."

"Cyanide?" Sophie asked, wincing. "I remember reading that in school. They used the same chemical that our country used in prison gas chambers."

Edmund shook his head. "Some of the work camps that were converted into death camps used cyanide, but not Treblinka. This place had all of German ingenuity behind it. When it was built, it was built for one purpose: to kill Jews efficiently. They learned from all the other camps. So the gas chambers didn't use cyanide which was expensive and dangerous to transport. They used exhaust from giant diesel engines.

"And over there is where they piled the bodies." He pointed to the large ditches, simulated firepits where the Germans burned the corpses in troves. Now, the memorial had 'mock pyres' with fake bodies wrapped in swaddling to represent humans.

Sophie said, "I'm still amazed that such a thing could happen. How the Germans could trick so many people to march unknowingly to their deaths."

"Wouldn't you do whatever it took for your family to have a better life?" asked Edmund. "If your sister needed a life-saving operation and the only way she could get it was for you to commit to living in Russia for a year to pay it off? Would you do that?"

She silently nodded.

"That's the position all these people were in. They were promised a better life. It wasn't ideal, but people chased those trains. They wanted to ride because—" Edmund's voice trailed off when he remembered the paper from the gas station.

People followed the Ghost Train.

"Ed?" said Bill. "Ya alright, bud?"

He just nodded. "Sorry, lost my train of thought. Anyway, let's look around, shall we?"

The rest of the afternoon was filled looking over the various memorials spread across the seven-acre viewable area of the camp. Edmund tried to imagine it—imagine the pure evil that lived in wooden shacks while the indentured workers slept in cold bunkhouses. For every stone in Treblinka, there was a name scribbled upon it. Much of what the public learned of the camp was from survivor stories, and those only totaled sixty-seven. The Germans were quick to tear down the camp to hide their crimes, but the Soviets couldn't help but find human remains in the pyres' pits. Human teeth, jawbones. It was hard to make so many deaths simply vanish.

After their visit, they walked past the car and up the dirt path, through the arch and near the main road where large work trucks still trundled by. There were tracks, but Edmund wasn't sure if they were the original ones that brought the train near the camp before running off the spur line. Although they didn't realize it, they were standing in the same spot where, almost eighty years ago, a small child touched a supernatural being, sending it into a panic and rushing back to its lair.

Edmund looked over into the woods, where the hill shot up with jagged rocks and a clean, albeit rough, path. Had he thought to walk twenty yards up the hill, he'd find, half buried in dirt, a railroad spike that should have been removed eighty years ago . . .

Treblinka

January 6th, 1943

Otto Herzog was a much worse man than Klaus Wagner had ever been. Both were among the first to arrive in Poland on that oddly chilly September morning four years ago but while Klaus was busy fulfilling his whoring and drinking vices, Otto was learning the enemy. He was watching them, listening to their pleas, understanding how they saw their overseers. And when the time came to drop the axe, Otto was one of the first to lend his aggression. The Entity knew an uprising was brewing in Warsaw—he was privy to the human spirit of rebellion—but if Otto were still there, in command, those unwashed animals in the ghetto would be too afraid to start trouble.

No matter. It was all coming to an end. War, strife, death, the camps. All of it. What the Entity needed to do now was become a bear, and store what he could for the long, horrendous winter. Unfortunately his stores were no more.

Otto had killed all of them with very little coaxing. After the first train, he emerged bloodied and downtrodden, hysteria running down the trainset like a virus. He'd killed before, but this was different. Even the Entity knew it wasn't the same, but he didn't care. This was food—and after that first car fed him, he couldn't wait for the rest to follow.

"They're not even fighting back," said Otto to himself. "Not a single one raised a hand to stop me." The alligator wrench was steadily dripping blood onto the tunnel floor.

Because every man, woman, and child accept fate for what it is. Just as you do.

"I suppose," he said, in a singsong voice.

Back to work.

It took all day to kill so many. Otto rested quite a bit because bringing down an alligator wrench on a skull was hard work, sometimes because it got wedged in squishy membrane and he had to put a boot on their shoulder to wrestle it free. But Otto also needed rest because, despite the Entity's influence, he still had reservations about such systematic killing.

Your people have been doing this for a year, the Entity whispered into his mind.

“The train was supposed to go to the camp,” he said, not for the first time. This was the loop in which his brain was stuck.

And they would’ve already been dead. You have done worse than this.

“I have,” said Otto, flicking the blood off his wrench as he stepped into the next cart. He slid the door shut in order to keep the killing contained. “There were those children in Munich.”

That’s right, the Munich children. So this should be no problem at all.

Otto, fresh out of Wehrmacht, was stationed in Munich at a fuel depot. One day a pair of children who lived in a house just up the road came looking for their mother. Every soldier in the depot knew Agnes Seiden, the vixen of Brower Street. She danced at a local pub and gained notoriety. Since she lived so close, she often ventured to the depot in hopes of subsidizing her nightlife with a little coin on the side. The soldiers often took her up on this offer, taking turns with her in a supply building just a few feet from the depot.

One day, she came down the road after a morning of drinking, insisted on seeing her favorite soldier, then proceeded to vandalize the depot when she was told he wasn't there. It happened at the worst possible time—when word came down that a field officer was on his way to inspect the depot. Not about to let some harlot be their undoing, the soldiers dragged her to the supply closet and tied her up until the visit was over. Unfortunately, she fell out of her chair, still bound, and asphyxiated. Otto was helping to drag her out and down to the river—

—when the children happened by. He looked at the other soldier who was helping move the body, then to the dirty kids. And then, without even thinking, drew his gun and shot them both dead. He'd never batted an eye over that, nor did the other soldier. They simply gathered up all three and dumped them into the river. No one ever mentioned it again.

"I guess I'm a very bad man," said Otto, jumping out of the dead train, wiping his sleeve across his bloody face.

That you are. But there is strength in being bad. Bad is the rightful state of the world. Goodness merely passes through.

That thought was probably too profound for Otto, but it worked. He went back to killing, bashing skulls, shoving bodies aside, cleaning blood from his eyes. The Entity simply followed behind, letting the sweet smell of death permeate in the air before sucking it all in.

For two days Otto killed, in the end racking up a death bill, while not as impressive as the commanders in the death camps, was still noteworthy. The Entity had consumed over four-thousand lives in just forty-eight hours and still he was hungry. It would have to do for now. Otto was covered in blood, and the man had been pushed so far beyond his natural limit that the Entity didn't think he would be of much service now. Still, he would find a job for him before the end.

Drifting further into the lair, the Entity discovered a series of rooms that had been widened and supported by whoever laid plans for this place. At first he wasn't interested—there was nothing here to kill, no morsels of life that he could turn into morsels of death. He was just about to float away when the far room caught his eye, and in it, a glimmer of hope. Most of it was smashed beyond repair—a few empty vials here, a microscope there. This place had potential. It was hidden and forgotten, and with that in mind, the Entity began to plan.

We have more work to do, he told Otto who had seated himself back in the engine. It was the only clean place left. The bald man nodded and stood.

Bring the wrench.

***

For the next two nights, Otto worked alone, outside the tunnel's entrance. In an agonizingly slow process, he used the wrench to pull up the railroad spikes, then dump them in a bucket. For half a mile—all the way to the junction where the spur line merged with the main line, Otto began to erase all evidence of the track.

If not for finding rats and drinking water from the reservoir in the engine, Otto would've died days ago, for the Entity pushed his body to the limits. Luckily the rails were segmented, and although they were each two meters of solid steel, the burly man used every ounce of his strength to lift them, then drag them into a pile inside the cave. After the tracks, he carried in the wooden ballasts which were equally as heavy and in far greater numbers. He brought in all evidence of track—the fish bolts, the spikes (except for one), the sleeper plates, all of it. And after this work was finished, he used a rake and broom to get rid of the ballast pattern in the dirt that told that a track once cut through the woods and into a cave.

And after all was done and the Entity was sure the place would remain hidden until he could put it to use, he allowed Otto to come back inside and sit in the engine. The man was tired, defeated, his body and mind near broken. Upon a closer look, the man's heart was going to fail in a few days, but the Entity was sure he'd be dead before then. Otto looked through the window, to the track that was no longer there.

"I'm hungry," he said. Two mangy, uncooked rats were not enough to sustain such a large man.

No, you're not.

"No, I'm not," Otto echoed.

The Entity wasn't sure if it was thirst, hunger, too much brain suggestion, or the heart like he'd originally suspected, but Otto died the next day, slumping over the controls as if he were merely sleeping. And as the creature that had existed for millennia sucked out the last bit of death he'd taste for at least a few weeks, he wondered how his plans would ever come to fruition, especially if he were confined to the cave.

It would take time, he thought. *Perhaps I just need to sleep like before. And when I wake up, the world will be sick, and I will be strong.*

It was an inviting thought, but it was also upsetting. He hated to be asleep. He hated to miss the world as it passed by. Although he was infinite, he still didn't like feeling at a disadvantage. Last time he slept, he missed the advent of penicillin, and that caused problems for a being who thought he understood the human body's failings.

He drifted out to the mouth of the cave. The sun was coming up. A train was headed to the camp, no doubt the tenth or so to arrive at Treblinka since he'd decided to bring this one back to his lair. He would wait, and grow weaker, but he would wait. And one day, he'd see death wash across the Earth in a way the man in Berlin never thought possible.

Poniatowo

January 10th, 2019

The evening of the day they'd investigated a mere half-mile from the Entity's lair, the trio of Americans decided they didn't want to have dinner at Krakus House. The food wouldn't be to their liking anywhere this far east in Europe, but the company of the common room had grown somewhat stale. Edmund's insistence on knowing about the Ghost Train, or at least the location of where Addey was found, presented an odd barrier between Lena and the rest of the group, as if she were afraid that her grandmother would kick her out onto the snowy streets. The old woman on the other hand, was creepy without even trying to be—and oddly mobile for someone who sat in a wheelchair and watched black and white reruns of some old Polish sitcom. So the group decided that they would venture to the closest town to find food, which turned out to be Poniatowo, a half mile east.

Poniatowo was a small town, like all the rest, but this one had the distinction of being thrown up along the 627, a major highway throughout eastern Poland. On the other side to the south, the beginnings of the dense forest that hid Treblinka. Most of Poniatowo was burned to the ground when the Germans were fleeing and covering their tracks as the Soviets pressed from the east, so the town lacked the 'old as the hills' facades featured in most of the architecture in Poland. All of the properties were fenced in with neat wrought iron or treated wood, and almost every business was right along the poorly maintained, but paved road.

There were no parking places on the main road, so they pulled off in the mud about two-hundred feet from the small huddle of businesses and walked to the only restaurant they could find via their internet searches. It was a two-story eatery simply called the Palace, although its Polish name was written above that on the swinging oak placard over the door.

A van was straddling the sidewalk just beside the front doors of the Palace, the words Polsat-Vega in faded letters on the side. Inside the restaurant they were treated to an establishment much larger than they would have guessed from the outside, but then again, most of the properties here seemed to favor narrow storefronts but deep buildings, much like the single houses back home in Charleston.

As soon as they entered, the smell of seafood made Edmund's stomach grumble. He wasn't much of a fish eater, but he could eat endless shrimp from Red Lobster all day, and often did on his birthday when his mom and dad took him out. But the wonderful aroma of shrimp, coupled with some eastern spicy flair went unnoticed as they pushed past the trio of men in jackets that matched the logo on the van outside.

One was a reporter, obviously by the microphone he shoved in a seated man's face. The interviewee worked for the Palace, as was evident by the apron and the little castle embroidered on the breast. His hair was greasy and he wore thick glasses—what Edmund's mom would have called 'pop bottle' glasses on account of the lenses being so thick that they magnified the eyes. He was telling a very animated story with his arms over his head, to which the reporter simply nodded while the cameraman and sound tech captured it all.

A hostess escorted them toward the back of a surprisingly busy restaurant, but Edmund lingered behind, listening to the man tell his story. It was all in Polish of course, but the way he told it meant that something big had happened. Then again, this was a one-horse town. Someone could have gotten their wallet stolen at the grocers and the story would dominate the local newspaper for a week.

But as he was about to turn his attention away, to follow his group deeper into the restaurant, he caught a snippet of the seated man's testimony, and out of his mouth came the word Sonderzüge—Special Train. Edmund slowed his gait, turned around and watched. The guy being interviewed locked eyes with him for just a moment, sensing that the story had gained interest from a passerby, but he quickly resumed talking to the microphone. Edmund didn't understand what they were saying so he simply followed his group and seated himself across from Bill.

Edmund thought, for lack of a better term, that he was chasing a ghost. And not in the sense that excited him. This ghost was simply a shadow—something that wasn't there. Sure, there may be a Ghost Train out there, but what business did he have with it now? Addey was alive and accounted for, albeit in a sad state. What could Edmund possibly do but go on and enjoy the rest of the trip? Wouldn't Addey have wanted him to do that?

"You alright, dude?" asked Sophie, looking at him quizzically.

"Yeah," he said. "Say, how about we head out in the morning?"

Bill looked up from his menu as if he didn't hear him correctly. "You sure? We can stay another night or two."

"Nah, there's no sense. Whether we find this train or not, it's not going to make Addey miraculously wake up."

"We can visit him again," said Bill. "We're shooting down to Romania and we'll need to backtrack to Warsaw anyway. Would you like that?"

Edmund nodded.

"Seriously?" asked Sophie.

"What?" Edmund asked.

"You came all this way to hunt the Ghost Train and you're going to just bail like that? Addey would be so disappointed."

"Addey didn't want me to go anywhere near it, remember?"

"True," Sophie conceded, just as their server arrived. "But remember what he said? Something's going on here and no one will talk about it. Maybe you need to be asking questions."

He thought of that for a moment as he mindlessly ordered a plate that he wasn't even sure he'd like. They made small talk again as they waited on the food, with Bill reiterating his desire to propose to Sophie when she trundled off to the bathroom after their drinks arrived. The interview at the front wrapped up only a few minutes after they were seated and the man, a commis waiter by the looks of him, started bussing tables. He and Edmund made eye-contact more than once during his jaunts through the restaurant but the man kept to himself and worked dutifully with his head down. Perhaps the interview did not go well.

They ate the best meal they'd had since arriving in Poland just two days ago. Edmund had Forszmak, a very salty fish garnished with melted cheese and onions. Sophie had a large cut of Baltic salmon, boiled in some sort of lemon and dill sauce, and Bill, not in the mood for seafood tonight, had a dish of Pierogi and venison.

"How is everything?" asked the commis waiter in surprisingly good English. He must have heard their conversation because there would be no reason to assume the three kids were American. Until now he had not been serving them, so perhaps he was only interested in the way Edmund was interested in *him*.

"Fine, thank you," said Sophie.

"Just great," chimed Bill.

"Pull up a seat," said Edmund, garnering strange looks from his companions as well as the waiter. "I'm curious about the interview, is all."

Sophie and Bill continued to fix him with odd stares because this was uncharacteristic and still seemed a strange subject to randomly bring up.

"They'll post it on their website and Polstat will air it but none of them believe me. I'm a joke to them. I'm a joke to everyone I tell."

"You won't be a joke to us," said Edmund. "Please, sit." He used his foot to kick out the one empty seat at their table.

The waiter looked around, as if worried he might get in trouble for skirting his duties, but he wiped his hands on his slacks and took the seat, nonetheless.

"I'm Edmund. Edmund Riley. These are my friends, Sophie and Bill." Both of them politely nodded, but said nothing else.

"Emril," he said. "Emril Jablonski."

"Emril, did your interview have to do with the Ghost Train?"

He nodded. "I saw it, sure as I'm seeing the three of you now."

"When?" asked Bill.

"Four nights ago. When the zoologist went missing."

The three of them exchanged glances, Edmund feeling there was a large part of this story that he didn't know, that Emril was dropping them *in medias res*.

"What zoologist?" asked Sophie.

"It's just now hitting the papers. A guy named Piotr Galin went missing. Big, important professor from the University of Warsaw. No one gave a damn about any of the missing people until someone like him got took, no they didn't."

"Got took?" Edmund asked.

"Yeah, got took. By the damned train. I saw it. Saw it as sure as I'm seeing you right now." He was getting agitated, probably because no one believed him thus far. "You all think I'm joking, don't you? That I'm trying to get my spotlight or somethin'?"

"No, we don't." Edmund pulled out Addey's cellphone and showed Emril the video. The man's eyes lit up and he pulled a cigarette from his pocket and struck up a match, seemingly out of thin air. By the time the video was over—the first seven, action-filled minutes anyway—he had tears streaming down his face.

"I saw it, dammit. I saw it." He shook his head, almost defeated.

"We know," said Edmund. "We believe you. Please, tell us about it. Tell us what you saw."

He settled back into his chair, flicked ashes onto the table and then scooped them into the floor with his hand.

"So the professor was having a late dinner a few nights ago. News said that he'd been visiting a colleague in Belarus so he stopped here on his way back into Warsaw. We weren't busy at all, not with the snow we had that morning.

"I brought the bloke his drink and he says to me that he has a train to catch. But his face is all weird."

"Weird? Weird how?' asked Bill.

"I dunno. Like he isn't aware of anything around him. Like his body is making the noise but his brain isn't there.

"Anyway, I laugh it off because we don't got any trains down this way. They all stop before the Malkinia line. But this fella is insistent—keeps saying he has a train to catch, even though no one else is talking to him.

"Then it gets strange. I bring him out his food and he pays right there. But he doesn't eat it. He just gets up and says 'I hear her! I hear her playing her piano!' and walks right out the door."

"So he just disappeared into the night?' said Edmund, thinking back to the newspaper from the gas station.

"That he did," said Emril, putting out his cigarette on the table's surface. He scooped the ash into the floor and immediately lit up another. "But it doesn't end there. My shift was ending, so I followed the bloke.

“He walks out and turns south, heading right into the woods. Now people always park down by the car lot or up the street by the old soccer pitch, so when someone heads south, there ain’t nothing that way but trees and more trees.”

“Did you try to stop him?” Sophie asked, just as engrossed in the story as the rest.

Emril nodded. “I didn’t touch him, if that’s what ye mean, but I called out for him. He barely acknowledged me. He said his sister was playing the piano on the train and that he was going to listen closer.

“So the bloke takes off running with me running after him. I got the asthma, so I start falling behind. He’s screaming from the top of his lungs ‘Hanna! Hanna! I’m coming, keep playing!’ I keep following him because by now I figure the old fella has either had a stroke or some kind of fit and I’d need to be there for when he eventually collapsed. There’s no phone service out here, anyway.

“And then, that’s when it happened.”

The Americans exchanged glances and that’s when Edmund realized that this was the part of the story that

Emril had no doubt repeated many times over the last four days, the part that no one seemed to believe.

"What happened?" Edmund asked.

"As sure as I'm seeing you right now, I saw the train. I was chasing Piotr, probably twenty or so paces behind, and then it slides right in front of us, the ghostly glow of it lit up the forest! Piotr stopped dead in his tracks. If he was afraid, I couldn't tell. He was still blabbering on about Hanna and her piano.

"The faces . . . oh, God, there were faces everywhere!" he said, voice growing frantic. "I couldn't stay. I couldn't watch. When that train appeared out of thin air, sitting on tracks that weren't there, I fell, got up, then got the hell out of there. I went straight to my car, drove home, and didn't come out of the house the next day." He put his second cigarette out on the table and left the wadded butt there. "I'll never go into those woods again. Not for nothing."

"What do the people around here say about your story?" asked Sophie.

He blew air out of the corner of his mouth and rolled his eyes. "Some believe it. But most don't. His family, all of em's back in Warsaw. They got money, too. I worry I'm going to be linked to this thing. The smarter ones don't seem to believe in ghosts and all that."

Sophie said, "Could be bad, especially since you were the last one to see him alive."

Bill nodded. "And if he turns up dead."

At this, Emril just laughed. "Turns up dead? That's not how the train operates. He was *taken*. And he'll never be seen again, lest it's through the window slats of the train car."

"This isn't the first story like this," said Edmund.

"No, it isn't," said Emril. "They all get promised something, don't they? Just like them Nazis back in the day with their hollow promises. Get on the train, and all you need will be provided. Horseshit." He pulled out another cigarette and stuck it in the corner of his mouth but didn't light it. "Say, why you so interested in this anyway? You're American right? Or Canadian? I can't imagine this story has jumped the pond with enough force to make a ripple."

Edmund briefly told him about Addey and the strangeness surrounding what happened. Emril just nodded and gave a curt chuckle.

"Then I say your friend is the lucky one," he said, mirroring what Lena had said back at Krakus House.

"Could I get your number?" asked Edmund. "In case I can think of anything else to ask about the train. Or Piotr?"

"Sure," he said, then pulled the pencil from behind his ear and scribbled a number on a clean napkin. "But if you have any questions about Piotr, best look up the tip line his family set up. That would tell you more than I could. I only saw the bloke for ten minutes. Last ten minutes of his life, I'm guessing." He gazed down, a morose look in his eyes. The cigarette still wasn't lit, only hanging limply from his lips.

"Thank you. I appreciate you talking to us," said Edmund.

Emril stood, and finally struck up his third smoke. His eyes dug into the three Americans as if he didn't really know what else to say. But it was to Edmund that he directed his warning.

"Don't go looking for this train, fella. Let it be. Whether it calls for you or not, give it a wide berth and you might'n just stay alive."

Edmund just nodded, this advice starting to stack up.

"Who is Hanna?" asked Sophie. It was a tiny tidbit of information Edmund found unimportant but was now curious.

"When I started talking to the news, word got back to Piotr's mum so she gave me a ring the other night. I asked her that same question. Know what she told me? Hanna was Piotr's sister. Girl loved to play the piano. And she played almost every night while Piotr was in the bath and he could hear it through the floorboards and it relaxed him.

"I asked the old lady if there was any reason why he'd think his sister was playing the piano on the train. You'll never guess what she said."

Edmund and his friends just shook their heads.

"She said 'I can't think of any reason why he'd think that. The poor girl has been dead for ten years.'"

***

Early the next morning, Edmund awoke to more snow, another dusting, which was enough to cover the tracks of the car leading up to Krakus House. There was no breakfast, per se, but either Lena or the old woman had left a large basket of fruit on the downstairs table. Edmund didn't want any of it, despite this being one of the few times to have normal, world-standard food. His head was hurting, his brain fuzzy, and he was having trouble understanding what had happened last night.

Emril's story helped to solidify the train, if only a little. There were still so many unknowns, but at least he didn't feel as though it were a wild hunt, that he was back in the *Nun Hunters* and taking pictures of willowisps and streaks of lights that were to pass as ghosts. At least now there was an independent party who at least followed Edmund's train of reasoning.

He wasn't sure why he even came downstairs so early—it wasn't to eat, that's for sure. Maybe he thought that since someone else had substantiated the Ghost Train, he might take another stab at Lena. The girl was holding back, this much was sure, and Edmund wondered just how much he could press her before she or the old woman told them to get out.

Just before heading back up to his room, to shower and get dressed, he heard a sound from the new world—

something that took him back home, made him forget for a moment that he was standing in a place that was old as time. It was the incessant pecking on a computer's keyboard.

He followed this normal, yet strangely placed sound toward the back, beneath the stairs, and found a room secluded far from the front doors and the main eating area. Above the doorway hung a sign with a computer screen and keyboard on it, along with a string of polish beneath it. Edmund followed the pecking into Krakus House's public internet café, although that was a broad, far-reaching term. It was just a folding banquet table covered in a black sheet, and upon that a pair of aging desktop computers.

On the one closest to the doorway was Sophie, on her screen, an assortment of wedding dresses. She was lackadaisically scrolling through pictures, her chin resting in her hand. Edmund felt like he was watching something he shouldn't, as if he'd just stumbled upon her researching porn rather than what she would wear once Bill popped the question. He moved back out of the doorway, grunted, paused for a moment, and then entered.

“Mornin’,” she said, turned around to greet him. The rolling green hills of the Windows XP background had replaced the online closet of dresses.

“Morning. Where’s Bill?” he asked, moving past her and taking a seat at the next and only other computer.

“Sleeping. That food didn’t hit right and he was up and down most of the night.”

“He just ate potatoes. Who gets sick from potatoes?” Edmund laughed.

She just shrugged and pulled up another browser on her computer. “This food isn’t for everyone, that’s for sure.”

They sat alone in silence for a few minutes. Edmund, normally proficient with computers, had trouble initially figuring out how to change the language pack on the desktop. It was tough finding English when everything was set to the odd crossings and accents of Polish. The room was chilly, heated only with a tiny, antiquated ceramic heater. When they built Krakus House, whoever *they* were, the builders probably didn’t envision it would one day include a small internet lab.

Sophie pulled up a games site and promptly went to chasing a ball of yarn with a cat whose body was long like a centipede. There was no sound, but Edmund wondered if relics like these computers even supported audio.

"You can go back to looking at dresses," he said, without looking over at her. He didn't want her to feel embarrassed, and he knew he'd feel awful if he saw even the slightest tinge of red hit her cheeks.

"I just feel weird, ya know?" she said, but put the dresses back on the screen, nonetheless.

"Weird? Why?"

She just shrugged, her frown turning up so that it balanced in such a way that she could turn to a laugh or a cry. Edmund didn't know what he'd say if it became the latter.

"How's that saying go? Putting the cart before the horse? I don't know what's on Bill's mind these days. I never do. I know I love him and I want to marry him. But on this subject, I don't even know if we're on the same page."

You're definitely on the same page, Edmund thought. What he said was, "I'm sure he feels the same way as you. They say school sweethearts who make it past high school tend to always stay together."

"Who says that?" she said, eyebrow cocked.

"You know, experts and stuff. Official researchers."

She laughed and shook her head, then resumed looking at the dresses. "I like that answer. Thank you, Ed."

He slowly turned back to his screen, hoping that placated her. For most of his life, he'd been a great keeper of secrets, but this one was different. A part of him wanted to tell her that *hey, if only I could figure out what really happened to my comatose friend, you'd get your engagement and subsequent wedding. But we gotta play in Poland for a bit longer, girl.*

Edmund turned his attention to the interconnected world that lay at his fingertips. There were answers out there—maybe not about the Ghost Train, but perhaps its origin. Records from the era abounded, but you just had to know where to look. He thought for a moment about what he *did* know.

A train left Warsaw one cold morning in January of 1943, bound for the Treblinka death camp, but never made it. Already, it was sounding like one of those horrible math questions from the SATs he all but flunked in his senior year. Still, he kept thinking, kept compiling all the data he had thus far.

He knew they were called Special Trains, so that was his entry-point, the spot where he would launch his search. But that was too broad a subject because the Special Trains were in and out of all the concentration camps, from Treblinka to Belzec, from Sobibor to Majdanek. Information specific to Treblinka was difficult to find—that wasn't where the movies and television and literature chose to show the dark side of Nazi Germany. The spotlight inadvertently always fell to Dachau or Auschwitz. So when Edmund used search parameters of 'Special Train', 'Treblinka' and 'missing', the results narrowed to such a thin band that he grew hopeful.

Holocaust trains didn't exactly adhere to standard rules and practices. They were hidden from the world, and thus paper trails were hard to follow. Edmund did come across several trains that were logged by the Germans, but only two of them from Treblinka, the majority, Auschwitz. Even then the information was restricted to what the Jews were carrying on their person, inventory records so that Berlin would know what to expect. Edmund wasn't sure what he could do with the right information even if he found it. He knew nothing about the train, none of the passengers, nor the conductor. Holocaust trains, for research purposes anyway, were *all* ghost trains.

But then a year came to mind, a date that Marcus Davies, the PI from Surrey, had mentioned. That year was 1948.

About sixty people had gone missing, he'd said. *All the way back to 1948.*

That led him to the local sites about the Ghost Train. Many people claimed to have photos, but the train was this part of the world's Bigfoot or Chupacabra. He didn't think any of the amateur photos were the real thing, certainly nothing came close to the quality of video that Addey had captured. A few puffs of steam beyond the mountain, limned by an ethereal glow was the only 'proof' that he thought was halfway viable.

The local sites that spoke of the specific train—a steamer built in 1933 by the Rudnicka company—connected him to the one source that he thought was credible. There *was* a record of a train, bound for Treblinka, vanishing, but the experts had reason to believe that it simply kept heading east, disappearing past Soviet and German contested Belarus where it was no doubt scrapped, the passengers sent to work camps or press-ganged into the army.

Aboard the train was a notable officer by the name of Otto Herzog. Many years before the War, Otto was caught up in criminal proceedings that involved the killing of children. Many people assumed he was innocent, but just as many did not. What made this story survive was the fact that Otto was catching a ride on the train, hopeful to disappear in the already secretive Treblinka. The going story was that he wasn't satisfied with Treblinka—it was German run and thus he'd be handed over to a German tribunal. So, he ran. He took the train across the Polish lines and disappeared into the unknown region of Soviet partisans.

Edmund found a picture of him, most likely many years before the fateful ride on the train. Naturally, it was old and monochromatic, faded a stark white at the corners like some negative fire had burned it away. He was wearing a dark, button-up suit. His jaw was set, eyes narrowed to slits, as if he was untrusting of the photographer. Beneath his arm he held his field hat, little glitters of metal shining.

"That's him," whispered Sophie, so unexpectedly that Edmund jumped. "I'm sure of it."

"Maybe," he said. He'd taken to carrying Addey's phone around everywhere he went, knowing he would want to show anyone who cared to look at the video. He scrubbed it to the brief clip where the man came into frame holding the alligator wrench. Edmund paused it, but too much time had passed between the man who became the ghost and the bright-eyed cadet in thc photo. The bald head matched, as did the nose and the chin. Either way, Edmund chose to believe that Sophie was correct—this was the man aboard the Ghost Train.

He shared all that he'd just learned with her, bringing up the very few credible sources. Lots of people claimed to see the Ghost Train, but not everyone's story fit. Edmund had a knack for telling when someone wanted their fifteen minutes of fame and those who were telling a story simply because they wanted people to hear it.

"Listen to this," he said as Sophie moved her folding metal chair over. "In 1948, in the town of Borowe . . . which is just a few miles from here, a pair of kids, brother and sister, were walking home from choir practice. As many as ten people saw the train that night. Two of them knew it firsthand because they'd been in Warsaw, in the ghetto. They literally saw it leave for Treblinka."

"And the kids?" Sophie asked.

"Were never seen again," Edmund said. "Look at this one." He pulled up another entry on the website. "In 1950, in Klukowo, a woman told her husband that she had a train to catch, that it was going to make her family rich. Husband said he laughed it off, but she went out the door and he never saw her again.

"There's so many more stories like this, Soph. In 1956 a man named Horace Szuba is heard screaming in the middle of the night. Several people go outside to see the Ghost Train sitting there, and a man dragging Horace toward it with a hook." Edmund turned to look at his friend and added, "But we know it wasn't a hook, was it?"

She shook her head. "So why a ghost?" she asked.

"What?" He had no idea what she meant.

"If we look at this missing train from a paranormal point of view, we have to ask that question. It didn't cross to Belarus where the Soviets or the Germans controlled. Hell, I don't know the history like you do, Ed. But it never made it to Treblinka. So what happened in between? A real train of metal and wood filled with flesh and blood people went missing. How did we get from that to a ghost?"

He really didn't know the answer to that, but his amateur work with the *Nun Hunters* had helped to understand the pseudo-science of ghosts. And by pseudo-science, no science whatsoever.

"We went to an old chapel in Ritter once," he said, meaning a small town just outside of Lynchburg, Virginia. "Me, Bill, Addey and a couple of other guys who were part of the *Nun Hunters*.

"Local legend was that a bunch of kids went missing about a century ago, under the watch of a Sister Helena. Lots of people accused her of killing them and hiding their bodies. A lot of angry parents got together, dragged her out of her home and hung her from an old oak tree."

"I remember hearing this story," said Sophie, eyes lighting up. "That oak tree is still there, and it's a huge party spot on Halloween."

"Right. So anyway, after she's hung, the real murderer is found. A crazy old man who leads them right to a bunch of shallow graves up in the woods. Whole town feels awful about Sister Helena now. But that's when people start to see her. You know, normal ghost stuff. Some see her hanging from the tree, some see her walking the streets. My point is this: Something has to *make* a ghost. I don't know how the other side works. But when something awful happens, it leaves an imprint on reality, like bloodstains on a shirt. And it's there forever. Something happened with this train and that's why we still see it all these years later."

"Makes sense, I suppose. But one would think this whole area would be overflowing with ghosts if that were the case. Poland has more awful history than anywhere in the world."

"This is true," he said, just as he peered over her head and noticed Lena sweeping the floor back in the common room.

Sophie followed his gaze, turned back to Edmund and fixed him with a half-scowl that meant she was partly serious in what she was about to say. "Don't scare her off or get us kicked out of here, please?"

He stood up, started to walk out. "I like the dresses without all the frilly stuff on the sleeves."

Lena didn't see him approach—she'd had her back to him from the beginning and had since stopped sweeping to look out the window. This side of Krakus House was pressed up against the forest.

"Where's the old lady?" he asked.

The broom clattered noisily to the floor and she whirled around. Edmund did not feel they were off to a good start by the way her normally pale face reddened.

She stooped over to pick it up. "She's asleep. She's more of a night owl."

"Does she speak English as well as you?"

Lena smiled, most likely figuring that it was always best to keep up a ruse to outsiders that you didn't know what they were saying.

"Perhaps."

"I didn't mean to make you uncomfortable the other night," said Edmund, daring to take a few steps closer. He leaned against the underside of the stairs.

"You didn't," she responded curtly. "I just didn't want another fight." She turned and started sweeping toward the front of the common room.

Edmund slowly chased. “Another fight?”

“My grandmother. She doesn’t like outsiders. People who come looking for the train.”

“Why not?” And then, playfully, “It’s just a legend, right?”

She stopped sweeping and turned around, braided hair swinging out far. “You don’t believe that any more than we do. I’ve seen those who fancy themselves as ghost hunters before.”

“Another person went missing,” said Edmund, mind skipping over what she’d just said. “A zoologist from Warsaw.”

Lena nodded. “I know. He won’t be the last.” And then, as if it didn’t matter, she resumed sweeping.

“So why don’t you like it when people search for the train? Seems to me that the more people who understood it, the better.”

“We understand it just fine,” she said without looking back at him. “And we have enough people being taken away without would-be investigators and ghosthunters coming to be added.”

"Just how many people does this train take?"

Her shoulders slumped, and he didn't have to see her face to know it had softened with sadness. "A lot more than is being reported."

Edmund dared to approach.

"Look, my friend Addey, the guy who stayed here? He was on to something. I just know it. Please, just tell me where he was found or point me to someone who can."

She turned back around, and this time Edmund thought he'd pushed too far. Her face was bent into a scowl that he was yet to see on such elfin features. Lena placed the broom against a table and came up to him, and for the first time he noticed just how small and delicate she appeared, as if she were no more than ten, playing make-believe at being an adult.

She said, "Don't you get it? Don't you see that I'm trying to *protect* you?" Her voice had turned pleading.

"I don't need your protection, I need answers."

Her eyes studied his for a moment, and when she saw this was the end of his reason, said, "I have to go chop wood."

"No, don't," said Edmund, voice defeated. "I'm sorry. I'll go." He circled around her, giving a wide berth, and then mounted the first step to the second floor. He stopped halfway up and said, "Look, have you ever had a friend you loved? A relative? That was Addey. And now I'm going to be home in a few days and he's going to be in a coma for God knows how long." He didn't think his eyes were going to well up with tears, but they were. He didn't care. And he didn't care that when he continued, his voice was starting to break down. "I have *zero* closure. All I wanted was to see where this video was taken." He'd pulled Addey's phone out of his pocket.

Lena gave him a curious look.

"What video?"

***

She had said nothing else after seeing Addey running through the woods, coming upon the Ghost Train, then dropping the phone. Her face barely showed any sort of emotion at all, as if she were either incapable of comprehending what she saw or simply didn't care. Maybe she just didn't believe. But after the video was done, after Otto—for that was most certainly who he was—had brandished the slightly bent alligator wrench—she just shook her head. Edmund was too spent to follow-up, to make his corollary case when the evidence was so strong. As the saying went, there was no use in flogging a dead horse. She turned to sweep and he turned to go back to his room, the stalemate making his blood boil.

He didn't go any further than Bill and Sophie's room that evening, where the three played cards, just as they did on the train from Berlin, what seemed like ages ago. They didn't go out, as the snow had picked up throughout the day, so Lena—clean slate as ever—presented them with meal choices, and the Americans ate lunch and then dinner in their rooms. Edmund heard water running in the eastern bathroom, so he headed to the opposite one to shower, just as he entered into the one closest his room.

That night, after Krakus House, Ozelki, and Poland all went to sleep, and the hush of gently falling snow blanketed the land, Edmund got up and went to the bathroom. As his hand graced the cold wood of the railing, he peered down into the common room and saw Lena sitting at the table, alone, polishing an assortment of figurines who normally lived in the curio cabinet by the fireplace, its door now hanging open. She glanced up because all of Poland could hear the squeal of the floorboards as he walked, and offered him a curt smile which he simply returned.

After his business in the john was complete and he was making the same route back to his room, he glanced over the railing and saw only the chair pushed out, the figurines still on the table, but no Lena. A crackling fire blazed in the hearths. He yawned and closed his bedroom door behind him.

As was his usual bedtime ritual, he responded to the collection of text messages he'd received throughout the day, during American hours of operation. And just when he was about to place the phone where it would charge alongside Addey's device, the hallway outside his door came alive—footsteps, light but quiet, as if someone were tiptoeing. He watched as the line of light was broken by the shadow of feet and then, something was sliding beneath his door. Then, the light was once more unbroken as the squeal of floorboards danced away.

Edmund took his time throwing back the covers and standing up. Surely it was Lena—who else in this place was so small and so quiet? He stooped down, picked up the folded scrap of paper and looked at it. This was a printout, and Edmund brought it back to the bedside light to see better.

At first he didn't realize what he was looking at, for the black and white photo wasn't easily discernable because of the garbled pattern of what turned out to be trees. He was looking at a satellite map, the coordinating planes at the sides marked off in degrees of 10. A large, black circle had been drawn around a square about halfway up the page, right in the middle of the dense forest.

It was a location—close by.

Edmund raced to pull his phone off charge, simultaneously accessing his EarthTrotter app. He used his finger to find the intersection of coordinates—the latitude and longitude, then punched in the numbers, separating them by a coma.

Immediately the app showed a globe, and upon it, a little blue dagger that represented Edmund's location. Then, the globe was spinning, a tiny turn, not even enough to jump continents—not even enough to jump countries. The coordinates he input only moved the globe a millimeter, for the location that Lena had marked on the map was but a mile away.

It was just north of the Treblinka camp.

After all that back and forth downstairs, Lena was showing him where Addey fell.

***

After dressing, he grabbed both phones, his IR camera, and the spare key to the car that the good people at Nomad gave him. It was currently half an hour past midnight, but that didn't matter in a place like this, with a chill in the air and snow on the ground. Edmund wagered that even in warmer months, the dead of night was still just as empty.

Out in the hall, he lingered for a moment by Bill and Sophie's room, listening to someone (he didn't know which) snore softly. Going out alone was a bad idea, but he'd rather see the spot where Addey fell by himself, rather than drag his friends along. He'd done enough to ruin their trip already.

The logical part of him said to wait until morning, but the logical part of Edmund Riley was often like a train itself, and these days it always pulled away from the station just as an important decision was to be made. Tonight would be no different, and should things pan out, he'd go there, snap a few pictures, and come back in the morning with his friends but armed with more information.

Down in the common room the fireplaces were on the wane, but central heat cleverly hidden behind brown-painted faceplates kept the room reasonably warm. The army of figurines had been returned to their curio cabinet and Lena was nowhere to be found. Her chair at the table was pushed in. But just as Edmund was about to let himself out the door, the sound of the small counter television caught his ear, and he turned to look at it.

The old woman was propped in front of it, a blanket covering her legs. She wasn't watching the bygone black and white show—she had her head turned back, and she squinted at Edmund, as if trying to figure out if she'd ever seen him before. He didn't like her stare one bit—in fact he compared it to the narrator in Poe's *The Tell-Tale Heart*, completely vexed by the eye. But rather than chop her up and stow her beneath the floorboards, he gave a curt nod—it was his only way to get through difficult pretext—and headed out into the blistery cold night.

As he slid into the driver's seat of the Fiat for the very first time, a conundrum stopped his quest in its tracks. Sophie had done all of the driving in Poland, as he nor Bill had any idea how to operate a manual transmission. He'd seen her do it many times, had even seen his dad all those years ago when Edmund got to ride along in various construction vehicles on equally varied construction jobs. How hard could it be?

He learned rather quickly to try further down the hill, as the noise of the constantly stalled engine was sure to bring the whole of Krakus House out to see what was happening. When the ground leveled out, he held the clutch down, moved into first gear, then started to let it up just as he pumped the gas. Edmund didn't need to go far, and he didn't need to go fast, so he didn't bother trying to move to a higher gear. Every few yards, the car was stalling out and he found himself having to turn the key all over again.

Just like any other night, the street was deserted, only tonight it was so cold that even the tealights weren't lit around the Catholic church. Edmund had his phone sitting on the dash, the EarthTrotter app telling him that he would be at his destination in only two minutes.

It was near impossible to stay on the road, and he only hoped his silver arrow on the app was accurate to where it said he should be. Even without a soft blanket of untouched snow, the dirt paths would be hard to see at night since there were very few lights out this way. He was just happy that somehow, his phone was getting service.

For a brief moment he touched industry, an overlap of passing traffic near Poniatowo as he turned onto the 627 and off it again only half a mile down the road. Now, he was on yet another dirt path—snow covered, of course—and was only another mile from the stone arch that would lead into the Treblinka Memorial.

He'd come to the end of the road on the EarthTrotter app—if he wanted to continue, it would look like his car was floating in a virtual, green void. But that was for the best, because as far as Edmund could see, the road in front of his high beams was growing rough, and most likely wasn't even there after a few more feet. No, this was where the beaten path ended and the Polish wilds began.

Edmund pulled over to the side, felt the wheels disappear from the road and land on crunchy dirt, and killed the engine. He circled to the passenger's seat and pulled out his backpack, then turned on his phone's flashlight.

Currently, he was standing in the middle of nowhere. The sound of the highway could be heard far off, but only because the snow muted all local noises. It was dark out, but the moon was up there, playing peekaboo with the thick clouds as they dumped snow. He could hear his breath, could hear his own heart beating in his ears. The Fiat made little popping sounds as the engine settled but for all intents and purposes—it was silent. For the first time in all his years of hunting ghosts, he was unnerved.

He leaned against the car and pulled out Addey's phone and watched the video. His eyes had to focus each time he looked up from the bright, unnatural light of the blue screen. There weren't many identifiers in the video, and if there were, they didn't look much as they did tonight, with a sheen of confusing snow covering everything.

Without having much to go on, he turned to his own phone, where the spot highlighted on the map lay waiting a hundred yards or so up the hill. That was a good start since Addey seemed to be scaling a hill in the video.

He kept his light trained on the ground, careful to watch for fallen logs or jagged rocks. Remembering one of his first thoughts upon coming to this area—it wouldn't do to be injured. If he fell and broke a leg or punctured a lung, there's a good chance he'd just have to bleed out right then and there.

Edmund Riley's third rule of travel: Don't die in the Polish wilderness.

The sound of the highway was lost as he entered the woods, replaced by the crunch of his boots on the snow. Somewhere to his right, far off, a dog howled, and then to his left, two more of them joined in. There were birds in the trees, angrily braying, unsettling snow as he walked beneath. He sucked in air, cold and frigid, and his lungs burned.

That red checkmark on his map suddenly separated from the top corner of the screen and now shared space with Edmund's current location. He was getting close, but how accurate could a circle on a printout be? As he neared the spot, he stopped long enough to consult Addey's video and did his best to line up a shot. It wasn't perfect, but he thought just up ahead was where Addey's video began. Edmund looked back and could no longer see the car, between the curvature of the hill and swirling snow.

This was the right way—an abnormally thick tree amongst a throng of skinny ones was standing just to the right in the video and Edmund was able to match it because of the way the hill slanted off to the left. It pained Edmund to think that he was walking the same path his friend had, just before falling into a coma.

He nearly dropped his phone when the EarthTrotter app spoke, telling him that he'd arrived at his destination. Edmund did a full circle, looking at the ground where his friend must have fallen, as if a ghostly apparition of Adlai should still be prone against the snow. There was nothing here, but then again Edmund wasn't expecting anything. This wasn't the only spot shown on the video—Addey had continued on for several yards before being confronted with the train and turning around to run, so Edmund pressed forward, feeling the chill run down his spine.

The dogs' howls turned to barks and then to shrieks so suddenly that Edmund stopped and listened, expecting to hear them fighting. Were there bears in these woods? He didn't know. But just as his feet started to shuffle forward again, the dogs began to whimper, running off down the mountain and away from him.

He came to the apex of the hill, the place in the video where Addey confronted the train. Standing there, looking down the decline, Edmund saw nothing special. There were no tracks, but of course he didn't expect there would be—the Ghost Train didn't need them. The ground leveled out, however, so he supposed there could have been tracks there at *some* point.

His whole body shivered, and not because of the cold. It was disconcerting knowing that he was standing where Addey stood when his friend saw it. The train. The reaching ghosts. Otto Herzog with the alligator wrench. On a night like this, the train had appeared.

In his mind, or perhaps not, he heard the distant whistle of a steam engine.

Edmund did a full circle, juggling the two cellphones as he did. The world was on mute. There were no train whistles, not even a dog anymore. The only thing he heard was his heart beating in his ears and the adrenaline to go with it. Part of him wanted to go back to the car, and the smartest thing he could do would be just that, but the ghost hunter in him, now over the perfunctory jump-scare, pressed on.

Since the train's engine was facing the left in the video, Edmund took the logical step and began walking that way, hoping that he didn't lose track of himself in the woods and that he would be able to find the car should he take too many turns. As he'd thought earlier, this part of the hillside was relatively flat, so he followed along, trying to put logic behind a ghost sighting.

If the train was headed this way, where would it go? Perhaps it had no destination. Perhaps it simply rode in circles, terrorizing all that it came across. As long as Edmund had his wits about him, didn't see people who weren't there, didn't hear offers from the train, he knew he'd be safe.

He'd walked over a hundred yards along the flat part of the hillside, had considered turning back because all he saw ahead was more trees and not much else, but his boot kicked something hard. The way it felt against his toe made him think it wasn't a rock, certainly not dirt. Edmund turned his phone to the ground and almost didn't see it until he used his heel to clear some of the snow and mud away. It was metal, that much was certain in the red-tinged rust along the smooth, curved top that protruded from the ground.

Edmund used his fingers to dig it up—cold metal for sure—and when he pulled it from its grave and held it up for the light to fall across it, his jaw went slack because there was no logical reason why this should have existed here.

It was an old, rusty railroad spike.

A railroad spike from a train track that was no longer here. Edmund remembered how all the railroad spurs leading to death camps were dismantled. But Treblinka was in the opposite direction. Why had this one been taken up? The only logical answer was because whatever lay at the end of the tracks needed to remain hidden.

Just then he had a thought, so he stuffed the phones into his pockets and pulled out his IR camera and waited for the boot screen to disappear so he could switch over to heat mode. He was using his ghost hunter instincts—the callback to the *Nun Hunter* days when he knew he needed to look at things from a different perspective.

He held up the camera, moving it back and forth but saw nothing because this was a frigid land with nothing at all giving off heat. For a moment he caught sight of something high up, but it could have been a glitch in the lens as much as it could have been a bird.

Just when he was about to turn it off, he lowered it toward the ground—and found two streaks of red, moving off ahead of him. Two streaks—like railroad tracks, only there weren't any here. Edmund bent down with his knee in the snow, still using the IR camera to look at the heat signature. But when he touched the spot that should have certainly been warm, if not hot, his fingers didn't detect even the smallest trace of heat.

Edmund walked a little longer, his mind hearing a steam engine, somewhere far off. The part of his brain that didn't believe in ghosts told him that it was simply a trick of the mind, or perhaps it really *was* a steam engine—weren't those still used from time to time? Surely they were, in a backwater country like Poland, where there was barely any Wi-Fi, no people, and the only car you could find was of the three-pedal variety.

Another hundred feet past the railroad spike and the hill started to move upward. Still, he could follow the eerie, red lines of a train track that was no longer there. Although it was dark out and the snow was swirling about his head and through the trees, he was sure that the mountain was growing much steeper because the stars were gone, as were the clouds. Far ahead, perhaps another hundred feet, the mountain moved up, and he squinted to make out what he saw toward the top.

Could it be lights? He wasn't sure. As he stood there in the snow, his heart raced because he was nervous—and unnerved, not to mention he was tired after such a trek. But Edmund squinted his eyes, and through the snow and darkness he made out several squares of golden lights. Could it be a house? No, the squares were too spread out to be one house. Maybe a town? That seemed more plausible, but he didn't remember seeing any sort of town this close to Treblinka, with the exception of Poniatowo and Ozelki. Even through the camera's lens, and even zoomed in, he couldn't tell what he was seeing.

That's when he noticed the chain link fence directly in front of him, veering off to the left and right and eaten by the darkness. It blocked his path and aiming the IR camera high, he saw there'd be no going over it either. This fence rose at least ten feet and was tipped in barbed wire. A thick, knobby mass sat atop the post in front of him, probably a surveillance camera.

The red streaks on the ground disappeared abruptly, as if the train, not so long ago, had pulled to the fence and then stalled.

He wondered if the IR camera was glitching—it did that once a long time ago, during a ghost hunt near Williamson. It was an older model and he probably should have replaced it, but such things were expensive. Edmund wanted to test it out on himself, so he turned it around, held it out at arm's length to snap a selfie, then looked at the photo.

It was a mash of all reds and yellows in the form of his face, the heat signature from an IR camera that, despite what he originally thought, was not glitchy. It only made him look like a bloodied monster of light.

But there was also a train in the background, just behind him.

He whirled around, dropping the railroad spike but somehow, miraculously holding the IR camera. The night was still dark, the train sitting directly in front of him gave off a muted, ethereal glow that shimmered with mist, but he could see every single car as it stretched out behind the engine, like a long, dreadful snake.

The engine faced him, the heat coming off its metal pilot shimmering against the cold air. Edmund fell to the ground, crawling back a few steps by its sudden appearance. A hush washed across the hillside, and in the next moment, it was filled with an assortment of awful noises.

The steel wheels, as if connected to steel rails, screeched so loudly that snow fell from tree branches. Each of the cars sitting on the invisible track rocked back and forth as those inside clambered to get out. Ice filled his veins—he was more afraid than he'd ever been in his life.

But that fear only expanded when Otto Herzog, as substantial as any living man, hopped out of the engine, landing solidly in the snowy grass. His eyes, dead and milky orbs of light, found Edmund, but this apparition's glare was so much more awful than the old woman's could ever be. In his hand was the long, jagged alligator wrench, bent slightly to the right. Otto was a mountain of a man, and the video on Addey's phone hardly did his size justice. Slowly, he was approaching, snow crunching and mist swirling beneath his boots.

Edmund didn't know if ghosts could hurt the living—all of the pseudo-science suggested that they could only be viewed, just noncorporeal beings. This whole notion went up in flames the moment the brute swung the wrench, just where Edmund had been before rolling aside, sending up tufts of grass into the air. A wide, yet deep divot remained.

Again, he swung, the wrench coming inches from Edmund's throat with such force that if the ghost had managed to connect, it would have ripped his head clean off. It took the third swipe, a deep slash against a great oak that left a foot-long trench in its bark, to get Edmund to his feet and running away.

When Otto drove the wrench across the tree, he turned his back, and in that brief moment Edmund hurtled past him, running alongside the train because the hillside was level enough for him to gain speed. For a flicker of a second he threw his head back to see if the man had recovered, only to find him giving chase, and closing fast, like a steam engine himself, running at full speed. The wrench was held high, the little jagged teeth catching glimpses of the moon.

Edmund veered off course as he quickly turned back around, smacking into the train—it was as much metal as any ordinary trainset, but when he collided, he became entangled. At first he thought the train held some sort of cosmic power to adhere the living to it, but there were dead, awful faces, and dead awful limbs pawing at him, holding his jacket, pleading for him to let them out.

They reminded Edmund of his little sister's dolls—the rubber ones meant to look like real babies. When you pushed on their foreheads, the whole thing collapsed. That's what he was seeing now—ghostly men and women with heads that had been crushed. Some were missing eyes, some were missing teeth. Many had brains, pulpy and pink, running down their faces. Still, they grabbed at him and still they cried out in a language he didn't understand.

This happened in the span of a heartbeat because as soon as Edmund realized it was groping hands that were holding him fast, he slithered out of the jacket, one of the phones dropping to the snow, and continued to run as fast as he could. A loud, metallic twang blasted behind him and the sparks on his neck meant Otto had been close enough for another swing.

The enormity of the train dawned on him as he continued to run alongside it, like an ethereal Great Wall of China. Although his mind was too taxed to do the math, forty-nine cars and one engine at around thirty feet each meant he'd parallel it for another five-hundred yards before he'd be able to get around. Edmund wasn't entirely sure, but he thought the car was on the same side of the train as he was running, so without thinking, he left the leveled hillside and darted back into the rough, uneven forest.

As he pulled away from it, the voices started to grow faint. Most of them were in Polish, but a few were not. He turned, locked eyes with a ghostly woman who was hanging halfway out of a car, reaching for him and yelling for help in English. Edmund paid her little attention because Otto stepped up, put a hand on her face and pushed her back inside, and then followed him into the forest, regaining his pace in half a heartbeat. Edmund turned and ran, hoping no fallen trees snagged his pants because the moon was the only light he had.

As he reached the apex of the hill, lungs like storehouses of hot embers, he knew that no such affliction bothered the dead conductor. He was blindly running and wondering if the ghost would chase him until he caught him. Or perhaps it had to stick close to the train. He prayed that was the case.

He stopped for a minute to get his breath, and it was a good thing he did because as he turned around to see if Otto was closing, he spied the car, about a hundred yards away. He'd come out of the forest a long way from where he'd entered it. Edmund ran a straight line, kicking up snow.

He was already fishing the key out of his pocket before he even got to the Fiat, which had already accumulated enough snow to blot out the windshield. Edmund ripped open the door and flopped down into the driver's seat. He put the key in the ignition, did his best to remember the order of the pedals—

—and lurched forward a few feet before the engine stalled. The dash lit up in angry lights, beckoning him to try again. Just before he turned the key over, Otto emerged from the forest, right behind where Edmund had a few minutes ago. The brute looked around, seeming to have lost his mark for the moment, and somehow not seeing Edmund's hurried, jagged footprints.

Edmund just sat in the car, torn between the safety of silence and the riskiness of starting and stalling and alerting the ghost.

It did not matter, for Otto quickly spied the car sitting on the side of the road and started for it, slowly at first, then running. Edmund frantically turned the key over, held the clutch, eased his shaky foot off and hit the gas—but he stalled again, knowing all sense of timing had gone out the window. Driving this car was an artful balance, and currently he didn't have the wits for it. Otto had halved the distance.

Edmund tried again, the car lurched forward, but again it stalled.

"Shit! No, no, no! *C'mon*!" he said, punching the wheel. Otto was still running, now only twenty yards out, the alligator wrench held high.

Edmund was about to get out of the car, to run off and leave it, but then knuckles were knocking on his window and he found himself away from the steering wheel and into the passenger seat, kicking off from the door as if in a swimming pool. The window was foggy, but when the person bent down to look into the car, he felt strangely relieved.

It was the old woman from Krakus House.

Edmund reached back across and held the button to lower the window. Her skin was pale, white hair stuffed up in a knitted toboggan. She looked in the car to see if he were alone, then fixed him with that dead eye.

"Stay in the car," she said, in English far better than he would have guessed, then she walked off, straight toward the lumbering Otto.

He was slowing down, as if the sight of the old woman gave him pause. The alligator wrench fell to his side, and he stared at her with a mixture of curiosity and something else . . . could it be fear? Edmund didn't know. He didn't know a lot of things tonight.

It was the first time he noticed headlights behind him, and another person, silhouetted against them. From the small frame he had no doubt it was Lena. She was leaning against the grill of another car, and seemed mildly interested in what her grandmother was doing.

The old woman stepped in front of the Fiat, the high beams blasting her shadow across the mountain. Edmund fully expected Otto to rip her in half with the jagged teeth of the alligator wrench, but he did not. Instead, it looked like they were talking. He couldn't hear any words, but by the way they stared, like gunslingers in the old west, he thought for sure this was about to get bloody.

But were they conversing some other way? Seeing them standing there, stoic, unmoving, Edmund couldn't help but wonder if something more were happening, as if they had some kind of telepathic link. As absurd as it sounded, it made more sense than the old woman and the ghost having a stare-off.

The train rushed down the mountain with a great whistle, snapping trees and plowing snow aside. It stopped right behind Otto, a puff of white belching from the smokestack, and it was the first time Edmund noticed a second conductor in the window—his head blown open and one eye completely gone. The trainset snaked through the trees, as if they could turn and pivot in whichever way suited them. The old woman and Otto faced off a few heartbeats longer before he grudgingly climbed aboard the train. She turned back toward Edmund.

Otto gave the American a scowl before the steam whistle screamed, as if to say, *this isn't finished*, and then the train was moving off, the horrible, horrible faces looking down at him until they were gone.

The door of the Fiat suddenly opened and Lena got behind the wheel. She slammed it and put on her seatbelt just in time to see the headlights behind them back up, then head away.

"What are you doing?" asked Edmund, feeling like it was a dumb way to start his questions.

"Taking you back to Krakus House because you obviously can't drive this car." She put it into gear and easily pulled away. His cheeks flushed and his eyes fell to his lap.

"What the hell just happened? What did I just see?" he asked, nose now pressed to the window, wondering if he could catch a glimpse of the train. But it had vanished, returned to wherever it went whenever it wasn't terrorizing Poland.

"I told you not to go hunting for it. Didn't I tell you that?" she said, shaking her head. "If she hadn't shown up . . ." Lena let that hang in the air.

"Why didn't the ghost hurt your grandmother?" he asked.

"It's a complicated story. And she will tell you, if she wants to. But I think it would be a good idea for you and your friends to pack up and leave. Things are only going to get worse."

"How do you know? Worse how?"

"Just worse. Trust me. You don't want to be here for this." And then as if to herself, "God, it just doesn't care anymore. Ripped up the whole damned forest back there."

"I don't understand. I don't get any of this."

"How far did you go?" she asked, turning off the 627 and back onto the first dirt road.

"What do you mean?"

"How far did you go up the mountain? Did you see the town? Did you go to Polvec? You didn't climb the fence, did you?"

"Climb? No. What is Polvec?"

"Nothing. Don't go anywhere near that place again."

Edmund wondered if she was referring to the squares of light he saw just before the train showed up.

"You wanted me to come here. You left me the note under the door."

Her eyes crinkled at the sides. "You can't prove that. And let's not talk about it anymore. Grandma's furious."

"But why would you help me now?"

"Because we share something. Because I know what it's like to lose someone. The train took someone from me, too."

"I'm sorry."

"It's fine. And it's my fault the train almost got you. It was on the other side of the Bug an hour ago. It's becoming . . . unpredictable."

"How could you possibly know all this?"

She just looked at him and grinned, but there was something else behind it—sadness? A resigned duty? He didn't understand how he knew that.

"The Ghost Train is shrouded in mystery, but my grandmother knows a lot about it."

"God, I have *so* many questions."

They had just turned up the hill past the Catholic church. A small garage sat at the foot of Krakus House, unseen by Edmund until now. The old woman was walking up the hill with her head down and hands stuffed into her pockets.

"She looks so fragile," said Edmund. "Like if she fell over she'd break into a million pieces."

Lena waited for the old woman to kick off the snow from her boots and then let herself in the door before driving the Fiat and parking where it had been before Edmund grew adventurous.

“Don’t let looks deceive you, American. My grandmother is one of the strongest women in this world. She’s survived a lot to be here today.”

“She must have if even the Ghost Train won’t hurt her.”

Inside, the fires crackled but they were dying without the only two employees there to tend them. No, Krakus House had emptied in order to come rescue a dumb American who went looking for trouble.

Edmund’s eyes fell to the kitchen doorway, which was standing open, and the old woman was inside, stripping down. He wanted to turn away—seeing the backside of a naked, elderly woman was at the bottom of his bucket list, but he couldn’t because of what he saw on her exposed skin.

Her whole backside, from the nape of her neck, to her back, to her buttocks and thighs, were covered in scars. Little ones, like the remnants of a thousand bug bites that never healed. They were ancient, but also so plentiful that it made her pale, motley skin look like a Picasso.

"It's not polite to stare," said Lena by his ear, so sudden and so close that he recoiled. This brought a snort from the girl that he found far more annoying than endearing.

"Sorry," he said.

"You know what all that is?" she asked, nodding forward, indicating the scars.

"Motorcycle accident," he said, not sure why he chose a joke at that moment. The old woman shut the door.

"The doctors would call it scars from body lice. But to those who lived in the ghetto, they call it Typhus scars."

Edmund didn't know much about that, other than lots of the Poles and Jews suffered from it due to being so overcrowded in the ghetto. Lice, fleas, and other vermin spread it rapidly.

"I'm sorry," he said, not sure of what else to say.

"For what?" she said, her voice slightly playful, an edge that he didn't like after what he'd just come through.

"I don't know. For her trouble, for tonight. I'm sorry. Look, I just want to go to bed. Can we all just forget about this?"

"Sure," said Lena, simply enough. "Goodnight."

He nodded it back, then mounted the steps. As soon as his boot came down, the old woman opened the door and stepped out, now in a house robe and a brightly colored quilt draped across her shoulders.

"American, a word," she said, stepping up to the counter and putting her hands on the surface. Her fingernails were long and yellowed, flesh covered in age spots. But she was steady.

Edmund turned around, came back down.

"No more hunting the train, eh?" she said, eyebrow cocked.

"Yes ma'am," he said. "I won't go looking anymore."

"Good, good," she said. She shivered, pulled her quilt tighter. "Because next time, it might come looking for *you*."

***

He wasn’t sure how long he slept, only that he’d been so exhausted that the bed came crashing up to meet him before he’d even had time to change. A siren, a weird warble of unfamiliar emergency personnel drew him from sleep, and immediately he rolled over onto his back because something in his front pocket was poking him painfully in the groin.

It was daylight out, and even thought the single window had its shade drawn and curtains down, the idea that night had passed made him feel a little calmer. Those awful thoughts of the train, of Otto and his swinging wrench swam in the forefront of his brain and wouldn’t let go. He hoped he would never be face to face with something so terrible ever again.

Edmund reached into his pocket and pulled out his phone, tried the only button so that he could see the time, but naturally the device was dead. He was getting worse about charging it. He felt his other pocket for Addey’s phone, and immediately tears burned his eyes, because he knew it was gone, knew he’d dropped it in the scuffle with the train.

He moved over to his bedside table and plugged his phone into the charger, then stripped down to change.

Edmund peered out the window from behind the shade, seeing nothing but countryside, alternating from forest to field and far off, a lake looking as calm as a giant mirror. The snow was starting to melt into a dirty slush.

His phone read that it was an hour until noon, but the clock was quickly replaced by a missed call alert. He tried to make out the weird number, and it didn't occur to him that it was local. His addled mind assumed it was a telemarketer. When he placed the phone back onto the nightstand, his wrist brushed his wallet, sending it to the floor where his bank cards, rail pass, and money spilled out like confetti.

Edmund stooped down, started putting his cards back in their preordained slots, folded the money, inserted the rail pass—and then he opened the flyer that the British investigators had given him the other night at the gas station.

And just like that, he was back with the train.

Edmund's mind raced to something that happened last night, but he was too frazzled then to realize it. All of the Poles and Jews on the train were shouting for him in a language he didn't know. But there had been one voice that drew him because of all the motley words and cries coming from the car, hers had been the one he understood. It was Katherine Walker, the same face on the flyer as the woman last night on the train. Otto had put a hand against her face and shoved her back in, as if she were one of the very prisoners who'd been riding around for the last eighty years.

Edmund didn't know what he would even say, but without even thinking, he'd dialed Brian Harrick's cellphone. This conversation wouldn't go well, but Edmund didn't think he could just sit on this information.

The phone rang twice, and then a scruff, but recognizable voice picked up on the other side. "'Ello, this is Brian Harrick. Whom am I speaking with?"

"Uh, hello Brian. This is Edmund. Edmund Riley. We talked a few nights ago in Warsaw?"

"Ah yes, the American." There had been music playing in the background—heavy metal that sounded like one of those Scandinavian rock bands Addey listened to in high school. It abruptly ended when Brian recognized him. "What can I do for you Edmund?"

"This isn't going to be easy for me to say. I have information on the girl you're looking for. But you aren't going to believe it."

"Try me," he said. "We've exhausted every lead. We're actually a few miles north of Poniatowo and contemplating heading straight for Warsaw."

"Okay. Here goes. I saw her last night. On the train."

Silence.

Then, someone nearby, most likely his colleague, Marcus, "What's he saying?"

"Quiet," Brian told him. And then, "Edmund? You're sure?"

That was a turn he didn't expect. Edmund fully assumed the man would hang up the phone, the mention of the Ghost Train the icing on the cake of his mound of dead ends and lack of information.

"I'm sure. I had a run in with the train. I know you don't believe me. I hardly believe it myself. But I did, and I saw the girl. I saw Katherine Walker. Tell her parents that she's dead."

"It's a little hard to explain a ghost, mate. Her poppa isn't the type to roll over at that news. But . . . I believe you."

"You believe me? A few days ago you thought I was crazy for thinking the Ghost Train was real."

"Yeah? Well a few days in its backyard opened my eyes."

"What did you see?" Edmund asked.

Again, another silence.

"Enough. That damned thing is cruising around eastern Poland and it doesn't need a track beneath it. What the hell does it want? You're the ghost expert, ain't ya?"

"I don't know what it wants. But it's getting stronger." Edmund hadn't really thought about it until now, but that was the truth.

"How do you mean, mate?"

"This thing used to only show up a few times every January. There's been years where it wasn't even seen at all. And now, it's taking people almost every week. It's getting stronger."

"That's a right terrifying thought."

"Yeah. I'm sorry she's dead. Katherine, I mean."

"Don't sweat it. It's just work. Besides, we may be staying longer than we'd anticipated. My firm just texted Marcus here and it seems someone else would like to hire our services while we're in the area."

"Someone else went missing?"

"Yep. Some zoologist."

Edmund told him all he knew of Piotr Galin.

"Bloody hell! We're never going to get paid if the damned train takes all the bodies."

Something in the way he said it made Edmund's mind switch gears. He'd never really given any thought to the fact that the ghosts had to transition from the living, and the living left behind bodies.

"The corpses are out there somewhere," said Edmund. "Katherine Walker, Piotr Galin, those two people who disappeared a couple weeks ago. They're all buried somewhere, right?"

"Buried? Why would the ghosts on the train bother to bury them?" Brian asked.

"Okay, so maybe not buried. But none of the train's victims have ever been found. They're out there somewhere. Hidden."

"Interesting theory, my friend. If you figure out where, do ring us, please?"

Probably aboard the train, he thought. Wasn't that the most likely place? Still, the train wasn't the only location shrouded in mystery, that much was clear by the way Lena avoided talking of it.

"There's a place near the Treblinka camp. It's called Polvec."

"Polvec? What's Polvec?" asked Marcus, listening in on the call.

"Yeah, Edmund, is that a town?"

"I don't know. I think so. But there's a fence surrounding it and cameras guarding it. I saw it just when the train showed up. And had I not been there, the train would have probably ridden straight for it."

"I'm not seeing anything online about a town called Polvec," said Marcus.

“We’re looking at satellite maps all around Treblinka,” said Brian. “We don’t see a town anywhere by that name.”

“I don’t know,” said Edmund. “*Some*thing is there.” He pulled up the EarthTrotter app on his phone and zoomed out to where the fence had started. Edmund was probably looking at the same geodata that those Brits were seeing, and there definitely wasn’t anything there. Nonetheless, Edmund tapped the spot, then took a screenshot of the coordinates and sent it to Brian. “That’s the spot. Or close enough for you to see the fence.”

“Alright, Edmund. Thanks. We’ll check it out.”

“How? There’s a fence and cameras so I doubt they want people snooping around.”

At this word, Brian began to chuckle. “My dear boy,” he said, “we are professional snoopers.”

“Just be careful, please. I have a bad feeling about it.”

“Duly noted, my good man. Thanks for the lead. We’ll be in touch.” And then, he was gone.

Edmund sat there, feeling uneasy about the conversation but knowing there wasn't much he could do about it. His phone was teetering on one percent battery, so he powered it down to expedite the charge and headed downstairs to the common room where he hoped he could eat whatever it was he'd started to smell.

Halfway down the steps he found the common room full, or at least full by Krakus House standards. The largest table, the one where they often had their dinner was filled with a banquet-sized breakfast. Both of his friends were eating and talking with Lena and the old woman, who had wheeled her chair right up to the edge of the table.

Bill was the first to hear the creak on the steps and turned to see his friend coming down, still wearing the clothes from last night.

"Ed?"

Sophie got up, briskly walked over to him and wrapped her arms around him. He wanted to cry, not because she was showing him such warmth, but because he knew he didn't have to explain what had happened. They knew what he'd been through.

"Morning," he said, unsure of what else to say.

Lena said, “We’re just bring them up to speed. Are you hungry? I made kasza manna. It’s like oatmeal in your country, I suppose. But with blackberries and—”

“You don’t know how lucky you are to be standing there, boy,” said the old woman. Her eyes were stern, reproachful.

He took a seat at the end of the table, away from the group. Whether it was subconscious or not, he couldn’t tell. “I’m sorry. I didn’t mean to put anyone in harm’s way.”

“Just yourself,” said Sophie, shaking her head. “Why didn’t you wake us?”

“I honestly don’t know. I saw the map . . .” Edmund glanced at Lena, not sure if she’d told everyone her part in all this, “. . . and it made me impulsive. I had to see it for myself and I had to see it that very moment.”

Bill had taken on a more serious tone, his friend becoming ever more irritated by Edmund’s actions. “You’re lucky this nice lady followed you or else you’d be just like Addey. And we would be just as clueless about *you* as you are of him.”

Lena said, “We’ve been talking about your friend and we understand this is important to you.”

The old woman leaned in. She coughed into a fold of her blanket and then put her piercing gaze to Edmund. Whenever she did that, all signs of age disappeared. When that eye found him, old and brittle flitted away, replaced by a vigor he didn't understand.

"But *you* have to understand why it's dangerous for you here. Why it's dangerous for anyone to be here. And if it's answers that will send you home, I'll tell you." She took a breath, hacked into her blanket again, then continued. "I know what happened to your friend. Because just like last night, I was there."

"You were?" Edmund couldn't help but notice his friends were hardly surprised by this news, probably already having heard the story.

"Lena, be a doll and put a log on the fire," said the old woman, another fit of coughing unsettling her frail lungs. She turned her attention back to Edmund. "Your friend checked into Krakus House and he stayed for three days. He asked many questions about the train, as people often do when they come here. For most, it's a passing interest. The Ghost Train has always been rare, coming out only at night and only in January. Our house is unbothered for most of the year. But your friend was determined to find the train. On the eve of the last day we saw him, he spoke of the town. Said he got inside, that he found a secret way past the fence and that he'd thought about going back to take pictures." Edmund thought of the strange buildings in his photos, the armed guard, the lab and the train track that looked like it was inside a tunnel.

Lena nodded toward the old woman as she sat back down. "Babcia told him that would be unwise, that he would get into trouble. She told him it was a military base and he'd be shot for trespassing."

"Is that true?" asked Sophie.

The old woman shook her head. "That it's military? No. That he'd be shot for trespassing? Yes. Anyway, we were at the bar, he'd just come in . . .he stayed gone for most of the day, and then immediately started to talk about his grandparents and how they were on the train."

So goes the story of all the others, thought Edmund.

Lena said, "He left out of here, got in his car and drove off."

"My battery was dead when I got behind the wheel," said the old woman. "Damned relic, it is! So I borrowed the neighbor's truck down the street and followed as best I could. I got out of the car up in the woods because I could hear your friend shouting for his grandparents. I'm old, can't move like I could before, but I chased the boy as best I could. The Ghost Train was on the prowl—damned thing doesn't care who hears its whistle when it's angry—and your friend was headed right for it. But then I came upon him. And he looked as dead as dead could be."

"Otto came looking for him," said Edmund. "That's the big guy with the wrench. We could see him in the video."

The old woman chuckled, revealing a mouth full of yellowed pegs. "Yes, boy. I know all about Otto. And had I not been there, Otto would have taken your friend onto the train."

"So you just left him there," said Edmund, his voice coming out far more hostile than he intended. It didn't matter because he wasn't sorry.

She just stared at him for a moment before answering, as if choosing words that wouldn't exacerbate conflict. But in the end, she only looked defeated. "I had no choice. I can barely lift my bread out of the oven. Surely not a twelve-stone boy."

“She didn’t just abandon him,” Lena said, jumping to the old woman’s defense.

“No. I didn’t. After I was sure the train was gone, I called the police from a phone kiosk near Poniatowo. Told them I saw a boy running into the woods and where they could find his car. He was picked up within the hour.”

“I don’t understand what’s wrong with him,” Edmund said. He always circled back to this. “Why is he in a coma?”

The old woman shrugged. “Your friend showed incredible resilience to the train. Some of us have that. Most do not.”

Lena reached out and touched her grandmother—her babcia—on the hand. “And some of us have a *lot* more than others.”

Bill chimed in with the story of the zoologist, of how that man had simply gone into a stupor when he thought his sister was on the train, playing the piano of all things. He said, “Addey seemed to have his senses in the video. He wasn’t like . . . what’s the word?”

“Zombie,” answered Lena. “You Americans love that word. Brainless, moving without thinking.”

"Right," Bill said, "like a zombie. He had enough wits about him to film while he was running after it. And he even ran away when Otto stepped off the engine."

The old woman pursed her lips and shook her head. "I've never seen anything like it. But coming in contact with the Entity has caused stranger things to happen. Your friend just fell into a shock that can't be mimicked any other way. He came face to face with a dark power, and unlike everyone else, is still alive." She turned to Edmund, a move that was so rigid and robotic that he was sure it caused her great pain. "I know this is a small consolation, but your friend is extraordinarily lucky. This is not the words you want to hear, but take heart because it's the truth. He is safe now. You all are not. You need to leave this place at once."

"I think we can all agree on that," Bill said. He rapped his knuckles on the table. "Ed?"

Sophie, unsure, looked at him also. "How about it, Ed?"

He didn't hear any of it. Instead, he focused on what the old woman had just said.

"You called it an Entity."

"Yes," she said.

"Why that word?"

"Because that's what it was before the train."

"Before the train?"

She said, "A ghost must have a catalyst. It wasn't always a train, but it's always been just as evil." Edmund recalled a very similar story he'd told Sophie.

"So what was it before it was a train?"

"And how did it even become a train?" Bill asked.

The old woman exchanged a look with her granddaughter and then answered. "Because I made it happen."

Treblinka

January 21st, 1948

When he picked this place as a lair in the years leading up to the construction of the Treblinka camp, he assumed the Nazis would be smart enough to keep it running until the *Final Solution* was carried out. That would have been enough death to satisfy him while he plotted to move elsewhere, find the next holocaust. Man had so many aspirations when it came to being evil, so surely he wouldn't have to wait long.

But now the lair was little more than a crypt. Five years had passed since the girl walked away, and in those five years he waited, hoping enough death would float on the wind, bolster his spirit, and let him leave this place once and for all. There was promise here, oh yes—with its hidden location and the laboratory at the far end, but what good was it all? He was weak, in no shape to govern the minds of the mortals to his will. The Entity had always been a scavenger but now he'd become a bottom-feeder, scrounging in the trash for whatever scraps he could find. The girl had broken him.

The only things keeping him from falling back asleep were the deaths that happened by chance. A few years ago, the first spring after the girl had left the cave, a two-vehicle accident claimed the lives of two drivers and three passengers. The Entity lingered at the mouth of the tunnel and breathed in the sweetness of fresh death. A couple of months after that a farmer, for whatever reason, walked across the field in the distance, sat down on the back of a wagon, and put a shotgun in his mouth. That death wasn't filling, but it was tasty, all the same. These were the scant offerings that wafted by his lair, and it was nearly torture. Just like the warriors of old, it was better to die in the heat of battle than linger past the world's turmoil only to live as an old man. And right now, he *was* an old man.

A year after the girl left was the last time he got a decent meal. He'd looked around his tomb that morning, finding a solace in the remnants that were once people. To be an Entity as old as he, was to forget the passage of time, to be content in the moment, and to be immune to the boredom that plagued man. His tomb was silent. The smell of rotten meat had long since dissipated. Now that he thought about it, nothing ever came to eat the bodies—his wickedness made the lesser creatures of the world keep away.

As the morning light filtered through the gap where the train tracks used to run, it cast an eerie glow across the four-thousand skeletons sitting in the cars, as if still waiting on the fateful night the train headed to Treblinka. Even Otto hadn't moved an inch since the day he crawled up to the engine and collapsed. True, he was smaller now, the meat all gone and his face sunken like a mummy. A fine sheen of cobwebs covered him from head to toe, as if to wrap him in a full-body cocoon.

But then, death started to enter his lair in droves.

He was bolstered, the power returning to his noncorporeal form. In an instant he had materialized outside the cave. The path Otto had cleared was now so overgrown that no one would ever suspect a train spur had led here. But from his perch, he could see the fields in the distance, and they looked nothing as they did five years ago. Now, green grass had grown back, saplings were pushing through the ground, fences had been reconstructed, and then, on the horizon, a line of tanks were punching to the west.

War machines all looked the same to the Entity. He cared about the results far more than the means, so at first he didn't recognize the tanks were of Soviet design. For the last couple of weeks, there'd been a steady stream of death floating through, and as he stood outside the cave at night, he could see the smoke billowing into the air. The Germans, in their retreat and in their effort to hide their horrid war crimes, had started to burn everything around the camp, including the nearby towns. Most were abandoned, but sometimes he would get lucky, and death was added to the air.

Now, the Red Army was pushing west, toward Warsaw, and mowing down any resistance that got in the way. As long as they were here, he would eat. However, this was short-lived, as the opposition had fled as far west as it could. The Germans were pulling back, Poland was lost, and now the Entity was living in a land where a new government was being installed. He cared little for the politics of man, but at any rate, the winds of death barely fluttered, and he had been begging for morsels ever since.

And then one morning, a few weeks after the five-year anniversary of the little girl fleeing the cave, cold, confused, barefoot, and clutching a straw doll—she came back.

At first he thought his perception was on the wane—he was incredibly weak, after all. But he could taste her on the air, just as he had all those years ago when Otto put her on the tracks and told her to leave. Why on God's green Earth would she have returned?

It was after dark when a trio of bouncing lanterns began drawing close to the tunnel entrance. A white vortex blew the flames aside, the wind and snow whipping the barren landscape beyond. His eyes could clearly see the visitors—or was invaders a more proper term? The girl was filled with blinding, white light, but he knew it was her, even if she had somewhat doubled in size.

What stood before the mouth of the cave now was a child, obviously around ten years old, but looking into the abyss with a certainty he'd never seen upon a child's face before. The confident stare, the slight grimace at her lips, told him that she knew she had power—and the two who'd accompanied her back to this place had most likely taught her all about it.

An older man with sandy brown hair flipped his hood back and reached out a shaky arm to survey the cave with his lantern. It was silent inside, as it had been for many years, and he hoped the trio would turn around and leave, but the Entity knew it wouldn't be so simple. Just as he could sense the good in her, so too could she sense the evil in him.

The man turned back and said to the girl, "You're sure?"

"There's no tracks here, love," said the other adult, a woman who was probably the older man's wife. The Entity tried to dive into their minds, to see what they saw, to perhaps unseat them and make them run off, but he couldn't. He was too weak, so all he was afforded was flashes of light, names, childhood traumas. None of the information he gleaned while floating around in their minds proved useful.

"I can't explain that," said the girl. "But the train is here. And *he* is still here."

The adults glanced at one another and then to the child. Finally, the man nodded, leapt past the rocks and then helped his friends inside. They made the first discovery which was the tracks—Otto didn't take those up because what use was it? If anyone happened inside the cave, they would see the train almost immediately.

"It's here!" said the man, as predicted. The lantern's glow was reflecting off the train's pilot. The child came up behind him and the woman put a hand across her shoulder. Who were these people? How did the child even survive—five years! Only to come back here. The Entity swam away on what little bit of energy he had left, and watched them from the back of the train.

"You can wait outside if you'd like," said the man to the girl. "We won't be long."

"Nonsense. I want to see him," said the girl with more resolution than someone her age should've possessed.

"Matilda, you do not have to do this. We've dealt with evil before," said the woman.

"Not like this. You need to let me go first." The girl named Matilda pushed her way past them and held up her lantern.

"So many dead. Look at them," the man said, pausing at each train car and peering inside. "Look at their heads. All beaten in. What kind of monster?"

"That monster," said Matilda, pointing up to the man in the engine. The alligator wrench lay at his feet in a nest of webs.

How did the child know such things? The Entity sensed a pressing at his metaphysical head, and knew he was being invaded. This little girl . . . was looking into his mind.

"He's here," said the child. "He's back there." Her shaky lantern—shaky only from the weight and not fear—pointed right at him.

"Right, let's do it," said the man, placing his lantern on the ground. He removed his robe, and that's when the Entity saw the medallion hanging around his neck—the spiral with the line through it. He'd seen these people before—they called themselves the Order of the Opeikun—and although they had no power over him, they could make life hard nonetheless.

"Can you bind him here?" asked Matilda.

"We shall try," said the woman, likewise removing her robe.

They didn't have the power to bind him. What they *could* do was offer a blessing on this place that would prevent him from ever coming back. And seeing as how he barely had the strength to leave in the first place, he didn't know what would happen when they placed the wards. For the first time in generations, the Entity panicked.

Matilda, still a hundred yards away, fixed him with a threatening stare. "Do you hear that?" the girl screamed in the otherwise still tunnel. The sound reverberated from both ends. "You are going to be stuck here forever! Never again will you hurt people!"

"Calm down," said the man. "Let's do this and be done." He'd already started burning a thin reed of incense while the woman dumped a straight line of some pale powder by the train.

The Entity was growing both fearful and angry because a mere child should not be addressing him in such a way! He was *immortal.* He'd been there in the red waters of broken ships as the Trojan War thundered against the walls of Troy. He'd watched from atop a fountain as Tacitus played knucklebones while the Great Fire of Rome sprouted behind him. And he'd been there, whispering suggestions to a young, shaky Gavrilo Princip that he shouldn't just shoot the Archduke but also his pregnant wife. The Entity had been privy to all this and more, and now was ready to flee at the coaxing of a ten-year-old girl.

In his final, last-ditch effort he attempted to poison the man's mind—perhaps make him turn on the woman and convince the child to run off, fleeing into the night a second time. He rushed forward, ignoring the searing light that was the girl and pushed all his malice and anger and fear into the man, but if he had even a slight chance of coaxing him toward suggestion, it was snuffed out when the girl stepped into his path, dropped her lantern on the ground, and grabbed him with both hands.

And in that awful moment, he knew he was dying.

What else could it be? His power was seeping away, like a ball of yarn chaotically unwinding in a hailstorm. The adults stared as if she'd lost her mind because no one could see the Entity but the child. Her face was contorted in a mask of rage, perhaps an underlining fear, but he'd never been troubled by a mortal's appearance before. Now, her eyes were haunting him.

"Leave!" she screamed. "Go from this place and never return!"

Go where? the Entity asked in her mind.

"I don't care! This world. Go back to wherever you were before you ate death."

I don't know where that is.

"Then just die!" She was screaming even louder, the stillness of the cave shattered. The Entity thought he would do just as she asked, for what choice did he have? It would have been better to be lulled back to sleep, but with the way she was draining his energy, he didn't think that was possible. Anything was better than not existing. Anything was better than death. This was uncharted territory, a state of being never encountered.

But she wasn't killing him. She was changing him and didn't even realize it.

Something curious happened.

Perhaps the prolonged cohabitation between good and evil made it happen, like two magnets with reversed polarity forced to touch. The creature he'd been was no more. His mind, noncorporeal body, and his essence turned to the train, and in that moment he didn't see steel and steam and wood and decay. In that moment, he saw a vessel, and its engine was a beating heart that offered him a new life.

The Entity collapsed through the girl's fingers and somehow shucked off the old life. It washed over the train, reaching from one end to the other. He was certain the girl was dumbfounded by what just happened, but then again, so was he. But the quick return to his strength told him that it wasn't necessarily a bad thing. His mind and form were changing—not just himself but also the train.

In the span of a human heartbeat, he knew all about the train and all those inside it, in more depth than ever before. He knew about Pawel Zak in car eighteen, and how he cared more about leaving his cats behind than his two sons. He knew about Lidia Baros in car thirty-one, and how she worried about her husband's dry cough, who may or may not have been forced onto the train. He was—and only three cars up. The Entity knew all about Otto, how his mother died in a housefire while he was spending the day with his father and sisters at the market. And he knew that deep down, a part of him enjoyed killing the children, both back in Munich and in the lair.

The Entity even knew all about the train itself—because the train had become just as substantial as those occupying it. He knew it was a 1933 steamer from the Rudnicka company and that over seventeen-thousand Jews and Poles had ridden it one-way to their end. He knew the wheel bolts were made in Romania, the cylinders in

Belgium. There was a total of 117,994 rivets holding the whole thing together. But that wasn't entirely true—the Entity was holding it together now.

And, also rebuilding it . . .

The girl screamed as the Entity filled the dead with life. Bony arms and legs shook off the cobwebs and the grime of disuse as four-thousand skeletons stood at once. The ripple sounded like dry leaves crunching across stone. They looked out through the window slats, hollow eye-sockets peering down at the only three warm bodies in the cave. In learning his new body—the train—the Entity lost interest in the mortals, and was more intrigued by what he could do. The train groaned as it changed, rust flaking off, bent metal from long trips across unforgiving rails pushing back into place. The train healed itself, but the Entity cared little for aesthetics, so the dull luster of the cars remained, shrouded by a misty, ethereal haze.

The trio of mortals were slowly backing out of the tunnel, unsure of what the bony men and women would do. Even the Entity was unsure at that point, feeling the fit of this new development like a mortal tries out a new suit. The skeletons started to plump up, gaining enough meat back on their bones to be substantial. After only a few seconds the victims looked much the same as they did before Otto crushed their heads with a wrench, although dead was still dead. They looked on with dull, lifeless eyes that saw everything but stared at nothing.

Having omnipotence all across the train was helpful but the Entity chose the head of Otto to settle. The dead eyes flicked open and found the trio of mortals attempting to escape. With stiff joints, Otto leaped from the engine, dragging the alligator wrench with him. It was the first time in his whole existence that the Entity knew his sense of touch. The cool metal of the wrench, the cold air coming in from the tunnel behind. He could get drunk on these human experiences but he chose to funnel his rage into the three who dared make him weak.

Or should he thank them?

The man, having abandoned the lantern, ran blindly toward Otto and was met with a swing so hard that it nearly ripped the top of his head off. The light from the tunnel behind caught little sparkling shapes after the swing, and the Entity realized this was the man's teeth flying free of his jaw.

The woman was leading the child out, and neither saw the man until they were standing over his corpse, still spurting blood across the gravel. She made half a scream before Otto brought the bloodied wrench down hard against her mouth, hooking her jaw with such ferocity that he ripped it clean from her face. As she collapsed, dangling tongue flapping in the wind, he buried the wrench so deep into her skull that he had to put his foot against her shoulder to pry it back out.

Now, the child.

He raised the wrench, blood dripping atop Otto's bald head, but his arm wouldn't come down. The Entity gave a guttural cry that was both anger and anguish. Still, the child had power over him. Still, he could not touch her. If this girl was going to be killed, he would have to find another way.

She scrambled to her feet and stood before him, slowly realizing that he still couldn't harm her.

"What happened? You . . . possessed the train?" All of the silent, sunken faces were watching her from the windows.

"I will kill you child," said the Entity through Otto's lips. "One day." He tossed the wrench onto the engine and then hopped up.

The whistle blew in the confines of the tunnel and the child dropped to her knees, holding her ears. The Entity had work to do. And now, he wasn't so limited. If anything, the chance meeting with the girl had improved his situation. He had a new set of rules.

But he couldn't bury the hatred he had for her, and he knew he'd never be able to rest until she was dead. When the smoke cleared, she was still standing there, more curious than afraid.

There was no track past the mouth of the cave, nor was the opening large enough now for the train to pass. But that didn't stop the engine from screaming, wheels turning, barreling out of the tunnel will all forty-nine cars. It disappeared into the Polish countryside.

Ozelki – Krakus House

January 12th, 2019

There was so much information to digest that Edmund wasn't quite sure where to begin. With all hauntings, the origin story was usually brief and tied to a single incident. But the Ghost Train had a rich past, sprinkled with Nazis, girls with power, and secret orders. The only thing he kept in his mind was how awful it had been for Addey to be caught up in something so big. The guy only wanted his grandparents and a chance meeting with the train had landed him in a coma.

After the old woman—Matilda rather—had finished her story, the group simply sat around, as if unsure of what to say. History painted an awful picture of the war, but she had fought another battle, one that waged alongside the one most talked about in the books. How could anyone's spirit remain intact after so long?

"So you were there," Edmund said. "You were on the train, headed for Treblinka." She'd said a lot of things, but this was the piece to which he kept returning. Matilda was a holocaust survivor.

She just nodded.

Bill said, "God, what a nightmare."

"You have no idea, boy," said the woman, eyes growing cold and distant.

"I just think about you, a little girl, no shoes, cold, wandering." Sophie shook her head, almost fighting back tears.

Matilda held up a hand. "It was an awful night, from start to finish. Otto put me out of the cave because the Entity didn't know what else to do with me. He was scared of me, as he still is. But I was lucky. Or maybe it was just God.

"I wandered out of the cave, having an equal chance of running into bad people as good, but fortune shined on me. My parents found me—not my real parents mind you—my tata and matka, the ones who would raise me. The Germans had burned everything. And then the Soviets did the same thing. I moved around Europe a lot. But when I was nine, the Order of Opeikun found me, and helped me to learn more about myself, and the Entity.

"I learned that I wasn't alone, there were others like me, although rare. I also learned that there were other

Entities in the world, although they are even rarer. This place where we're sitting? This has been in my adoptive family for generations. And it goes back the Legend of Krakus and the defeat of the dragon. Which some might think is mythology. And others think was the Entity long ago, simply in another form."

Edmund remembered the relief over the door to Krakus House—the man with the sword held high, as if to slay an awful beast.

"Krakus killed the dragon of Wawel," Edmund said. "I remember Addey telling this story. The dragon killed lots of people and livestock and King Krakus tricked it by feeding it a lamb stuffed with sulfur."

"Correct," said the old woman. "But Opeikunites know it was the Entity, and so it grew weak and lingered for a while, and then, with all the death surrounding the Treblinka camp, it stirred. It gained strength, and it woke up, ready to devour the world. I made it weak again."

"But that didn't last," said Sophie. "By going into that cave all those years ago, you set it free."

"They wanted to contain it," said Lena. "The Opeikunites, I mean. But they made it stronger."

Edmund had expressed the same thing to Brian and Marcus just a while ago. It seems as if the Entity, Ghost Train, whatever it was, continued to gain strength throughout the years.

"It makes no sense," said Edmund. He thought he knew ghosts, and knew that they were static—hardly ever changing, the legend of them remaining virtually untouched as they were passed down.

"It makes perfect sense," Matilda said. "Supernatural beings still adhere to the laws of nature, as ridiculous as it sounds. They still make evolutionary strides. Just as panda bears no longer have claws because they have become herbivore, the Entity is no longer limited to areas of mass death."

Bill shook his head and leaned back in his chair, as if the whole conversation was absurd. "You're saying it evolved."

"Yes. Survival of the fittest, even in the spirit world. It was faced with death or change."

"But now it continues to change," said Lena. "It feeds and it gets stronger."

"But how do you know?" asked Edmund.

Matilda cut off Lena before the girl could answer. "We just know. This is what we do. We try to be as vigilant as we can, but there will come a time when this Entity will win. My people, the Opeikunites, are spread too thin, and there's no one left like me." She said this last bit with a mixture of trepidation and relief.

"Like you?" Edmund asked.

The old woman nodded, her tight demeanor gave way to the hint of a smile, and for the first time she didn't seem to be taking herself seriously. "I'm the Font of Good, God's Hand, Krakow's Sword. I've had many names. The Entity cannot harm me. There's been a few like me over the years, but they are rare. And when I'm gone . . ."

"The Ghost Train will rule this land," Lena finished.

Sophie looked to both women, as if that answer couldn't be further from the truth. "You're not serious. What about the other Opeikunites? I know they're rare, but they can't let something like that happen, right?"

Matilda considered her words for a moment before a sardonic grin crept across her face. "I imagine some would come here to fight, but there's not much they can do.

I'm the only one immune to the train's call. And as my granddaughter said, it's getting stronger."

At that finality, Bill stood up, his chair noisily screeching across the floor. "I'm sorry that this is all happening to you. Really I am." He came around and sat in the empty chair next to Edmund, his eyes pleading. "Ed, we have to go. Don't you see that now? You have answers about Addey. They aren't the best answers, but the mystery is gone. What do you say, pal? Buy you a beer at Dracula's Castle?" Edmund stole a glance at Sophie just long enough to see her eyes light up by the prospect.

Before he could answer, Lena added, "Listen to your friends. This really is the best idea."

He considered their words and understood that everyone was right. There was no reason to linger here anymore. He'd been chasing a ghost all along, and it wasn't the train—it was his friend, Addey. It was madness that he even let his friends stay this long.

"Can we do something first?" he asked.

"Sure, buddy," said Bill. Now that he saw the tug-of-war was finally won, his tone lightened.

"I dropped Addey's phone when I ran off. I want to go back and get it before we leave."

Bill and Sophie both turned to Matilda, as if she were the divorce lawyer moderating a squabbling couple. Her good eye turned to the clock over the fireplace mantle, the one sitting next to a doll stuffed in a polka-dotted dress. She nodded.

"You'll be fine as long as you're away from there before the sun goes down."

Bill stood, an urgency in his body language. "Then that's what we'll do."

Both his friends put a reassuring hand on his back as they stood to dismiss this odd meeting. The old woman and Lena didn't seem to approve of the impromptu trip but everyone was on the same page at least—except for Edmund. Despite the old lady's words, he didn't think he'd ever feel closure, not with Addey unable to communicate.

But as Edmund had agreed, they took a last shower, ate a final meal, turned in their keys (including the one Addey had in his pocket), and then packed up all their belongings into the Fiat.

As they were headed out the door, the old woman appeared from the kitchen, pulling on a pair of gloves. Her mop of white locks was stuffed into a toboggan and she gripped the counter as she limped out into the common room. Edmund noticed how she just seemed to appear, like some sort of messiah when needed. But as they watched her hobble about, it was clear just how old and frail she truly was.

"Going somewhere?" Edmund asked, adjusting his bag.

"I am, indeed. With you." When Edmund and Sophie looked at each other and shook their heads, not understanding, Matilda clarified. "I want to see the train's destruction for myself, now that daylight will help an old woman's eyes. Come along, Americans." She turned without even waiting on the assured hesitation.

Edmund looked to Lena for support. "You have to come by here anyway, if you're going to Warsaw. Just drop her off at the front door."

He nodded. "I guess this is goodbye, Pole." It sounded silly in his head and he wasn't sure why he'd even said it.

"I guess so, Yank." She gave a toothy grin. For some reason, he thought he would miss the girl.

As he settled into the backseat next to Matilda, he pulled up his phone, dismissed the strange number that had called a second time, and found the spot on EarthTrotter where he thought he'd dropped Addey's phone. His mind raced back to the Ghost Train, crashing through the forest with the might of a dozen excavators. It would be a miracle to find the device, especially if the snow had continued overnight.

As the Fiat rolled away from Krakus House, Edmund couldn't help but feel a strange hush had fallen across Ozelki. True, they were yet to see a single person since their stay, but this morning, despite the cold, Edmund noticed more than one door hanging open. The old woman noticed it too, that was clear by the way she searched doorways and windows, but did not say anything. The connection wasn't there, but it would be later when he was fighting for his life. But in the backseat of the trundling car, he was filled with unease, despite the calm. And as they put the ancestral home of the Opeikun Order to their taillights, none of them knew it would be the last, restful day in East Poland.

***

Minutes later they were passing through the outskirts of Poniatowo, out of the forest and right back into it as they headed south, away from civilization and the busy highway. For a moment, they were aimed toward Treblinka—the site of the death camp and not the town with its namesake, and although only one person in the car would know it, this was the same path the train had taken when she was aboard it. Her eyes drifted out the window to the rhythmic, sentinel-like telephone poles that weren't there eighty years ago, and tried to remember the train tracks. Every time the old lady left Krakus House and came this way, whether it was to the doctors, the pharmacy, to get baking yeast, or just to watch Lena fish on the banks of Lake Uzek, she was reminded of the train stopping dead in its tracks. Then, it reversed and stole away to a hidden lair, near where the American was wanting to return.

"You alright?" asked Edmund, shaking the old lady from some sort of reverie.

"Fine, fine. Just admiring the snow, is all."

There wasn't much of it, and with another warm day or two, all evidence of it would be gone. Much like him and his friends after this trip was over. A part of him was relieved, but he was struggling to make himself change gears. He'd already been in many countries—why couldn't his mind leave this one?

"Up here," Edmund told Sophie. He leaned in and pointed out the steep incline where he'd pulled the car last night, and now that most of the snow was gone, he saw just how lucky he'd been. Had he driven up any closer to the treeline, the Fiat's muffler and undercarriage would have been ripped to shreds.

Ahead of them lay the ruins of the forest. On the edges, the trees were fine, skeletal branches still pointing up to the heavens, some crowding with large, dark birds that Edmund couldn't make out to be crows or ravens. But in the middle, as if a tunnel had been driven straight through the forest was the path the train had taken as it stormed down the mountain to pick up Otto. Trees had fallen, the snow had been pushed back into banks at least six feet high. Even a trench ran along the ground, as if the train had a rudder for a belly.

The group disembarked, with Edmund leading the way. Matilda followed behind, and even with Bill and Sophie offering to help her up the mountain, she refused. The snow had turned to rain overnight, and the rain had made the ground muck. Each of them wore heavy boots, the mud holding their feet hostage with each lumbering step.

Edmund explained what had happened as they walked. It was easy to follow the path back to where the train had first appeared, so jagged was the trail.

"How come there was no destruction in Addey's video?" asked Sophie. "Why didn't it knock down trees then?"

Matilda cleared her throat, coughed up a knot of green phlegm and spit in the snow. Then said, "We've told you. The train is getting stronger. The more people to succumb to it, the more powerful it will be."

"Then how do we stop it?" asked Sophie. Even Edmund thought it was a foolish, naïve question.

Matilda smirked. "You don't stop evil. You just change it. It'll always be here, some way or another."

"Then how do you change it?" Sophie asked.

Bill said, "Right, it became the train. How can it change again?"

Matilda considered their words for a moment, as if she'd never thought of such a thing before. "I don't know. But anytime something changes, there's the risk it'll get stronger rather than weaker."

"But isn't it odd?" Sophie asked, helping the old woman step over a fallen tree as they moved to the apex of the mountain. "We had a force of such evil. And you, a force for good. And you just so happened to cross paths."

"It is strange," said Matilda, swatting away help on the other side of the log. "I've always thought it was a coincidence. The good Lord has a sense of humor, eh?"

"I don't believe that," said Edmund. He wasn't facing the group. He was looking at the ground because Addey's phone had to be near.

"What don't you believe, Ed?" asked Bill.

"That it was a coincidence. What was the lesson Mr. Donnell taught us in world geography, Bill? The one about the wolves and the buffalo?"

"Right, so the buffalo in Alaska . . . or was it Russia? I'm not sure. Anyway, the buffalo were starting to thin out and everyone said it was because the wolves were killing too many of them. So what did the locals do? They started offering big money for dead wolves. Hunters showed up from all over to kill the wolves until finally, the buffalo had no predator left."

"And then the buffalo came back?" asked Sophie.

Edmund said, "Nope. The buffalo, in another ten years, were gone too."

"How?" she asked.

"I know how," Matilda said. She'd stopped to rest against a tree, but talking helped her to keep her pride. "Because the wolves had been culling all the old and sick and malformed buffalo. When they stopped doing that, the sickly buffalo started to procreate. And the sickly beget sickly and so on and so forth. The absence of the wolves killed the whole herd."

"Do you see what I'm saying?" Edmund asked.

She nodded. "You think that the Ghost Train and I are dependent on each other for survival."

"In a manner of speaking," said Edmund. "I think that there is a balance in the universe. Good and evil have always had it, and perhaps back in 1948, God decided that good had tipped the balance too far. He reintroduced wolves back into the herd of buffalos."

"I see where you're going with this," said Matilda, "and you're wrong."

"How so?" Edmund asked, feeling slightly embarrassed. He rubbed his neck and kept his eyes trained on the ground for Addey's phone.

"You think that if the train grows too powerful, the balance will be reset again. But that's not how the world works, boy."

"You don't know that," said Edmund.

She stretched out her arms, conceding the point. "Perhaps not. But I wouldn't put all my faith in God filing down the teeth of the wolf."

"You're the protector of this land," said Edmund. It came out silly but the old lady listened with intent. "You may think when you die, all is lost, but what if it's the opposite? What if—"

"Ed," said Sophie. She'd said his name with such trepidation that he feared to turn around because surely it was bad news. He did, though, and her eyes were just as forlorn as he'd suspected as they fell to the ground behind him. He followed her finger and there, sticking out of the snow was a bright sliver of green metal.

He bent down, plucked it from the grime and flicked off the mud. It was part of the faceplate to Addey's phone. If this piece was here, the rest of it was likely scattered all over the hill, smashed to pieces by the fury of the train. Edmund just shook his head and tossed it into the snow.

"I'm sorry," said Sophie.

"It's fine. I figured as m—" His voice trailed off when he looked into the distance, squinting to make out the boxy shape of a vehicle. If not for such a clear afternoon, he might not have seen the black SUV, nor the fence.

"We need to turn back," said Matilda. "I've seen all I need to see." She painfully pivoted around in a circle and started down the mountain, but Edmund paid no attention. He'd started walking off toward the vehicle.

"Ed?" Bill asked.

The SUV was parked alongside the fence, and it didn't take a genius to realize why.

"They couldn't get in, so they got on top of the car and jumped the fence," he said, getting closer. The barbed wire had been bunched together and ziptied.

"Boy!" Matilda shouted somewhere behind him. "Away from there!"

Standing by the SUV, he could make out the shapes of several buildings beyond the fence, although the incline was so steep that he only saw the edges of roofs. It didn't make sense—he'd been over so many satellite maps and there was nothing here. EarthTrotter even showed the tipped roof of Krakus House, but nothing other than trees here. It was almost as if the place had been hidden on purpose.

A steam whistle.

Far off, but the *chugga-chugga* repetition of steel wheels was getting closer. Edmund turned, in a panic, but saw the old woman standing on the side of the hill, her lips pursed, shaking her head dismissively.

"Not in the daytime," she said. "But come away. There's other dangerous things here besides the train."

He'd no sooner stepped away from the SUV when the trees on the far side of the mountain began to groan.

The group of four stood there silently, watching as they shivered in the wind, dumping snow from their eaves. It was as if a giant beast was on the other side of the foliage, waiting to pounce on unsuspecting prey.

And then, the trees snapped, the woods fell apart, and the train burst through the snow in a frenzy of gray muck. It was blowing steam straight up as well as to the sides, and all Edmund could think about was an angry *Popeye the Sailorman*. They could only see the engine, Otto and the co-conductor with his head blown out. The rest of the train was down the mountain, out of view.

It lingered there for a moment, no more than a hundred yards away, and looked up at the group as if it had just caught them in a trap. In a sense, that was exactly what had happened. The engine gave another ear-piercing wail, and then slowly started to stalk the hillside, crunching everything beneath it.

"Stay close to me," said Matilda. "And head back to the car. *Now*."

They wanted to run away, but the old woman simply couldn't. Edmund was more reassured than either of his friends because he'd seen firsthand how the old woman had stood against the train—and lived. But now, with it barreling down behind them, that was merely an afterthought. He was scared, whether the old woman was here or not.

The car was in sight—it was much easier to follow the train's path of destruction from last night, and just when they made it to the apex of the hill, Sophie lost her balance and went tumbling down.

"Soph!" Bill screamed, chasing after her. Edmund stole a quick glance, just long enough to see her picking up speed, her body summersaulting down the hill, away from him and the old woman. Bill was running as fast as he could and was barely gaining on her.

The train suddenly took advantage of the division of the group, and just as Edmund was about to veer off to the left, to go after his friends, the engine zipped by him so close and with such speed that he felt its unnatural heat slap him in the face. Matilda pushed him aside just in time to dodge reaching hands from the cars that followed.

Now, Bill and Sophie were on the other side of the train, which was picking up speed, the engine racing off ahead of both packs. Edmund didn't know what was happening, but as he saw the car in the distance, he understood what Otto was trying to do. The engine, now at least thirty cars past the running duo, veered back to the left. They couldn't see it, but they heard the noise—the impact as the pilot picked up their little Fiat and turned it into scrap. Edmund slowed his gait for just a moment as he saw the ruin of their rental go end over end, disappearing down the next mountain. The train continued on.

In both directions was nothing but cars, the trainset disappearing into a foggy haze. Edmund tried not to look at the people as he ran, but it was difficult. They saw him, and they pleaded. The kids were the worst—little boys and girls with half their faces hanging down, dirty fingers reaching through windows. Matilda shook him from his stupor and pulled him off the path, away from the car, and down another steep hill. In the distance, he could see buildings.

The only thing they had going for them was that the train still behaved like wood and metal. And even though it could appear out of thin air, run on tracks that weren't there, it didn't seem able to bend itself. If that theory held true, it would be difficult for Otto to bring back the engine—the threatening end—to where they now ran.

Halfway down the mountain, he grabbed the old woman's dry hand just before she went tumbling like Sophie. She allowed herself to be held, and as Edmund pulled her close, it was like holding a bag of feathers. Matilda was nothing more than bones and a hummingbird's heartbeat. They could still hear the train above, could still hear the whistle from the engine, almost a quarter mile away. A plume of smoke rose up to blot out the sky.

"Should we wait?" Edmund asked. "Sophie and Bill may have stopped."

"They haven't stopped, boy," she said through deep panting. "They're running just like us. Now c'mon!"

She took the lead and trudged down the mountain to where the landscape leveled out just before a narrow stream. The water was almost nonexistent, and they were easily able to walk across the bedrock to the other side. There were houses just a few yards away, and Matilda stopped to listen for the train before moving on.

"It's halted," she said. Indeed, they were finally surrounded by silence.

"Or maybe it disappeared. Went back to wherever it hides."

She listened a moment longer, then said, "No. It's stopped. He's out, looking for us. Or your friends."

"What do we do?"

"The train is blocking the way back to Krakus House. Your friends were luckier than us. They can run back to safety, provided they don't get lost. But us . . .we need to get inside one of those buildings and wait it out."

"For how long?" Edmund asked. He tapped his phone, then pulled it out to look at the screen.

"You won't be making calls out here, boy." She was right, there wasn't a drop of service.

"My name's Edmund. Stop calling me boy," he said.

"Fine, fine. Edmund, that's a warehouse. Let's go see if it's open."

She started off, not waiting for a response.

They were on a street now that could have passed for the same one where Edmund grew up, at least before his father took them on the first of seven moves by his twelfth birthday. He counted six houses, bookended by a warehouse on one side and a church on the other. An assortment of vehicles parked along the road, ranging from the usual farming trucks to one surprisingly modern sports car. But not a single person.

"Is this place always so dead?" he asked. Still, that silence.

"That's my friend Gus's house," said Matilda, pointing to a little two-story, white-thatched cottage. "He's ninety-six and never leaves the house. There's no smoke coming from his chimney." Edmund noticed that was the case of all the houses.

"And his door is opened."

She stood staring at it for so long that Edmund circled around and found her with her eyes closed, but they were moving beneath their lids, as if in deep, REM sleep.

"You okay?" he asked.

Matilda's eyes flew open and she swiped a single tear. "He's dead. Let's go."

"How could you possibly know that for sure?"

"I just do. Look, the warehouse door is open too. Come."

As they crossed over and headed through, something loud crashed up on the hill, and both decided that the train was on the move again. Edmund shut the door behind him, unsure why, but feeling a little better because he did so.

The warehouse was empty except for tiny feet running across the floor, snatching up whatever food was available. Someone lived here, at least until recently. Upstairs they found a quiet bedroom with a candle on the bedside table, burned down to a nub. A black and white television in the corner showed nothing but static. On the edge of the bed was a book and a plate with a half-eaten muffin on it.

"They left in a hurry, didn't they?" said Edmund, but he knew the truth of it already.

"They heard the call," said the old woman, moving over to the window that overlooked the street. "Seems a lot of people hear it lately. God, it's moving about in the daytime now. There'll soon be nothing left of Poland."

"So what do we do?" Edmund asked, sitting on the bed. He immediately stood up, not liking the feeling of complacency that quickly washed over him.

"I told you, boy. Sorry, *Edmund*. We are going to wait it out."

"It's a ghost. Can't it wait *us* out?"

"I suppose you're right."

Edmund didn't like the finality of her answer, so he turned to his phone again, desperate to see it connect to the network.

He was still checking his phone periodically as the sun crept behind the fog-enshrouded mountains and a fat, cotton ball moon loomed in the sky. Matilda had dragged a rocking chair into the room and was sitting by the window. From here, she could see both ends of the street, as well as the mountainside they'd scaled earlier that day. The moon's silvery glow glinted off something at the far end of the creek, and he was sure it was the ruins of the Fiat. But with the dark, it was hard to see anything beyond the little rings of orange lights that the streetlamps provided.

"If you're sleepy, then sleep," she said, catching him in mid-yawn. She looked up long enough to hike her thumb toward the bed.

"What about you?" he asked, letting himself yawn again.

"I sit with the owls," she said. "I won't be sleepy until the sun comes back."

"What would you do if . . . if I heard the call? Just got up and walked out like all the rest?" He hadn't really thought about it until now. But with the lack of people in the surrounding towns, it seemed the statistics were growing less and less in his favor.

She lifted her jacket and there in the waistband of her pants was what looked like a yellow gun. When she noticed he didn't recognize it, she pulled it out and turned it over in her hand. Now, Edmund had no doubt that this eighty-something year old woman was packing a taser.

She held it up, the little yellow door hiding the barbs pointed to the ceiling, once again making Edmund think she'd missed her calling at being a gunslinger.

"Then I change your body's current voltage of zero to fifty-thousand."

***

He didn't want to fall asleep but somehow he did, despite being scared out of his mind, both for himself and for his friends who could be in any sort of trouble right now. The thought of them being picked up by the train made his heart sink and he worked hard not to dwell on that particular nightmare.

When he woke it was because the old woman was gently shaking his leg. He started, but immediately found her eyes and she was holding a finger to her lips, instructing him to be quiet. She pointed toward the window, where the night was as black as could be, but some white glow lined the windowsill.

Edmund slowly rose from the bed and walked over to peer through the edge of the curtain. The streetlights were out, and Edmund wondered how he could have possibly slept through what he saw below, other than being far more exhausted than he knew.

The train was there, on the street beneath them, using the same path that cars had been using since the road was paved. But the trainset was too wide, and it had turned over telephone poles and street lights, and had driven parked cars into the sides of the buildings. The fancy sports car now looked like a tube of toothpaste after the wheels of the train flattened half of it.

Luckily the engine was long gone, the sounds of it but an echo far away. Now, the whole trainset was moving at a snail's pace, what Edmund's dad would have called taxiing speed, as if it were pulling into a station. The ghosts inside the cars were calm, simply sitting around in clumps, as if this was their naptime. In truth, as Edmund began to realize, they simply hadn't been activated by seeing a living person.

"What's it doing?" he whispered.

"The engine passed about half an hour ago. It's looking for people to take. And see that?" She pointed down to the destruction it was causing along the street. "It doesn't care to be seen. The Entity has grown the rooster."

"The what?"

"The rooster. That's your term, right?"

He thought for a minute, trying to connect the frayed wires of the language barrier. "Do you mean cocky?"

"Right, cocky. It has grown so powerful that it does not care who sees it."

Edmund looked down, and she was using a small pocket knife to make tally marks on the windowsill. So far she was up to thirty-three.

"Go back to sleep, Edmund. We'll leave when the sun comes up, if it's gone."

He did as she asked, and after he closed his eyes, the passage of time seemed to come all at once, and the next thing he knew the light was filtering in through the mesh curtains, tickling his nose with his eyes closed. The silence had returned and the rocking chair sat empty. His heart sank. What if the old woman wasn't immune after all?

The street below was clear, but still looked like a giant blade had swung right through it. Many of the cars were pressed against or into the houses, and those with parking brakes applied were flattened. A couple of the houses down the street had collapsed as too much debris—a delivery truck and a pair of telephone poles—obliterated their foundations. Before moving away from the windowsill, he took note of Matilda's tally marks.

Fifty-six.

He found her in the next room, standing by a window that looked out to the backside of the house. She sensed his presence and half turned, but continued to gaze out at the wide-open field, apple trees and hedge rows the only things noteworthy.

"Good morning," she said. "I found some coffee and it's boiling on the wood stove. The train knocked out the power last night." Now that she'd mentioned it, he could smell the coffee.

"Have you been to sleep?" he asked. He looked at his watch. Quarter past nine.

"I dozed after the train left. It was enough." But her eyes looked heavy, and just when he was about to suggest she rest before they leave, she said, "Are you ready?"

"What are you looking at out there?" he asked, joining her by the window.

"A whole lot of nothing," she said. "You'd never know it now, but there used to be a whole town out there. Right past those trees."

"What happened to it?"

"The Germans happened to it. We're close to Treblinka, so they set fire to everything around here to keep it secret. This would be nothing but a desert if not for the trees and their usefulness. Buildings and people could tell of your crimes. But the trees . . . the trees could hide them."

"Is that where you lived?" Edmund asked, pointing out.

"For a time. After I left the Entity's lair. Good people took care of me, helped me discover that I was special, and then I led them back and to their deaths."

Edmund didn't know what to say to that, so he just kept quiet.

"The Entity is evil, but it's the same as the Germans. The same as the Soviets. It's so hard to have hope in the face of such evil. Do you understand?"

"I think I do."

"Good. Because hope is all we really have, isn't it? I remember the night I was loaded into the train. I'd been sleeping, and I was sick with typhus. It was a miracle I even survived to the night of the train. People ran into our house, Poles, I mean, shouting that we were leaving. I had no time to get any of my belongings other than my doll and that was only because I was hugging her when matka told me we had to go."

"Matka?"

"My mother. My real mother. Sometimes I can still see her face. She was beautiful. Long black hair. Good teeth. A kind smile. But that's all I remember.

"When she put me on the train, she told me she hoped we were going to a better place. And that hope was all I had during those four agonizing days, crammed in with nearly a hundred other people. No food, no water, taking turns to shit in the corner. And even after the Entity took us back to its lair, I still had hope, because for the first time I felt strong. Nazis had been around for over half my life, at least the years I could remember, and I was finally able to stand up to something. And that's the hope that has continued to drive me forward."

"You're a strong woman. Stronger than any American woman I know," he said, hoping it sounded sincere and not as cheesy as he thought it did as it left his lips.

"But I won't always be," she said. "This old woman is ready for her rest. Ready to join those who have gone on before her."

Edmund draped an arm around her and gently pulled her away from the window. "But not today. Today she's needed to help a stupid American get the hell out of here."

***

The stillness of the morning unnerved him. When he opened the door, hinges squealing from years of disuse, he thought the whole trainset would barrel right through the buildings and land right on the doorstep. It didn't, and the old woman blew past him, taking the lead and heading right across the broken street and up the mountain where they'd come down only sixteen hours before.

She had a renewed vigor, and although she walked with a limp, Edmund figured that was ancient stroke damage and not from last night's horrid events. The taser bounced in her waistband as she took long strides to get across the trench dug by the train. Edmund moved far slower because he couldn't go more than a few steps without turning a full circle, making sure the train didn't slide out of the mist.

"Your car is wrecked," she said, as if that even needed explained. They passed it, a large jagged hunk that barely resembled an automobile at all. While gas was cheap in Poland, replacing a whole car was not. He didn't even want to think of how they were going to pay Nomad. Ghost train collision was probably not covered under the insurance policy.

Matilda wasn't leading them in a straight line, but rather a diagonal arc to the left of where they'd gone down the mountain. At the top, over a guardrail so overgrown with dead vines that he didn't even realize what it was until he'd crossed it, he knew why she'd taken them astray. The wind was blowing hard, picking up snow, but it wouldn't have mattered anyway for what he was looking to see. There wasn't a doubt in his mind that the black SUV was still parked by the fence.

"The train always appears when someone is near the fence," said Edmund.

"Yes."

"The town, Polvec? Why does it care so much?"

"Because the town sits around the Entity's lair. That's the very mountain I climbed down when it released me. Before there were buildings. A town. Come. Let's not linger here."

"Just wait, please? I'm trying to understand. You're saying that a town sprung up around its lair?"

"Yes." She had stopped, turned to face him, but her eyes kept lingering to the spot where the train had appeared yesterday. The trench was unmistakable. "The locals have known about the town for years, but it has remained hidden and untouched all this time. The Entity has sway over them."

"They do his bidding?"

"They are entranced, much like the people who hear the call. And much like Otto Herzog was after I left the lair and he turned his wrench against every person on the train. The Entity is powerful, and you would be wise to stay away from its backyard. Come on, Edmund."

She started to walk, he started to follow. But he couldn't shake the feeling that something didn't add up. Matilda sensed that he had stopped again, and that he was looking in the opposite direction, toward Polvec.

"Edmund?"

"Why does it care?"

"I'm sorry, boy?"

"Why does it care that we go near it? The train has shown up both times I came too close to Polvec."

"No one likes someone snooping around their house. That applies to supernatural beings, too."

"That's not it and you know it. Think about it."

"Okay, Edmund. I'm thinking about it, but why don't you just have out with it? And save an old woman the trouble?"

"It's protecting something."

Her eyes flashed with acceptance for just a moment but her natural, stoic face quickly returned. "Why would you suggest that?"

He shrugged. "When I was a kid we had this pit bull that lived down the street. Name was Jasper. Anyway, Jasper didn't bother anyone. You could go into his yard and pet him and he'd lick your palms like he was your best friend. But across the street, by this little abandoned turnabout, was a big oak tree. If you so much as walked near it, Jasper would lunge at your throat. He eventually had to be put down because some kids were riding bikes near it and he pulled one of them to the ground. Kid had to have a bunch of stitches."

"Where are you going with this?" Matilda asked impatiently.

"Sorry. What I'm getting at, is that a few years after Jasper was dead, they paved the turnabout, but they cut the tree down first. And buried all around it was at least a dozen squirrel skeletons. He'd been burying them over the years. And that's what I'm reminded of when I think of Polvec. The train is hiding something there and tries to bite anyone who comes near it."

"Interesting theory," she said. "But impossible to prove."

He nodded, in full agreement. However, the private investigators seemed to have gotten in, for better or for worse.

They moved away from all signs of the train's damage, but he couldn't help but think that it was still reaching beyond the physical destruction. The world had changed, at least to Edmund in his limited understanding of Poland. From where they walked, they could see the 627, and the traffic was much lighter than he'd ever noticed. He started to pull Matilda toward the highway but she shrugged off his hand.

"Don't bother the motorists with our troubles." She pointed ahead, where a building rose above the treeline in the distance. "We're coming upon Poniatowo. We can call from there."

But Poniatowo looked nearly as deserted. While they didn't see any doors hanging open, there was still a remarkable hush blanketing the town. There was a payphone outside the Palace, the same place Edmund had a conversation with Emril Jablonski about seeing the zoologist chase the train.

"Do you have any money?" asked Matilda, picking up the receiver. "I never carry any."

Edmund fished around in his pockets for a few coins and dropped them into the old lady's palm. "Just tasers, huh?"

She winked, a terribly disconcerting gesture with only one good eye, then turned to make her call. Edmund caught sight of someone moving on the other side of the door's frosted glass window and he pulled it open and stepped inside, wondering if it could be Emril.

The place was far more deserted than the other night, but that could be accredited to it being early morning. Emril wasn't around, but a tall, bushy haired girl at the hostess podium offered him a fabricated smile, nonetheless.

“Is Emril here?” he said. He always preferred to ask the first question so that they knew beforehand not to launch into a spiel about today’s specials through a language he didn’t know.

“Emril not here,” she said, picking her words because English was far back in her language rolodex.

“Oh, sorry,” he said.

“Not here yesterday either. Doesn’t call. Boss is worried.”

“Thank you,” said Edmund, not wanting to push it. Emril was probably riding around in a boxcar by now.

Edmund stepped out just as Matilda was hanging up the phone.

“Your friends are safe, although the girl hurt her wrist. Lena is coming in the car to pick us up. So we wait.” She pointed to the bench outside the Palace and the two sat down, a sense of normalcy coming back at once.

“I’m sorry, Edmund,” she said. Every bone in her body sounded like gunshots as she stiffly leaned back.

“For what?”

"For getting you involved in our fight. Lena should have never sent you looking for your friend. I should have just told you from the beginning. But we are scared out here."

"I understand. And it's fine, you didn't get me involved. I came here looking for answers and would have found them either way."

"I certainly believe it." She coughed heavily into her hand, turning away from him.

"Truth is, we need to be moving on. Bill is going to propose to Sophie in Romania. At Dracula's Castle."

"What? That sounds horrid. St. Mary's Basilica is right down in Kraków. Have him take the girl there."

"No, you don't understand. It's a pop culture thing. She'll love it at Dracula's Castle way more than some old cathedral."

Matilda looked like she didn't know what to make of that, so she crossed her arms and shook her head. "You Americans confuse me. But at least the two have each other. Do you have someone back home?"

"I do," he said. His mind had hardly drifted to Samantha during this whole trip. He pulled out his phone and a saw he had a few missed texts from her, all popping up at once because his cell was getting service again.

"Why didn't you bring her with you?"

"Because we don't have the same kind of relationship that Bill and Sophie have. We aren't . . . um, what's the word I'm looking for? Serious? I'll probably break up with her when I get home, anyway. We don't get along. We barely see each other. I'm okay with that, too."

"I see. That's a shame." She watched the road again, waiting to see the car come along, and even though it was yet to appear, it must have reminded her of her granddaughter. "I wish Lena would find someone."

"Are you all she has?"

Matilda nodded. "Both her parents, my son and his wife, I mean, heard the train's call."

"Jesus, are you serious?" The thought of it made a chill run down his back.

"Yes. My daughter-in-law in 2005, and my son in 2009."

"She was young during both of those,"

"That she was. Too young to lose one's parents."

Edmund nodded but he couldn't relate. Both of his parents were alive and well, and currently wondering why he wasn't responding to his texts.

And just as he'd made the mental connection, his phone began to ring. He held it up and saw it was that strange number again—the one that had already called, each day, at least once.

"You going to answer that?" Matilda asked, looking at the screen. "Might be important."

"It's a telemarketer," said Edmund, finger hovering over the dismiss button.

"I doubt it. That's a Warsaw number."

He took a moment to gauge the seriousness of her face and then shot up from the bench while pressing the TALK button.

"Hello?" he said.

For a moment there was only silence, and then, a clear, pleasant voice responded. "Yes, I'm looking for a Mr. Edmund Riley?"

“This is Edmund.”

“Mr. Riley, this is Agata Nowak from Copernicus Polana.”

“I’m sorry, who?” He didn’t understand the name, nor did he really recognize the voice.

She paused for a moment, and although her English was nearly perfect, she was having trouble coming up with the proper words to make him understand. So she simply said the easiest things to bring him up to speed.

“Adlai Chobot. You were here, to visit him? You told me to call you if any change.”

Edmund’s heart sank because what news could there possibly be if not bad?

“Yes, right, I’m sorry. Long day. What about Addey? Sorry, Adlai?”

“I really don’t know how to tell you this, Mr. Riley,” she said, her voice trailing off. And Edmund felt the tears stinging his eyes, felt the phone slipping through his sweaty fingers. Matilda had stood, noticing his sudden dismay, but did not approach him as he did little circles on the sidewalk.

"Go on, please," he croaked.

"We lost him, sir. I just don't know how."

"What do you mean you don't know how? Was it his heart? His brain?"

"Sorry? Oh, God no. I'm so sorry, Mr. Riley. We lost him. He's gone."

"Gone how? What are you saying?"

"I'm saying that one of the nurses came into his room early this morning and he was gone. His life support monitors were off. He dressed first . . . and then he just left."

"No one saw him leave?" His face was growing flushed.

"No. We assume it was sometime late last night, when there's only two nurses on duty. We have an extra eight patients since you were here. It wouldn't be hard for anyone to just get up and leave."

"Thank you for calling me. I'll try to get in touch with him," he said, then hung up. He didn't know how he would do that since he took Addey's phone, and the phone had since been destroyed.

Edmund turned around, and there in front of him was Sophie and Bill, tears in their eyes but he didn't know from which trauma—the one they'd survived or the one Edmund was experiencing in that moment. Lena was helping the old woman into the back of a small, red car.

Sophie reached out and put a hand around Edmund's shoulder. She was shaking.

"I'm so glad he's alright," she told him. Edmund separated and held her at arm's length.

"That's not what's important right now. I'm so thankful you are both okay."

"Not as much as us," said Bill. "We had it easy—Krakus House's roof can be seen from a long way out, so we just cut through the woods and found it. But you two . . . c'mon, we want to hear about it."

Edmund followed them to the car, unsure how they would all fit inside. Sophie on Bill's lap, most likely. She turned around and walked backwards, smiling at him. There was a white wrapping on her wrist.

"Looks like we're staying in Poland at least one more day."

Ozelki – Krakus House

January 13th, 2019

Three new people had shown up to Krakus House, making it look like a functional business for the first time since the Americans had arrived. Two of them, girls who looked so similar that they had to be sisters, and a man, maybe even younger than Edmund, with a bookish look who could've been writing a travel guide. Large parts of East Poland were without electricity, something that may or may not have been attributed to the train. But it would be eventually. Already the news channels were covering it, and there had been just too many eyewitness testimonies, too much video coverage, to simply explain it away as something normal.

"And now the world will know," said Edmund as he watched the small television set from the bar.

The old woman stepped out of the kitchen—she'd come to shower and change the moment they got back to Krakus House. Her good eye fell across the news coverage, to the grainy video of the train pushing a charter bus right off the road and onto its side. She shook her head, a solemn expression upon her face.

"No one will notice. This is the wilds, remember? Nobody but us cares about Poland's troubles. It's always been this way."

"Won't others be curious?" asked Bill. "I've heard that countries like Russia have always meddled in Poland's affairs."

"True," she said. "But they care more about Poland's politics than its ghosts."

They spent the evening in the common room, on the large sofas that surrounded the far-side hearth. Bill and Sophie had very little story to tell, as she had mentioned outside the Palace. After the train drove the groups apart, Bill grabbed the collar of her shirt and lifted her into the air, heroically carrying her up the hill and away from the train's fury. It continued on, not turning one way or the other. Edmund found this strange at first, but it made sense if it simply wanted to chase them away from Polvec.

It was Edmund and Matilda's story that everyone wanted to hear, but it was relegated to Edmund since the old woman chose to man the oven and bring out large platters of food for all the new guests. Lena, however, sat by his side and listened to the tale.

"She's a fighter, she is. Has been for my whole life."

He didn't mention the tidbits of Lena's history that the old woman had mentioned on the bench, but he was glad he knew it. Growing up here probably wasn't bad, but it wasn't ideal either. She'd only seen the world in the little pieces that flitted in and out of the common room. Lena probably longed for companionship her own age, and that sentiment would only grow as the old woman became more dependent on her.

After the story, the Americans broke into groups so they could make a few much-needed phone calls. It would become serendipitous timing. Bill, with Sophie lending support in the background spent most of the afternoon making calls to Nomad and to his dad back in Lynchburg. The way Bill's face went pale told him it couldn't have been a preferable outcome where the rental was concerned. It was in his name, after all, and Nomad hadn't been happy to rent to such a young person in the first place. Edmund would help out as best he could, but Bill wasn't in a very talkative, nor friendly mood. And why should he be?

Edmund had been the holdup for this entire trip, and although his friend said it was all okay, that generosity—and finances—was starting to wear thin.

Edmund also made a lot of calls. He sat on his bed with the curtains drawn so he could look out the window, sure that he would see the column of steam trailing the countryside. There wasn't much of anything out his window, other than the far-off shapes of two helicopters quickly racing across the sky.

The first calls he made home, to his parents and to his girlfriend, Samantha, and later he would be glad of it once all communication in Poland ceased to exist. His dad was worried, his mom was worried, and his girlfriend was frantic, despite the fact that Edmund was notoriously unfaithful to all of them about checking in. He explained away his flightiness by painting a much darker, much wilder version of Poland, assuring them there was no running water, no electricity, certainly no Wi-Fi, and that food had to be hunted first in order to be eaten. He had no clue how close to the truth all of that would be in just a few hours.

After he managed to get his mom to wind down a long story about the church's new pastor, he dialed

Addey's parents back in Warsaw. Their number wasn't easy to find, but he was able to call nurse Agata from the nursing home and, in a moment of clear medical violation, obtain their home phone number. Edmund never got an answer, it simply rang and rang and rang in an odd, incessant tone that sounded worlds away from American telephones.

The only other option was posting a message to Addey's Facebook, telling him that Edmund had his phone (leaving out the past-tense of that situation) and that they were all staying at Krakus House.

Edmund had an uneasy feeling about the whole thing. Why did he simply get up and walk out? Was he still under the train's call? That thought sent shivers down his spine because he had no way to prove otherwise. Addey could've woken up and promptly started walking toward Treblinka. And at this point, the train may have very well been powerful enough to meet him closer to Warsaw. Edmund just hoped he'd see his friend sooner rather than later.

Finally, he tried to call Brian Harrick but knew those gents were probably dead, more so than anyone else who'd heard the call. If the Ghost Train had chased

Edmund and his friends down the mountain just for being near Polvec, what did it do to those who hopped the fence and went right up to it? He didn't want to think about it, and the fact that the cell phone went straight to Brian's voicemail did little to alleviate that concern.

There was a knock at his door. On the other side of it was Sophie, a look of pure horror on her face. She said, "Come downstairs, you have to see something on the TV."

Edmund followed her down, and when he'd left earlier the room was rather lively with the sisters talking animatedly in the corner with the young bookish guy. Now, everyone, including Bill, Lena, and Matilda, were crowded around the bar, watching the tiny set by the kitchen door.

On the screen there was a reporter, a tall, lithe man with a pencil mustache who looked like he'd just stepped off a 70s gameshow. His jacket was red tweed but the quality of the television made this difficult to see. Behind him, several military men were moving sawhorses onto a paved two-lane road. Behind that, vehicles were either stalled or turning around and heading the other way. A quick pan of the camera showed no less than four, large tank-like vehicles that Edmund had never seen. Then again, he didn't know much about the military here. The reporter was speaking Polish, but it didn't matter—there were at least two translators in the room.

"That's the Bialystok junction," said Lena. "It's the main artery to Belarus and Lithuania. And they're blocking it."

"But why?" asked Sophie.

"Why indeed," said Matilda.

"Look," said Lena. The coverage switched from pencil-stache guy to a short, rotund woman with thick glasses and a shawl over her head. She was standing in front of a vehicle's grill, and when the camera zoomed out, revealed it to be some sort of large, troop transport. The coverage showed a similarly obstructed road with several motorists milling about, looking to armored men with rifles for answers.

"Ukraine and Romania," said Matilda. "They are cutting off Poland from the world."

"Because of the train?" asked Edmund. "It's hard to believe that anyone's government would respond in such a way."

Matilda was listening to the reporters, now back in a newsroom with the word POLSTAT 6 on the soundstage desk.

"They're saying that official word hasn't been received yet as to why the country is on lockdown, but they keep using the words *radical threat*."

"Like terrorists?" Bookish Guy asked. He was clearly British by the accent.

"I don't know," Matilda said, turning her focus back. "President Duda is supposed to address the nation in an hour." She switched off the set and placed the remote on top of it. "That one is full of hot air, so I don't care to hear it. Lena, a word downstairs?"

The girl made sure the guests were comfortable, that food was sitting in front of them, then followed Matilda through the kitchen and down a trapdoor. Edmund didn't realize the place had a basement but it was foolish to assume an establishment as large as Krakus House wouldn't have a subfloor. The kitchen wasn't very big, and on the other side of the wall was the makeshift internet café, so it made sense that storage was below.

"Well that's just great," said Bill, his hand running through his hair. The patrons who'd been crowding around the television were moving away now. Edmund knew what troubled Bill the most—the confirmation that Romania was among the routes to be closed off.

"I'm sorry," said Edmund. "We should have gone yesterday. It was stupid of me to want Addey's phone."

"Yeah, it was stupid, Ed. Really stupid," he said, shooting daggers at his friend.

"C'mon, let's go play cards," said Sophie, wanting to diffuse the situation. She tugged at her boyfriend's arm. Bill just shook her off, not once breaking his stare with Edmund.

"This trip has been about your stupid quest. You don't give a damn about any of us, do you?"

"Of course I do," he said, the words stinging. He said it again, but weaker. "Of course I do."

"Like hell you do. And now we're stuck here. I don't get to . . ." His voice trailed off as his eyes flashed to Sophie. Instead, he said, "Did it ever occur to you along the way that you were in over your head? God, Ed, we are beyond the train now. What if the country stays on lockdown? What if we don't get to go home?"

"You're being overdramatic, Bill. Things will settle soon, you'll see."

"You're a damned fool, Ed. Have you ever heard of a government shutting down a country before?"

Edmund nodded. "Yeah. A government once shut down *this* one. Look, I'm sorry, Bill. I really am. And I wish I could take back everything I've caused but I can't. But we're in this together."

"No, pal. You're on your own," he said, and then he stormed off. Sophie tried to pull him back but he violently shook her off and headed up to his room.

"He doesn't mean any of it," she said, face flushing with embarrassment.

"It's fine. I deserve it. I really am sorry for ruining the trip. And I'm sorry about that." He pointed to the wrapping on her wrist.

"This? Don't be sorry. This is a battle scar, dude. If we get out of this, it'll be one hell of a story to tell."

"I remember when Bill had that kind of attitude."

"He still does," she said, looking off. "But Bill's starting to grow up, ya know? His dad is pressuring him about school, he has to pick a career or get out of the house. Maybe it'll be different when we get married. *If* we get married. It's a weird time for him."

Edmund looked out one of the high windows to catch another helicopter zip by.

"It's a weird time for us all."

Lena appeared in the kitchen then came out to give the common room a once over. The girls were talking politely with Bookish Guy. To them, the naïve ones who'd not known about a ghost train terrorizing the countryside, this was all simply a hiccup in their backpacking adventure.

"You two, come downstairs. Babcia wants to show you something."

***

The basement of Krakus House was a lot warmer than Edmund would have thought, given that these places were usually kept cool intentionally so as not to ruin produce, dairy, and meat. But the proprietor of the house had enough foresight to divide the massive subfloor into two sections—one for goods storage, and one for the War Room.

There was no other word for it, because as Edmund descended the steps and saw the bank of large, flat-screen monitors, it was as though he'd traveled from the distant past to the near future. A large table dominated the center of the room, and upon it a very detailed map carved from wood, as if someone had constructed it from one, giant tree. Each of the monitors showed security footage, but none were on Krakus House's property. These feeds were out in the world, showing scenes from parking garages, mountainsides, towns, water towers, and tunnels.

"What is all this?" Sophie asked.

Lena was walking backwards as she talked, holding her hands out to the amassed technology. "Welcome to the Order of Opeikun. Here, we monitor the train, and we have been since the sixties, since it started to take more people."

"My family was much larger then," said Matilda, sitting in a chair at a computer terminal that looked silly in contrast. On the screen was a video of the train, moving in slow-motion. "Lena and I are the only ones left to observe."

"When's the last time you saw it on camera?" asked Edmund, looking up to one feed where, in the distance, he saw a trench surrounded by several felled trees.

"A few minutes ago. It's currently just south of Malkinia. That's new."

Lena said, "It's never traveled past the Bug River before. Its range is growing."

"Indeed it is," said Matilda. She stood up, her legs shaky, and walked over to the three-dimensional map on the table. Edmund easily found Krakus House, looking very much like a lighthouse since it stood on a higher point than anything else. The map covered many miles.

"Do you see this ring?" Lena asked. There was a red circle drawn around the map, encircling as far down as the Treblinka camp, as well as a few miles north of Poniatowo. Edmund nodded.

"That used to be the train's limits, up until last January. And our cameras just caught it here." She pointed to a spot past Poniatowo, about five miles away.

"It's also moving much faster," said Matilda. "When we can see it, it behaves like a normal train. But when we don't . . . it's as if it slips into another world, and it's traveling. It can appear miles away in a heartbeat. Our cameras have confirmed it."

"How many cameras do you have out there?" asked Sophie, gazing up at one that was angled to a very uninteresting field.

Lena said, "They aren't all ours. Some belong to the university in Warsaw. Some are live feeds from a television channel who set up a nature website. But we have eyes all over Poland."

"And now we have visual confirmation that the beast grows," Matilda said. She placed a clipboard on the edge of the table and Edmund saw the tally marks. She pointed up to the screen she'd been watching. "This was taken from a bridge outside the village of Glina." The quality was remarkable on this particular video. It showed a daytime shot of a little dirt path running straight into the distance with hardly any trees or buildings at all. The camera was mounted high, watching the train pass beneath it. Matilda had slowed down the video to count the cars, just as she had by the windowsill last night.

"Do you know how many cars this train carried when it left Warsaw on its fateful voyage?" she asked.

Edmund and Sophie just shook their heads.

"Aside from the engine, the trainset numbered forty-nine. Last night, it carried fifty-six. This morning, it carries sixty-eight."

"The more people who join the train, the longer it gets?" Edmund asked, but the answer was obvious.

"How much bigger could it get?" asked Sophie.

Matilda shrugged. "I'm sure it's bigger by now. But who knows? Maybe it will one day stretch from here to *your* country."

Sophie bleated a nervous little laugh, but neither she nor Edmund thought it was very funny.

"What does it want?" Edmund asked. He'd posed that question before, but every time something new happened, it was like the rulebook changed. Matilda just stared up at the screen, then looked down, searching her long, troubled past.

"When I was in the cave with him, the Entity I mean, he couldn't see into my head. He couldn't hurt me, couldn't make anyone else do it either. And that scared him. I don't think he's as scared now, but I'm still a burden to him. Anyway, when he tried to see into my head, I somehow saw into his instead. And it was awful."

"Tell them," said Lena, putting a hand to the old woman's sleeve.

"It feeds on death. The same way we eat oatmeal or sausage or whatever you Americans like. Hotdogs. It is sustained by death. And in that cave, it was growing irritated that there wasn't enough death feeding it."

"This was during the *holocaust*," Edmund said. "What more death could it want?"

"All of it. Every single person on the face of the earth. It wasn't satisfied. But then I came along, right when it was starting to plan how to end all life."

"Just how would it do that?" Edmund asked.

She shrugged. "I suppose it's doing it. Like that." She pointed up to one of the screens right after Lena switched channels.

A group of men—non-military by the looks of them—were firing at something offscreen. They nervously backed up, and then from the right side, Otto came running, the alligator wrench held high, and he lopped off the head of the nearest man. The others still fired, but the bullets had little effect on him. They turned and ran, but it didn't look good for them. No sooner did they flee from the corner of the screen did the train zip by, filling the whole video with dark smoke.

"You think if it kills enough, adds enough cars to the trainset, it'll wipe out humanity?" Edmund shook his head, unable to believe such nonsense.

Lena and Matilda just exchanged looks. The old woman said, "That's all we have to go on right now. But no, I think the train will be limited if that's the Entity's plan. I'm sure there's lots of places it won't be able to reach, no matter how powerful it becomes. This tactic didn't work too well for the Führer."

"How so?" Edmund asked.

"He tried to control too much land. And it was his downfall. By stretching himself thin, he left himself weak and open to attack."

"Do you think it could really cross the ocean?" asked Sophie.

"I wouldn't be brave enough to assume not," said Matilda.

"Are we safe here?" Edmund asked.

"For now," Lena said. "It's always been weak against Krakus House. We have what some would call dark magic, but really we only have power against Entities."

"So what now?" Sophie asked. Edmund had never seen the girl so scared, not even when the train was bearing down on them.

"Now, we wait," said Matilda. "We are quarantined, possibly because the government is trying to contain the train, but they don't know how it works. The more men who come to fight it, the more who die—and those deaths are as good as the coal and kindling that once fueled its engine."

Lena shook her head solemnly and played with the hem of her shirt. "I fear that the train will encircle Poland, without a gap in its trainset—the engine's pilot touching the bumper of the last car."

Like a giant ghostly snake, thought Edmund.

Matilda stood up, gave herself a stretch and then walked by Edmund, heading back upstairs. "You all are welcome to stay here. I wouldn't advise you going anywhere else right now. And we have prepared for such things. We have food and drink and plenty of firewood."

"I'm surprised Bill hasn't tried to get a taxi out here," said Edmund.

"He may yet. I should go check on him." She got up and walked out behind the old woman. Now, it was just Edmund and Lena down below.

The silence hung in the air for a moment, and just as Edmund contemplated following Sophie upstairs, Lena asked, "Have you already contacted your family about what's happening?"

"We've talked. But about the train? No."

"Is there a girlfriend back home?" she asked.

It was such a strange turn of questioning, but then again, that's the type of thing people asked when they were being friendly. Edmund hated talking about things like that—almost to the point that he acted embarrassed to have a girlfriend.

"There is."

"Are you sure?" she asked, playfully. "That was quite the hesitation."

"We aren't serious." It was the same thing he'd just told the old woman because it was his default answer where his love life was concerned.

"I see," she said. "That's unfortunate, I suppose."

"Not really. I've never dated much. My dad always said I was a loner."

"That's a sad existence," she said, pushing the conversation to a very grim tone. She saw how it had dismayed him and squeezed his knee, just before getting up. "Sorry."

"Don't be," he said. "I've learned to live with this sort of detachment."

"Is that really what you want with your life?" she said, hovering near the stairs.

He shrugged. "It's easier. If someone breaks your heart, you don't cry if you never really cared, right?"

"Heartbreak is good for the soul, though, Edmund. I know that's a crazy notion, but heartbreak separates us from things like him." She was pointing to one of the screens, where Otto was hanging out the engine's window and chasing down a group of pedestrians.

"Maybe you're right. But there's benefits to feeling soulless."

Lena rolled her eyes and smiled. "Oh, Edmund. You aren't soulless at all. If you were soulless you'd be in Romania by now." And Lena let that stew in the air as she climbed the steps, leaving Edmund surrounded by Ghost Trains.

***

That evening, things began to change rather quickly. At approximately four o'clock, a pair of motorists who'd been turned away at a checkpoint on the 655, south of Suwalki, saw the train hammer through a collection of houses and a parking garage before slamming headlong into a power substation. The explosion was felt for miles, the giant fireball rising into the waning sunlight, and beneath the cloud of black smoke, the train barreled through.

Initially, electricity flickered out for almost sixteen-million people.

Three minutes later and over seven hundred kilometers away, was the tiny ski resort town of Karpacz. Alexi Jelenia watched from his office window as the train headed up the mountain toward the POL-1 uplink site. The train was billowing black from the smokestack as it climbed a near-vertical pitch, engine screaming for blood. It charged right through the main building, collapsing the walls and knocking over enough towers and dishes that people came out of their homes to watch them roll down the mountain. Alexi couldn't be sure, but he thought the train simply melded with the cascading snow and fog before it made it up the mountain, and when the debris collected at the bottom, the Ghost Train was long gone.

In only five minutes, half of Poland was without communication and electricity. By the time the sun went down at Krakus House, the whole country would be a desolate, black island.

***

They were sitting in the common room when the power finally did blink out. They still had enough light to see by, enough to find candles and become secure in their surroundings to get up and move. The girls—who Sophie had learned were here from Sweden—were named Gerta and Margo, however they were not sisters, but school friends who just had an uncanny resemblance. Bookish Guy turned out to be one Timothy Baker, who was on holiday from Leeds, and oddly enough, passing through East Poland on his way to Lithuania to attend a concert by his favorite Scandinavian metal band. Edmund was perplexed that he'd got such a bad reading on both parties, but that was hardly anything new.

They lost the television when they lost electricity, but the small radio Matilda produced from behind the bar lasted a whole twenty minutes before it too drowned in static. But in that short time, they had gathered a few bits of local happenings, like looking through the keyhole for the bigger picture.

The government was spinning the Ghost Train as a coordinated terrorist attack. This seemed to work for most people because the train was so fast, so agile and all encompassing, that it was almost as if it were attacking multiple places at once. Large parts of Poland were on fire, and troops were coming across the border from Belarus and Czechia. The news scared Edmund because for the first time he saw the train as a thinking, calculating Entity and not just the blunt edge of a club. It had the forethought to attack telephony services, to cut the power, to make people panic. It was doing exactly what Lena had feared: Creating a giant, ghostly ring around Poland.

Edmund didn't fully trust the information from the radio. Back home, three out of four news stations were pure garbage—the worst propaganda since the Cold War. That could be the case here. While he did believe the train was out there causing all sorts of problems, he thought—and hoped—that the frantic voices on the radio were embellishing. He didn't get to wonder for long because the radio died, just after they'd said the Ghost Train (referred to as the extremists' weapon of destruction) had rammed straight into another passenger train, sending cars flying all over the place.

Timothy was the youngest in the group, and as darkness crept across the land, and the shapes that were once harmless in the day became long with shadows, he started to panic. His car sat just in front of Krakus House—a tiny two-seater that was so nondescript that Edmund couldn't even begin to figure out the make and model. Timothy lingered on the porch, arguing with Matilda as she pleaded that he stay inside.

"You don't have to pay for your room or food. Please, just stay till morning. This old lady wouldn't sleep well tonight if you left in the middle of all this."

"I would rather take my chances in Lithuania, ma'am. No offense. This is a beautiful little pla—"

And as everyone had gathered around him on the porch, to see this fool really run off into the night, his words were cut off by two screeching shapes flying high overhead. By the time they were a mile out, Edmund realized they were jets—and just like jets were wont to do in such uncertain times, they rained down death and destruction against a faraway enemy. The firebursts were clear on such a dark night—two giant plumes of red shot into the sky as they dropped bombs and then parted in opposite directions.

Even from miles off, they could see the ghostly line of the trainset, unblemished by such conventional weapons. It slithered across the Polish landscape, cutting a line of spectral essence between the ground and the sky. The silence returned, and then the steam engine blared so loud that they held their ears. Timothy's face had gone as white as those crammed on the train, and he just nodded to the old woman without saying anything, and went back inside.

Edmund watched the train until the end, until it was completely gone from sight.

It may move across Poland but it's never far from Polvec . . .

***

For the next three days and nights, they did all they could to stave off boredom. Edmund looked at photos saved on his phone until the battery died and he had no way to charge it. He and the girls played cards, an assortment of games, some of which he knew and many he didn't. Playing cards seemed to be the universal language of all societies.

Bill hardly said anything to him, nor to Sophie which troubled Edmund more than he cared to say. It was one thing to be mad at the guy who prolonged the proposal, but don't take it out on someone whose only crime was being caught in the middle. Edmund stepped in to let Sophie vent and, on the second night, cry. Bill had shut down on them both, and Sophie was lonely. It was an alien concept to Edmund but he never left her side until it was bedtime. Everyone was scared, and rightly so.

The third night, most of the group was playing cards at the main common room table, thick tallow candles arranged so sporadically that they looked as if they were ready for a séance. Lena and Matilda had already gone to bed—the two proprietors of Krakus House did most of the day's work, and Lena slept in a room on the third floor while the old woman often fell asleep in the chair down in the War Room. There was nothing useful down there now, not without electricity. Edmund thought he saw the old woman with her head bowed, as if praying.

Bill was also absent. He wasn't much for socializing now, and to Edmund's recollection, hadn't even spoken a word to the Swedish girls and Timothy. Most of the days (and nights) he spent in bed, reading one of the few English books that Lena had available.

Gerta and Margo were trying to teach the group how to play a card game called Vändtia. It was confusing to Edmund because it seemed to borrow from many familiar games like Rummy and Poker, but also had sprinkles of a classic game from his youth that his dad called Crazy Eights. Only in this game the tens were special.

Both Edmund and Sophie threw their cards down, not sure what they were doing, but having fun pretending they could keep up. At least Timothy was just as clueless, probably never having held a deck of cards in his life. It was comical to see how serious he took the game, and how when he was unsure of a particular rule, he'd question the girls. They found him just as humorous as the Americans.

"Do you remember playing Go Fish on the train?" Sophie asked.

The word struck him funny for a moment, because these days whenever someone mentioned a train, it wasn't a normal one—it was the one currently swimming the waters of Poland outside their door.

"Yeah. Seems like a lifetime ago."

"It wasn't even two weeks ago," she said. "Dammit, we were supposed to be having fun." She was trying to keep her voice steady, but Sophie was coming undone.

"We couldn't anticipate this," he said, drawing from the pile of cards. "Bill will come around."

She nodded and swiped tears away from her eye so fast that Edmund barely saw them.

The world was quiet. Poland had always been remarkably silent but now, there were no sounds of industry, nor of nature. The train had made it all go away. And because Krakus House was so still, they all heard the floorboards as Bill emerged from the room and looked over the railing. Both Edmund and Sophie gave him a warm wave of the hand, but he barely threw his own up before turning and walking off to the bathroom.

Sophie looked at Edmund and just shook her head, as if she were about to cry. He turned to Margo and said, "Deal me out this hand, please." And then, to Sophie, "I'm going to have a chat with him. Be right back." Her eyes were pleading and he couldn't tell if that meant she was begging him to do it or imploring against it.

He pushed out from the table, headed up the steps, and caught Bill just as he was on his way out of the bathroom. Seeing Edmund on the steps gave him a slight pause, but he still offered up a weak grin and a nod before he headed off to the room he and Sophie shared.

"You should come check out this game," Edmund said. It was mostly to Bill's back since his friend was walking so fast, obviously trying to put distance between the conversation and himself. "It's hard as hell to figure out but Sophie's getting a kick out of it."

"No thanks," Bill said, about to close his door.

"Hey man, can we talk?"

Bill lingered with his foot in the doorway. "I don't really know what there is to talk about, Ed."

"You don't? How about the fact that we're all stuck here because of a train full of ghosts?"

"Stuck because of *you*," he said. It came out more venomously than Bill had meant, and the flash of regret in his eyes was quick, but it had been there. They'd never argued like this. "Look, I'm sorry. I don't want to fight. It's not your fault. I'm just having a hard time with stuff." He tried to shut the door but Edmund moved closer and held it open.

"What stuff?"

He relaxed, let go of the door and breathed a little easier. "Life, Ed. Life. I don't know what's wrong. I just feel like this whole ordeal has made me realize that I'm not a kid anymore. That dad can't bail me out when things go wrong. For all his money, it can't do a thing for me right now."

"Same with me." Bill had pushed back into his room a little and now Edmund was standing in the doorway, the sounds below becoming quiet because he was so intent on understanding his friend. "It happens to the best of us. We're growing up, and we can't stop that no more than we can stop the train. But you know what we don't do? We don't give up. And we can't shut down. We have each other and we can't let the train take that away."

"I'm sure you're right," Bill said, sitting on the edge of the bed.

"You know I am."

Just then, the train whistled, but it was distant. Bill and Edmund walked over to the window—it looked out in a different direction than Edmund's room and the scenery was just as uneventful, more so now that the train was prowling. They couldn't see it though, and the whistle went dead toward the end of its cry, as if it had slipped into that otherworldly dimension.

"I guess it's making its rounds again," said Edmund.

"I wonder if the military could airlift us out of here?" Bill wondered.

"Who knows. How many people do you think are left? We're here, right? Could be lots of others."

Bill shook his head. "I think we're special. The train doesn't like to come near Krakus House. But it's gone manic, just ramming into stuff. Like a vampire under bloodlust."

"That's a colorful way to describe it," Edmund said.

"Sophie would love that."

"Yeah, she would. Do you want to come down and play with us? No sense in anyone being alone right now."

He smiled gently and sat back down on the bed. He pulled out a thick, red paperback as if that should have been enough of an explanation. "I'm good. I just want to sleep and wake up in a different place."

That one made Edmund snort. "Good luck with that." He was backing away, sensing that Bill was done talking. The hostilities were over with, now his friend just needed a little space.

"Ed?" Bill said as he turned to leave. "Tell my girl I love her?"

"Sure." He pulled the door shut and headed back downstairs.

His first thought upon entering the common room was that it was rather cold but the two fireplaces were both burning fiercely, so perhaps it was the added electrical heat that was causing a nip in the air. Edmund's attention was drawn to the bottle sitting between the girls and Timothy—it hadn't been there before so he assumed one of them (probably the red-faced man from Leeds) had hopped the counter, found the old woman's stash of vodka, and helped himself. The girls' shrill laughter was akin to skinning a cat. Because all of these things had first grabbed his eye, he didn't realize until he'd sat back down that Sophie wasn't in her chair.

She could've possibly gone to the bathroom—it would have been easy to head up the steps and down the hall while Edmund and Bill talked inside the bedroom. But wouldn't she have stopped by the room first? A shiver, both inside him and against his flesh, made him hyperaware, and he turned toward the door—it was standing open.

Edmund stood up and walked over to it, the trio of foreigners barely noticing that he'd even sat down. A strong wind had picked up and was rushing inside, threatening to put out the nearest fire.

"Shut that, would ya?" came the cry of one of the girls, just before going back to the game.

Edmund stepped onto the massive, wraparound porch and looked out across the deadened Ozelki. There were no candles in windows, no chimneys sputtering smoke. They were truly alone at Krakus House. The smell of far off fires stung his nostrils. Edmund was trying to stave off a panic.

He raced back inside, stopping short at the trio of travelers. "Hey, did you see Sophie? Did she go outside?"

The girls both burst out laughing.

"What? Tell me!" He was growing frustrated.

Gerta, or maybe it was Margo, for who could tell, wizened up and said, "Yeah, she went outside. Just got up and left."

"What did she say? Anything?"

Timothy said, "It was something about getting married, right girls? No, not that. Her boyfriend was going to propose to her. On the train!"

Again, the girls were laughing, but Edmund barely heard any of it. He'd already spun on his heels and launched through the door.

He wasn't thinking clearly. The rational thing would have been to go get Bill, to possibly wake Matilda and Lena, but he had no clue how long Sophie had been gone. The conversation he'd had with Bill upstairs only lasted a few minutes, but if she left the house in a run . . . God, she could be anywhere.

It was difficult choosing a direction. The warming weather had brought with it rain, and so the snow had washed away. He was following what he thought could pass as footprints, but that only took him down the hill and to the church. The dirt road became paved and if she'd left a trail, it ended there.

He stopped, did a full circle, and screamed her name. Krakus House looked like a tall, looming monster with its lit windows and door still hanging open. If only he'd brought his IR camera, he could've possibly seen her in the dark. But that luxury didn't exist, so he ran in the only direction where he knew the train would be, and that was toward Polvec.

His lungs in this cold weather would never let him reach it, and he only prayed that this was the direction his friend had gone when she heard the call. If not, he was running further away from her.

The damage of the train was spectacular, even though he could barely see it in the darkness. There was no moon out, no stars, and the sky was a canvas of dark purple. In fact, the only light he did have was something burning in the woods. Fire would probably light the darkness for days to come.

Edmund called out her name again, and just when he was about to repeat it, the train whistled far off, in the direction he was headed. If Sophie was going toward it, then so was he.

It whistled again, and it was the first time Edmund had noticed that it was changing. No more did it have the high, ear-piercing cry of a normal train. Now it was lower, demonic, like when the batteries in the cassette player his dad gave him started to die. Any lower and it would sound like a foghorn.

Edmund cut through the woods, doing his best to keep a line of sight with Krakus House but failing because the terrain turned sharply downhill. Through the trees he could see the train's slightly spectral glow. He caught faces in the cars, moaning wails and reaching hands. They didn't see him—they saw the girl in front of him. Sophie was walking right toward it, not running, but quick enough that an exhausted, panting Edmund had trouble keeping up.

"Sophie!" he screamed. His voice came out raw and ragged. "Sophie, stop!"

She didn't hear him, or at least didn't *want* to hear him. She was enthralled, as so many others had been. This had been the march of anyone caught under the spell, and it was breaking his heart to see her running headlong into certain death.

Sophie's foot caught on a rock and she went down, but only for a moment. Immediately she regained her stride and started toward the train again. It was enough time, however, for Edmund to catch up, grab her arm and pull. She shrugged him off, as if he were some minor annoyance.

"Sophie? Sophie!" he said, circling in front. Her eyes were filled with starlight, as if under some trance. She wasn't blinking, but tears were running down her cheeks as if her mind was trapped inside a body working on its own accord.

"I'm getting married," she said. Her voice was steady. "Bill is waiting and he's going to propose."

"No, Sophie, he's not here! It's the train. We have to go."

Edmund put an arm around her waist and dug in his heels but she kept marching forward. Sophie was small—not more than a hundred and thirty pounds—but she was moving with unnatural resolution, and when Edmund tried to wrestle her to the ground, she slammed an elbow into his back so hard that he coughed and dropped to his knees. Sophie broke his grapple and trudged on.

They were nearing the train, and Edmund's body was wracked with pain, both from the exertion of chasing after her and now the blow against his back. Sophie was limned in bluish-white light as she still marched toward her death. The engine was sitting quietly, the hiss of steam the only sound. Sophie would die in the next thirty yards.

Edmund found his strength, found his feet, and took off running after her again. They cleared the treeline and were now back on a road, or at least what served as one now, days after the train had left trenches all over the place. Sophie stepped up to the edge of one such trench and went tumbling down the side until she reached the curved bottom, landing in a mud puddle. Edmund was able to make the same trip with less struggle, and that time allowed him to catch back up again. Sophie was climbing up the far-side of the trench and Edmund grabbed her foot. She wasn't wearing any shoes, her toes frigid beneath the wool sock.

She kicked back, but he was expecting it. One foot came down close to his head and he narrowly dodged her slamming it right into his jaw. The dodge made him lose his hold on her, and he fell back on his bottom, still clutching one of her socks. Sophie scrambled up the side and continued on.

Twenty yards to go.

Edmund lifted himself out of the mud, and on the other side waited Otto, standing by the engine, a wall of machinery at his back. Sophie kept going, closing the distance between herself and the man who would rip her head off with a wrench.

Ten yards to go.

He was about to yell her name again, but knew it was useless. So Edmund made one last-ditch effort to save his friend. He broke into a sprint, ran around Sophie and put his back to Otto for longer than he'd ever wanted, and grabbed her around the waist. Edmund lifted her off the ground, like a linebacker, and carried her away from the train.

The sound the engine made almost caused him to drop her, so loud and close it had been. Edmund couldn't carry her down into the trench and make it up the other side, so he ran alongside the unending trainset, dodging reaching hands and cries of help, much like when he first encountered the train. Sophie was kicking him, slamming fists against his head and back but he did his best to ignore the pain. Otto was chasing him down, and would be on him soon if he didn't get around the trench.

Luckily it ended abruptly and he was able to head back toward the trees. When he stole a glance back, he found Otto, a look of pure rage on his face. Had anyone snatched a victim so close to death from him before? Edmund didn't think so, and if he didn't put some distance between himself and that wrench, the ghost would have them both.

Optimistically, they made it another twenty yards before Edmund's arms started shaking and he knew he'd never carry her back all the way to Krakus House. His body was so taxed, and that was without the girl fighting to get free, as if he were some rapist who'd pulled her into a dark alley. There was going to come a point, probably in the next few steps, when Edmund was going to have to drop her. What would he do after that? Simply run off or wait his turn?

Edmund wasn't a runner.

He had managed to pull away from the slow-moving Otto, and the man trailed them by at least thirty yards. Edmund put Sophie on the ground and tried to hold her face so that she looked at him. Her starlight eyes were speckled with madness, and she didn't see him, nor hear him. Her attention was on Otto, the Entity, the one who promised her that Bill was on the train with a big, shiny ring.

"Sophie, please! Listen to me! It's Edmund. If you're in there, please stop running. Please stop going to him. You're going to die, Sophie!"

She wasn't looking at him. He had her arm, and then his fingers slipped to her hand, and then she was gone, walking toward Otto. The big German man had stopped and slung the wrench over his shoulder. He kicked his leg out and locked it, as if telling Edmund that he'd won. His hand stretched out, and it looked for a moment as if he were going to ask Sophie for a dance.

Light quickly flooded the forest as Edmund's blood turned to ice. The train was coming to meet its conductor and latest victim. But Otto dropped his hand. He looked toward the light and the wrench fell to his side, a look of bewilderment upon his dead face. Edmund also saw it, and quickly realized this wasn't the light of a train—this was two lights—headlamps—and they were coming right toward the ghost.

A black SUV raced in front of Sophie and plowed right into Otto with such force that the ghost went flying off into the muck. Edmund couldn't believe what he was seeing, couldn't believe that a ghost could be affected by the grill of a car, but either way he was glad that it could.

The window was down and Brian Harrick stuck his head out and said, "Well don't just stand there, mate, grab 'er and get in!" The hatchback lumbered open.

Edmund didn't wait around for Otto to come back, so he grabbed Sophie, who'd changed directions to follow the flying ghost. He pinned her arms to the sides and dragged her to the back of the SUV. Hands reached out and helped him load the kicking woman inside, and the vehicle started rolling even before Edmund hopped in on top of her.

"Hang on, we're going back to your place!" said Brian from behind the wheel. The SUV jerked around, and for a brief moment he caught Otto standing back up and running toward their taillights.

"Hey, Edmund."

And there in the backseat of the SUV was his friend.

It was Addey.

He couldn't process what he was seeing because so much was happening at once. Sophie was still fighting them, still screaming out for Bill. And just when the SUV left the dirt path and the wheels landed on pavement, the train was back, coming up behind them with a stream of smoke and fury. It let out a guttural growl, flames belching from the wheels.

The pilot rammed them in the bumper, and because it was angled—and because they were designed to not-so-gently nudge cows from railroad tracks, it lifted the vehicle off its back wheels. Had Brian not quickly pumped the gas, the SUV might have tipped over, but instead it slipped off the train with a frenzy of sparks and kept on going.

There was no beating the train, no outmaneuvering it. They could go no place where it couldn't follow. The trees provided no cover, nor the buildings, nor the bridges. If the SUV wasn't hindered by the terrain, then neither was the train. If they could've turned around, run alongside the trainset in the opposite direction, they might have stood a chance, but it had chosen a strategic spot to pin them—train cars on one side, trench on the other.

They were fortunate that the rain had caused one end of the trench to collapse, so Brian was able to jerk the wheel hard left, putting them on course to arrive at Krakus House. The train was still coming, but as Edmund held down Sophie's hands, he noticed through the tinted back windshield that it was falling behind.

Brian pulled the SUV right up to the front door, parking next to Timothy's tiny car. Edmund could see Matilda standing in the doorway, a throng of people behind her, but his attention was snatched away as the train came just feet from their back bumper and then veered off to the right, heading down the hill behind Krakus House. He was about to hop out, but then the engine appeared on the other side, having circled around the building like a giant constrictor about to squeeze the life out of its prey.

Edmund now noticed for the first time that someone was lying across the next row of seats in their SUV, holding a bloodied hand to his side. It was Marcus, Brian's associate. He'd either been shot or stabbed, and now that Edmund had seen the wound, he couldn't shake the stagnant, coppery smell of blood that permeated the SUV's interior. The cars kept moving outside, the engine disappearing back down the mountain. Edmund could see no end to it, no beginning. It had become a giant ring.

"Sophie?" Bill screamed, pushing his way past Edmund when he saw his girlfriend. The starlight disappeared from her eyes, as if the veil brought on by the train could no longer stand while proof otherwise was in front of her. She collapsed, her body going limp in his arms.

"Get her inside," said Matilda, stepping out into the cold, hair whipping around her face. "All of you, get inside."

"Addey?" said Bill, carrying Sophie inside. "What the hell is going on tonight?" He looked to Edmund for answers but found none.

The train still circled as they gathered together and went inside. Addey and Brian carried in a very weak, very pale Marcus, and placed him on the floor by the fire. Both the Swedish girls looked as if they'd been crying, probably after a heavy reprimand from the old woman. Edmund pushed his way into the common room, thankful for the warmth, and was about to start his long, unending barrage of questions when Matilda hobbled past him and stood on the porch.

"You, boy!" she yelled. "Back inside!"

Edmund peered back out into the night, and if not for the slight glow of the train, he might never have seen the man standing twenty yards down the hill, past their cars. His wavy hair and long jacket gave him away.

It was Timothy.

"Tim!" yelled Edmund, but he was feeling an eerie déjà vu. "Get back inside, bud. That thing will snatch you right up."

Timothy had heard Edmund, but he'd heard the train first. He turned around, looked at him with little galaxies in his eyes, and said, "Crimson Halo is playing a concert just for me! They're on the train!" He turned back and started off.

Edmund knew it was a losing battle the moment he stepped off the porch. The engine had circled back around and came to stop just in front of the awestruck, oblivious man. Otto stepped off and Edmund froze in place, still twenty yards away and powerless to do anything. Timothy ran right toward the towering ghost and was met with a quick slash across the throat. A spray of blood cascaded off to the side as the man's knees buckled and he slammed them into the ground before falling over on his side. Otto looked up at Krakus House and flung the blood off the wrench. A chorus of screeches and cries erupted behind Edmund. Clearly there'd been an audience.

Otto scooped up the dead man—hell, dead *boy*—and carried him toward the first train car. Timothy's head lolled back and forth, hanging on by only a thin strip of sinew. Otto chucked him over the edge and then went back to the engine.

There were many things that night that would haunt Edmund forever. But the one that struck him the hardest was seeing the dead man pitch over the edge of the window and then, stand right back up, now bathed in an eerie mist.

Timothy's head was still hanging by threads, but he was able to look out and see Krakus House, see the assembly of those still living, and realize he was dead. He put his hand through the window, screaming for help, and then the others in the car swelled around him—ghosts of different times. Most had been there for eighty years, but tonight, Timothy joined the fray as a recruit.

The engine's whistle blared so loudly that the windows vibrated, and then it was circling Krakus House once again. Edmund wondered if it even planned to ever leave.

Polvec

January 16th, 2019

In all the years he'd been prowling the countryside, he never felt so strong as he did in the last month. As he hung from the side of the engine, curtesy of Otto Herzog's body, he watched the winding form of the train as it went on for miles. Three to be exact, as there were currently just over five-hundred cars connected to the trainset. No real train could pull so many, not a steam engine at least. The Entity was still bound to Poland and didn't know how the world had progressed outside the borders. Perhaps there were flying trains by now, eighty years after he'd melded with his current body.

He'd been smart enough to cripple Poland because of what had happened back in the lair. After all these years of dealing with mortals, they still managed to surprise him. And even though he was careless sometimes—it was hard to remain so vigilant and cover so much area—the Entity always regained control.

But tonight he knew something bad had happened, something to do with the Pole and the two Brits who'd fled with his latest two would-be victims. The Entity knew the hearts and minds of those aboard the train, and could sometimes read those he called, but it was sporadic, hardly reliable. That was one of the tradeoffs to becoming the train. He might have gained much power, but he'd also given up a lot. If he'd been able to read the minds of those fleeing in the large SUV, perhaps his mind would be put to ease.

But no matter, he encircled Krakus House, that hive of ungodly madness, and headed back toward Polvec. The countryside was barren, the people gone. He was confident most everyone around had either come to the train under the spell, or had been killed and loaded onto it just the same. The Entity fancied himself a siren, singing a lullaby that lured the humans and crashed ships. The destruction wrought by the train was beautiful, but no longer could he hide. Eventually, word would get out. His only hope was that by then, it would be too late.

Polvec was on high alert, as every person there was a thrall under his spell. Whenever he chose not to kill someone, to add them to the train, he could beguile them to do whatever he wanted. And early in the fifties, he began to build a town around his lair, painted to blend in to the natural wooded landscape. He'd been smart enough to know spy planes would always take pictures of Poland from the air, so he made sure Polvec was always invisible.

Currently there were around thirty men and women who lived in Polvec. It operated like a real town, and for the first time the Entity was seeing new generations of people populating the streets. No one ever came looking because no one cared. Poland was wild in the 40s, and it was wild today.

The Entity didn't have much use for humans, but they served two very important purposes at Polvec. First, there were the guards. Many of those that the Entity chose for this came from military backgrounds and were adept at small and long rifles. They patrolled the mountainside, within the border of the fence, and made sure the lair was never disturbed.

The second group was the scientists. They were the most important people in the world. He always looked into the heads of those who heard the call, if he could, to see if they knew their way around a laboratory, had any experience with infectious diseases, biology or virology, then he put them to work rather than kill them outright.

As the Ghost Train pulled down the deserted street of Polvec, up the hill that the child Matilda had walked all those years ago, the Entity saw something was very wrong. Two of the guards were down, shot dead and lying in pools of their own blood. They were wearing their white fatigues, as to match the snow-covered mountain, only now their backs were splotched red. He could have tossed them into the train and made them ghosts. They would have told him what had happened, but he was starting to put it together on his own.

Otto pulled the train into the tunnel, past the pile of railroad scrap that he'd disassembled all those years ago, and stopped at the end, right by the labs. The back of the train, some three miles away, was still wrapping around Krakus House.

The burly man stepped off the engine—the Entity used Otto's eyes and ears as short-distance surveillance. He couldn't move more than a hundred feet from the train, but he rarely needed to go any further than that. As he surveyed the lab, he was angered by what he saw, by what he'd allowed to happen.

All of his scientists were down—it had been a firefight. They were clutching guns, as every person who lived in Polvec was required to have one. But they had fought and died valiantly protecting the work that the Entity had started back in the sixties. All of the computer monitors were shot up, as were the testing chambers, the centrifuges, all of it. He glanced into the quarantine cell and found all the live subjects still there, lingering at the end of their lives just as planned, their skin mottled with so many sores that they look dressed in polka dots.

This place was little more than a processing room for silver panhandlers during World War 1. With the help of his thralls, he turned it into something magnificent, a biological research facility that would rival any other on the planet. And now it was gone.

Only one person moved inside the lab, and the Entity had felt his presence the moment he entered. At the rear of the room, collapsed by a filing cabinet was Piotr Galin, the zoologist who had single-handedly pushed the research to new heights. He'd done more in a week than the biologists had in twenty years. The formula was perfect. Now, he was on the floor, blood dribbling down his lips, a revolver still clutched in his hand.

"What happened?" the Entity asked. It came out in German but Piotr understood.

"The Brits," he said, voice cracking.

The Entity knew them—they were the last two healthy specimens, and Piotr had taken great interest in them because he wanted to see how the formula would react to their specific genome. They'd been kept alive but that had been a bad idea. They never should have been allowed to enter Polvec, but the Entity hadn't been able to detect them. Now that he was so strong and able to move into parts of Poland like never before, his range of detection shifted when he was far away. He'd been near Czechia when they hopped the fence.

"They . . . did this?"

"They had help. But it was a massacre. We weren't prepared."

"You're weak. The lot of you." The Entity grabbed the revolver and placed it on a table, then lifted Piotr up by the arm. The dying man stiffly rose to his feet, coughing a great glob of blood onto the floor. "Get on the train."

Piotr knew what that meant, but nodded his head and staggered away. He'd made it two feet before he half-collapsed against a rolling gurney and held himself up with shaky legs. He turned back around and said, “You should know something else.”

The Entity, by way of Otto, raised his eyebrows.

After the dying man told him of the ultimate slipup, Otto picked him up and tossed him over the window of the first car. The man wasn’t dead yet, but he would be soon. Right now, the Entity was growing angry because the last eighty years were about to be erased by a boy and two Brits who seemed to know their way around guns better than the thrall he employed.

But now they were all congregated at Krakus House. He had little power there, certainly none over the old woman. She’d never strayed far from his mind, hadn’t even strayed far from his location. He thought she’d died soon after the train was born, but then the house went up, the Opeikun setting up a base right in his backyard. That was probably the case all over the world where creatures like him roamed, but he had to remind himself that there were no other creatures like him. He was a beast from out of the shadows, and he would stay in the light forever or somehow be shoved back into darkness.

But how could he fix this problem? The old woman would protect them, and as long as she existed, he was powerless. Time had strengthened him—he was stronger now than he'd ever been. She had not changed since her youth. If anything, she was weaker now than ever, crippled by the curse of age.

He had a plan because one of the benefits of existing forever is the unmatched time to think. Humans were simple. Humans were predictable. And now that he had Poland in a vice, it was time to test them in ways they've never known.

The train's whistle blew and a large cloud of black smoke filled the tunnel. Piotr, now noncorporeal, stood up in the car and left the lair, the first time in many days since the train had taken him away.

Ozelki – Krakus House

January 16th, 2019

There was much to tell, but the immediate story Matilda wished to discuss was why there was a man currently bleeding out across her nice bearskin rug. Lena and Edmund searched the place over for medical supplies but were satisfied with hydrogen peroxide and clean towels.

"You, boy! Help me!" Matilda was pointing at Brian, who looked almost as bloodied as the dying man on the floor, but only because he'd carried him out.

Brian nodded and bent down to help the old woman move him onto his side so she could inspect the wound. He wasn't crying out, but Edmund saw a gush of blood ooze from his gut as they moved him.

"Was it a bullet or a knife?" asked Matilda. "I can't tell because it's a clean cut."

"Bullet," said Brian. "Must have went right out his backside."

They rolled him flat again, and Matilda doused two towels with hydrogen peroxide, then stuffed one beneath him and one on the frontside of the wound. She snapped her fingers to get Brian's attention and said, "Here, hold pressure." He did as she asked without question.

Bill had pulled Sophie to sit against the steps but her body was as limp as the man bleeding out. Her breathing was slow, but steady. Matilda moved over to her, pulled back her eyelid and gave it a thorough look. Finally, satisfied, said, "She's fine. The train stupor, is all. Let's hope she's not out as long as this one." Matilda hooked her thumb back at Addey who just stood by the door, as if unsure if he was invited to come in.

The girls, Margo and Gerta were sitting at the table, talking quietly. Neither of them had ever seen something like this, and the train had frightened them so badly that they didn't dare separate from the group.

"What's it want?" asked Gerta. "Oh, God, my mum will be scared out 'er mind! We have to get out of 'ere!"

"We will, darling, we will," Margo comforted. "These men aren't going to let anything happen to us." Edmund didn't like the shrillness of either girls' voice, so he paid little attention to what they said.

"Is anyone else hurt?" asked Matilda, turning a circle around the room.

Nine others, in various states of energy, said no.

"It's still out there," said Addey, looking through the window. "But it's stopped. I don't see the engine."

"Why isn't it ramming down our bloody throats?" said Brian, switching hands against Marcus's bloody stomach.

Matilda said, "Long story. But it won't bother any of you as long as I'm here."

"Believe her," said Edmund, just as the Brit's brow furrowed in skepticism.

"Lena, put on some soup," the old woman said. "We have guests who are undoubtedly hungry. And I'm sure they have quite the tale for us."

For some reason, all eyes turned to Addey, rather than Brian.

Edmund's friend simply nodded. It was almost painful to see him awake because he still didn't look like himself. The weeks spent in the nursing home had left him gaunt, eyes sunken and cheekbones poking through. He'd grown plump back in America, enjoying all the fatty delicacies found on every street corner. Now, his jeans hung from his hips and his shirt was so baggy that it was impossible to tell if he were hiding abs or a gut.

"I went to Polvec a month ago." His grin turned sheepishly toward Matilda. "It was a bad idea, just like you said. There's a spot on the far side of the mountain where the rain has washed out the earth beneath the fence, and I was able to slip in through there."

"Why, Addey?" asked Bill. "Why did you even bother to go there?"

"Because he was searching for his grandparents," said Edmund.

"That's right. Mama and Tata told me they heard the train. That was back when I was in high school. I was so depressed. I never talked about it. But I went back home because there were so many unanswered questions. I'm sorry, Edmund. I shut down on you. I should have told you what was happening in my life."

"It's okay. I can relate. We all can relate." He flashed a look to Bill who dropped his head and said nothing, only stroked Sophie's hair.

"Anyway, I did a lot of investigating. A lot of train searching. I found out all the things you probably found out as well, Ed. Otto, the train and the way it only comes out at night and in January—two things that are no longer set in stone."

It took Edmund a moment to realize what he meant, but now that he thought about it, Addey's video was shot last month, in December. That should have been an early warning that the train was growing in power.

"The more I learned, the more afraid I became. And this is all after I hyped up the ghost hunting to you, Edmund. I wish I'd never mentioned it. I sent you a message, telling you that I didn't think it was safe, but that was the night I heard the call. My grandparents were calling my name, and I was hearing them as clear as I'm hearing you now.

"I left, but I pulled my camera out because I knew I was going to die. I knew that the train had lured me. I don't know how I had the strength to fight the call, but I did. I filmed the train, and at the last minute . . ."

"Otto came for you and you ran off, leaving your phone," said Edmund.

"I dropped it in the snow, but yeah . . . how did you know?"

Both Bill and Edmund brought him up to speed, telling him of how they'd visited his parents and then the nursing home. They saw the pictures and the video—countless times until the phone broke.

"This was all a month ago right?" said Lena. "Why were you back there again tonight?"

"Because I had to see it for myself. When I woke up, I stumbled out into the hallway, and on the television was the train. It made my blood cold! I got dressed and hitchhiked my way back here."

"You didn't go home first? Call your parents?" Lena asked.

Addey snorted and rolled his eyes. "My parents don't give a damn about me. Never have. My grandpapa and grandma were who raised me. I know they are on that train. I don't need Otto's siren song to convince me of that. But I knew Polvec was hiding something. It's the source of the train's power, or at least a closely guarded secret."

"And now we know why," said Brian.

“You do?” Matilda asked. For once, the old lady was as clueless as the rest.

“Thanks to Edmund here, Mark and I learned about this Polvec. The locals weren’t friendly, they never are when they meet you with AK-47s, but that’s besides the point. We hopped the fence and started snooping around. We stayed hidden for little while but then were discovered.

“This man, that Piotr character who went missing a few days ago? He showed up right when we were going to be shot full of holes and asked them to keep us alive.”

“Piotr is alive?” Lena asked.

Brian nodded. “Oh yeah, lots of people were still alive. The train may call them, but it doesn’t call them to death. It calls them to serve. Anyway, thank God this here boy showed up and sprung us.”

“You helped them escape?” Bill asked Addey. He simply nodded.

“Damn right he did. We were to be experimented on, and I seen just what those experiments looked like. The boy let us out of our cage, Mark and I snuck up on a bloke and took his gun. Then it was an all-out firefight. We took down probably a dozen of ‘em, but Mark took a hit right in the gut. We were able to leave Polvec the same way Adlai here got in, packed up Mark in the back and that's when we ran upon Edmund here and the lady there." He pointed over to Sophie whose eyes were still clamped shut.

"Tell me about these experiments," Matilda said. She was looking down at Marcus and Edmund could see it in her eyes that she knew he wasn't long for the world.

"It was awful, mum. They had these injections, right? And after only an hour, the people would start to break out in horrible sores. Those would start at the trunk and move to the limbs. I watched people scratch so hard that they were bloody afterwards. They didn't suffer very long, that was the grace of God, because they got sick—some kinda fever—and died not long after."

"God," said Matilda, barely above a whisper. "He's done it."

"Done what, mum?" asked Brian.

"And who?" added one of the girls from the table. They had been hanging on Brian's words.

"The train. The Entity," she said. "He wants death and now he's found a way to spread it more effectively than ever before. He's engineered typhus."

"But isn't there a vaccine for typhus?" asked Bill.

"There is, but I'm betting this strain is immune," said Brian. "You didn't see the lab. These ghosts have worked hard to enslave smart people to build a research facility to make the typhus."

"We have to tell someone," said Lena. "The CDC or WHO."

"We're way ahead of you," said Addey. He dug into his pocket and pulled out a flash drive and a tiny, capped test tube holding a dingy green fluid inside. "We swiped their samples, downloaded their schematics. If we could get this to the right people, perhaps they could reverse engineer it. Find a cure."

Bill stood up and looked at the flash drive with wide, fearful eyes. "Shit, Addey. Does it know you took that? It's gonna be pissed."

And so it was.

Just as he said it, the train bellowed from outside. Noise sprang up all around them as the cars began to move in reverse, the ghosts inside springing to a frenzy. The trainset was moving so that the engine could once more reappear close to Krakus House's front door. Those inside gathered at the window and watched through the darkness as the *chugga-chugga* slowed down to a crawl and then with a hiss of steam the engine stopped just where it had earlier, when it took Timothy the Bookish Guy who would never read a book again.

Otto hopped off and stood in the muck, looking Krakus House over as if it were the first time he'd ever seen it. The alligator wrench was still in the engine, and to Edmund it looked like he was wringing his fists. He took a few steps forward and stopped, as if he were waiting on something.

"Stay behind me," said Matilda. "I think my old friend wants to have a talk."

Edmund couldn't believe that so many people were rallying behind the old woman because most hadn't seen the power she commanded over the Entity. Most of them didn't even know the train *was* an Entity. They all filed out the door except for Brian, who'd sat on the floor and kept a firm hand pushed against his friend's wound. Bill even leaned Sophie against the stair post and followed his friends.

Matilda walked toward Otto who only stood his ground, sizing her up. She stared at him, and he returned it with equal venom. Edmund realized that he had control over most everyone, but this woman had bested him since she was a mere five years old.

"Leave this place," she said. "You have no power here."

Otto smirked, then rattled something off in German and turned around, heading for one of the train cars.

"What did he say?" asked Bill.

"He said that he's not here to talk to me."

Otto picked up a child from the first car and placed her on the ground. Although Matilda wouldn't recognize her after so many long years, it was the second girl that Klaus Wagner shot dead when the Entity put the suggestion in his head. Now, the little girl with half her head collapsed stood there and spoke in English that wasn't perfect, but passable.

"The old woman is a hindrance to me," the child spoke.

"Who are you?" asked Edmund.

"I am Gertrude Panza. I am Otto Herzog. I am this train. I am death." When she spoke, it didn't just come from her lips. It came from *all* their lips. The dead on the train and Otto. They were connected as one voice . . . one *Entity*.

"And what do you want?" Lena asked.

The little girl made a creepy half smile because most of her cheek was blown out. "I want the old woman. Dead. And I want you to kill her for me."

"You heard the old lady. You have no power here," said Lena.

"I do not. And I can't force any of you to do it. But . . . I'm asking you to do it."

"Why would we listen to you?" said Edmund.

"Because I'm not going to leave here until you do."

"You just want this back," said Addey. He held up the vial, and for a moment the little girl and Otto both dropped their stoic faces.

"That belongs to me," the girl said. "And I will have it back."

"We're done here," said Matilda. She'd started to walk off.

"I have been here since the beginning of time!" screamed the child. The dead on the train held their ears. "You humans are nothing more than animals. You will run out of firewood. You will run out of food, water, medicine. And in the end these people will bring me your head on a platter and beg me to take it!"

Matilda turned around, and for a moment the light from the house made her look at least fifty years younger. She was a strong woman, to be sure, but that was the first time she'd ever really looked the part.

"You're scared," she said. It was such an odd thing to say at the moment but the ghosts standing in perfect unison, like bees in a hivemind, just stared. "After all these years you still can't control everything. You aren't all powerful. And you still fear change."

"Change made me strong."

"It also made you weak. What will happen next time? The two of us together—it's always interesting, isn't it?" Matilda started to stroll down the hill. Otto and the girl both took a synchronized step backwards. The old woman threw her head back and laughed.

He climbed aboard the engine while the little girl struggled to lift herself up and roll into the car. She peeked out from the same place that Matilda had all those year ago when she grasped the Entity, effectively spreading a cancer that ate away at the bad things of the world.

"Remember what I said," the little girl uttered. The engine came alive, blowing smoke, bellowing a warcry. "Bring me her head and I'll go away."

With that, the train pulled out, slowly at first, but then picked up speed. It wasn't going away, only circling Krakus House like a giant, ghost-filled merry-go-round.

Ozelki – Krakus House

January 17th, 2019

True to its word, the Ghost Train did not leave through the night. Edmund tried to get a little much-needed sleep but every time he shut his eyes, the engine, as if sensing his slowed heartbeat, blared its whistle. He shot out of bed more than once, only to look out the window and see nothing but a cloud of smoke.

Somehow Marcus survived the night, Brian using the cigarette lighter from the SUV to cauterize the wounds enough to stem the bleeding. He said he believed Marcus's liver had been nicked, and if that were the case he wouldn't get better until he had a professional tending his wounds. For now, he lay in and out of a drunken stupor, fevered and most likely still going to die, despite Matilda and Brian's best efforts.

His state of consciousness was a little better than Sophie's, who remained in a fitful sleep. Bill had carried her up the steps and put her on the bed, then fell asleep next to her with the door open. In fact, they'd all slept with their doors open. The train had united them—strangers no more.

Matilda gave Addey an empty room—the one he'd stayed in last month, actually—but he didn't even use it. Instead, he spent most of his time in the common room where Brian slept next to the fire alongside his dying friend. Addey kept watch, looking at the train through the windows and making sure no one attempted to walk out the front door should the Entity call them.

"You haven't slept any?" asked Edmund, walking down the steps and finding his friend sitting at the bottom.

Addey shook his head. "I've been asleep for a month. I'm scared to shut my eyes. What if I don't wake up?"

"I don't think it works that way, bud." But he didn't believe that. He very much believed that people newly awakened from comas often slipped right back in.

"It's good to see you, Ed," he said.

"You too. I guess we didn't get a proper hello last night."

"We didn't. I can't believe you came here."

"I just couldn't leave without knowing. I had to know what had happened to you. We had plenty of chances to be out of Poland. Bill and I are at odds right now over it."

"Bill will get over it," he said. "We're all safe. For the time being."

"Where's the vial?"

"In my room upstairs. Makes me nervous just carrying it around."

"Yeah, I guess it would. I wish we could get that thing out of here," said Edmund.

"Not sure that'll be possible," Addey said, pointing out the window. Currently the train was stopped, but the car in front of the house was filled to the brim with dead men, women, and children. Their lifeless eyes were turned curiously toward the BnB.

"Why do you think it stops sometimes?"

Addey shrugged. "Maybe it's still causing destruction out there. As many train cars that's in its set. . . the engine could be halfway to Germany right now."

"It's like one of those tree snakes, with its tail coiled around a branch."

Addey smirked. "And we are the branch."

“Hey, Ed?” called Bill from up above. “Come up a sec, will ya?”

The men on the stairs looked up and found him there, leaning over the railing, stuffing some kind of bread into his mouth. Addey threw up a hand to wave. Edmund nodded and left his friend there on the steps to watch a sleeping Brian and Marcus.

Bill had wrapped Sophie like a mummy atop the bed, but that had been smart thinking because the house was far colder this morning than it had been last night. Each of the rooms had a fireplace in them, but Bill, like Edmund, had trouble keeping one stoked.

“How’s she doing?” Edmund asked.

“She talked in her sleep last night. I couldn’t understand what she was saying, but that’s good right?”

“Yeah, I’d say that’s good.”

Bill walked over to the window and looked out. It was the only thing they could do—watch the train and wait.

“I just need to say I’m sorry for how I acted before,” said Bill.

“Not necessary,” Edmund said, voice rigid.

"Yeah, it is. If not for you . . ." His voice trailed off, eyes turning back to Sophie, sleeping as still as a porcelain doll.

"You would have done the same for me, or for Lena."

Bill smiled. "You mean Samantha."

"Yeah, Samantha. That's what I said."

Bill just shook his head, but he was still smiling. "Yeah. That's the thing I realized. I would do the same for you. We're all friends, we stick together."

"Damn right we do. Now we just have to figure out how to get out of here."

"Or how to make the train leave."

"Do you think any of the others would . . . you know, take the Entity up on his offer?" Edmund asked.

"Of our group? No. I've only had a few conversations with the PIs. Those girls . . . who knows. And certainly not Lena."

"Okay. Then I guess we do what we can to wait it out. Won't the military or someone come? A whole country can't stay cut off from the world."

"I think the train is far more capable of keeping things away than we give it credit for. When it's stopped like that . . ." Edmund pointed out the window, to where the boxcars sat motionless. ". . .I think the front end is raising hell."

"They'll nuke us," said Bill. It was so matter-of-fact that it caught Edmund off guard. He was probably right.

"Let's hope they took note of how ineffective missiles were and back off."

"That's asking a lot, but I pray that's the case," said Bill.

Just then Sophie turned over and Bill rushed to her side, lifting her arm and trying to wake her.

"Soph? Sophie? Wake up, baby. Please?"

"Bill . . ." she said, and his eyes lit up. Hers, however, remained closed.

"She's coming around," said Edmund. "Just stay by her side."

He nodded and started to say something, but the train lurched forward, the whistle far away, but loud enough to make Sophie tremble in her sleep.

***

The first three days they created routines and seemed to do a fair job living them. Lena and Matilda had inventoried their food and firewood and thought they could survive another two-weeks before things would become dire. Matilda told them that January was the off-season, even though Krakus House catered to the Ghost Train fan club. The heavy season for backpacking travelers was November when air rates were the lowest, and that's when the pantry would be stocked to maximum capacity. They had one strike of good luck though—the boy who sold them firewood had delivered a truckload the morning before the train wrapped itself around Krakus House.

"We'll hack up the tables and chairs before we freeze to death," said Lena one morning. She and Edmund were sitting by the fireplace. Marcus was only a few feet away, and he'd even woken up a few times to take in his surroundings, only to fall back asleep. His skin was a putrid yellow color.

"I hope that won't be necessary," Edmund said.

"It won't be. Besides, we'll run out of food before firewood."

He just shook his head. The Polish sense of humor left something to be desired.

"Where does the old lady stay?" asked Edmund. Matilda was hardly ever seen, only when she appeared in the kitchen to help her granddaughter prepare food on the small propane hotplate.

"She's been spending a lot of time downstairs."

"But why? None of the equipment works."

"That's where the voices are the quietest."

"Sorry?" he asked.

Lena smiled, and rolled her eyes a bit, as if she'd forgotten to tell him something. "Sometimes . . . she hears the dead."

A week ago, Edmund would have laughed, but not after having spent time around the old woman. She'd known her friend Gus was dead. It made sense now, the way Matilda seemed to step out of herself, the way she would look at him as if she weren't really seeing him. Those pauses weren't because of a stroke-addled mind. She was *listening*.

"Does she hear the ghosts on the train?"

"Sometimes," Lena said. "And when she does, it can be overwhelming. There's so many of them."

"What does she say to them?" Edmund asked.

"She says nothing. She can't talk to them. But they can talk to her, and they are scared and hate their existence."

"It must be horrible."

"You have no idea. Imagine living that life. Being born the wrong race, forced to live in a filthy ghetto. And then, instead of the mercy of the camp, the mercy of the *gas chamber*, forced to live eternally on the train. I wouldn't want babcia's 'gift.' It must be terrible to hear their cries."

"Imagine if they could fight back," said Edmund.

"What?"

He thought back to the picture of the holocaust train he'd seen in the newspaper on the night he met Brian and Marcus. All those people being loaded into the cars—thousands of them—and it was ordered by only a handful of guards with guns.

"What if all those ghosts just turned on the Entity? Decided they didn't want to be slaves anymore."

“I don’t think they have the option to fight,” said Lena.

Edmund looked into the fire, the flickering embers that reminded him of the fury of the train. “Maybe they do and they just don’t know how.”

She said nothing to that, only contemplated it with distant eyes that also stared into the fire. Edmund and Bill played cards on the floor with the girls—both Margo and Gerta were looking less kempt since there was no hot water. Indeed, they all had been a few days without a bath, but it was better to be filthy in icy Poland than sun-scorched Morocco.

Edmund watched them often, mainly because neither of the Swedish ladies seemed to click with the rest of the group. Whenever a conversation began, they found a way to exit it, and Edmund often caught them off in some remote part of the house, talking quietly.

He excused himself to go to the bathroom and noticed that the door to the kitchen was hanging open. Instead of going up the steps, he rounded the counter and went down, immediately feeling a shiver run up his spine because it was at least ten degrees cooler in the pantry-slash-War Room than it was upstairs.

Matilda was sitting in the room toward the back, the narrow space that separated the bank of computers from the stacks of dry goods. She was in a rocking chair, her motley-colored quilt draped across her lap. Her frail, splotched fingers were knitting by candlelight, and Edmund couldn't help but feel a little claustrophobic by the place she favored to live during this hardship.

"Are you hungry?" he asked. He didn't really know what else to say as a conversation starter. "I could warm you some soup or something."

She looked up at him, eye adjusting to the shape in the light. The room was pitch black if not for her pulsing, tableside candle. But Edmund could see her hands fold down across her lap, the smile spread over her face.

"That's sweet of you, but no." She coughed, and in the silence of the room, he could hear the rattle in her chest—what his dad had called the Death Knell when Edmund's grandmother had died in the nursing home, from complications due to pneumonia.

"Why don't you come upstairs? It's a lot warmer."

"I don't mind the cold, Edmund. But I do like the quiet. Come, sit with me." She waved a hand and for the first time he noticed there was a chair opposite of her, out of the candle's glow.

He pulled it closer to where she sat and seated himself. She put her needles away and turned to him, a slight adjustment that seemed to pain her. There was a soft, golden glow on her skin, making her look like parchment.

"It's still there," he said. "The train, I mean."

She nodded. "Of course it is. He'll not go anywhere until I'm dead, which may be sooner rather than later."

"Don't say that," he said. "You don't know that."

"People are predictable as often as they are not," she said. "One of those up there will be the death of me. I'd wager one of those girls. They're young, they haven't learned to appreciate life yet, and they may be just stupid enough to believe that the train will simply go away once I'm dead."

Edmund said nothing, because deep down, he agreed with the old lady.

"I need to ask you for a favor," she said.

"A favor?"

"Yes. When it's done. When I'm dead I mean . . . stop with the eye-rolling! Now listen. When I'm dead, the wards upon this place will not hold him any longer. He'll be able to come right in. When I'm dead, I want you to look after Lena."

"I will," he said. That favor was simple.

"That's not all. There's every chance that you will all follow me into death. I'm not telling you anything you don't already suspect. But if you can get out. If the Entity slips up at all and you can get away . . . head to Treblinka."

"The camp," he said as much as asked.

"Yes."

"Why?"

She turned away, as if she didn't know, or as if she were hearing something Edmund could not. "I don't know. You just need to go there after I'm dead."

"We will. But stop saying that. You're not dying on my watch."

"Such cliché, American," she said, then launched into another cough so horrid it made him cringe.

"Will you at least sleep up there? This chair can't be good for your bones."

"Safety in numbers, right?" She said it in jest, smiling crookedly.

"Normally, but the train easily thwarts numbers. Why do you think no one has heard the call?" Edmund didn't think the wards that she spoke of protected the house from that. Addey had heard it a month ago, and so had Sophie.

She shook her head, dismissively. "Because he doesn't need to call them. They're more useful alive. Right now he has several able-bodied people who could run a knife through my heart."

"I'm not going to let that happen," said Edmund.

She smiled and stood up, then placed a hand to his cheek. It was icy.

"I think I will take you up on that soup, boy."

***

Another four days saw the group becoming increasingly more agitated with each other. The girls—Gerta and Margo—were running out of what Edmund called ‘elective supplies’—makeup, hair and skin products, and little orange pills that Margo was fond of popping into her mouth when she thought no one was looking. Once those things were gone, they were truly ‘roughing it.’

The first fights didn’t begin over food as Edmund would have figured, but over firewood. True, there was plenty out back and you only had to go within eight feet of the nearest train car to grab it from the pile, but Lena and Matilda made the decision that it shouldn’t be squandered on individual rooms. So the whole group decided they would stack all the chairs and tables to a corner in the common room and put down bedding on the floor. That way they could feed the two main fireplaces and keep one room warm, rather than several smaller ones. Lena and Matilda normally slept in a joint bedroom on the third floor, and it was easier for the old woman and her knees to stay downstairs.

Sophie continued to sleep, and after Bill carried her down and put her in front of the rear fireplace (Marcus had the one up front because invalids came first), she was looked after by several people. Lena and Matilda took turns changing her soiled clothes while Bill held up a blanket for privacy. Even Edmund and Addey helped to spoon feed her chicken broth.

Marcus was starting to wake up, helped along by the bottle of antibiotics that Gerta found in her purse from when she had her wisdom teeth extracted. He was much quieter than Edmund remembered, but getting shot in the gut probably humbled someone. He listened intently as Brian explained their current predicament. Marcus just seemed content that Addey had made it out okay after risking his life to spring the PIs.

A few days into the holdout, Marcus was eating soup, spoon fed by Lena. He was sitting up, his lungs sounding as though they needed drained with a hose. His brow was sweaty, but it was one of the few times he was alert enough to have a conversation.

"Look after Lil for me, will ya, Brian?" he said.

Brain just shook his head. "You're going to look after her yourself, mate. We're getting you out of here soon. You'll see."

"Bullocks. Whether the train uncoils or not, I'm done for. You know this. You saw this kind of trauma in the war."

Brian said nothing.

"I just need you to take care of me baby girl when I'm gone. Her mum won't know what to do without me."

"I will always be there for Lily and Jean. You know that."

This answer seemed to satisfy Marcus, whose body went limp. He didn't wake much after that night.

On their eighth day, Marcus started to decline again, his skin staying an oily yellowish hue. His states of consciousness were fleeting, and he spent more time yelling out in fevered nightmares than talking in wakeful conversation. Even though Brian didn't say it, he was both worried and devastated over his friend. He kept a cold washcloth on the man's brow. Cold water was something of which they had plenty.

On their tenth day of interment, Margo started to unravel. This was brought on by the train's suddenly close proximity to Krakus House. Edmund thought that it was getting bolder, that Otto was steering it closer and closer with each pass, but that wasn't entirely true.

He noticed when standing on the second floor of Krakus House, he could now see the tops of the train cars as they passed. When the group ventured out to the porch, they learned the reason—after the train had made so many rounds, it had begun to cut a deep trench in the earth. The windows were nearly level with the dirt and mud surrounding the house. What made this more terrifying is that when the train was still, the car on the backside of the house leaned inward, and the dead inside could scrape their fingers against the windows of Krakus House.

Margo and Gerta disappeared upstairs, preferring their cold room to the eyes of the group. Edmund couldn't be sure, but he thought they came from money, and the thought of camping in the common room with the rest was beneath them, despite the current predicament. Still, the situation was making Margo seem a bit like a loose cannon.

"Good news," said Bill, sitting down on the rug between Addey and Edmund. He pointed out the backside window, to the stalled train and the throng of ghosts who were pawing at the windows. "If the train keeps cutting a trench like it has been, we'll be able to walk right over top of it and leave."

"Wishful thinking," Addey said. "It is lower, though. Do you think we could pull a car up to it? Climb onto the roof and jump over?"

"I don't want to think of doing that again," said Brian. "That bit of ingenuity's what landed me on that thing's bad side."

And as if in response to his friend's voice, Marcus sat up, vomited a greenish bile down his chest and fell back against his pillow. He was muttering incoherently and blowing snot bubbles from his nose. Brian sprang into action to clean him up.

Edmund said, "If only we could direct its attention to somewhere else. Give us a break in the trainset."

"Not going to happen, I'm afraid," said Addey. "I'd just be interested to see what's happening in the rest of the world. The rest of Poland, even."

Lena got down on her knees and helped sponge Marcus's bare chest with a cloth. Brian fell back on his haunches and thought for a minute, then stood up and said, "We have to get him out of here! He needs a hospital."

"The antibiotics will help a little," Matilda said from her rocking chair.

"It's sepsis," said Brian. "He's going to die if we don't have something stronger to fight this infection. I was just trying to help." His voice broke down and he aimed his hand out the door, toward his parked SUV. "I just wanted to stem the bleeding is all."

"And you did. If not, he'd be dead already," said Matilda.

"If only we could signal someone, reach a helo or something!" said Brian. Then, a thought struck him and he bolted out the door.

Addey and Edmund exchanged glances. It was raining out, the cold air that rushed in found Edmund by the fireplace and made him shiver. They could see Brian opening the back door of the SUV. He pulled out a black briefcase and then came back in.

"Gents, lady, follow me, if you will." Edmund, Addey, and Lena trailed him up the steps and then around to the third floor where Brian opened a door, as if knowing exactly where he was going. They passed through the old woman's bedroom and out a pair of double-doors that led to a balcony. From here, they could see the train, winding down the mountain like a colossal snake.

"Let's hope this thing still has battery left," said Brian. He knelt down and opened the case, then handed Edmund what looked like a cellphone, or at least a tablet with a large screen. Brian stood up, holding a tiny black drone in his hands. He powered it on and the little blades began to whirl around. “Got a signal?”

Edmund switched on the tablet, a little blue and gold logo popped up and was quickly replaced by a shot of their shoes. Brian took the tablet from Edmund, then tossed the drone up into the air where it hovered steadily. He assumed the controls and the rest gathered around him so they could watch the screen.

It looked like a trainyard from up high. The Entity had killed so many people, had lured so many unsuspecting victims that there were now so many cars that it couldn’t properly maneuver. Edmund wondered if there was a ghostly formula to it—did every hundred deaths equate to a new car added?

The Polish countryside looked like a scene from one of those post-apocalypse shows Edmund loved to watch on television. A nuke hadn’t gone off, but he couldn’t imagine it would be much different than what he was seeing further out, on the drone’s camera. There were no more forests. All of the trees had fallen, pushed aside by the train and its fury. This had caused wildfires, and now everywhere they looked were small piles of smoldering wood.

Even the towns were gone—Poniatowo was reduced to stone foundations. Brian moved the drone as far as the range would allow, until he was hovering over Polvec. If not for a pair of bloodied bodies against the fence, Edmund would have never seen the artfully painted buildings hiding on the mountainside.

If Brian had hoped there'd be life out there, a Med-Evac or a field hospital, it was dashed when the drone headed up the 627, now empty save for a few cars that were as dead as the trees in the forests. Krakus House was still standing, and it made him wonder if that was why no one had come to fight the train.

"The world has to be watching us," said Edmund.

"You think so, mate?" said Brian, sounding like he either believed that or just didn't care.

"Why else aren't they using deadly force? Maybe they know people are alive here. You can see this place for miles away, especially now that the trees are gone."

"You might be right," said Brian. He was bringing the drone back. "My granddaddy always told me that the Luftwaffe let St. Paul's Cathedral stand because it was an excellent navigation landmark. Maybe that's the case now."

Lena said, “The Opeikunites have influence in Europe. They could have arranged for the powers-that-be to hold off on attacking their main Polish headquarters.”

“The Opei-what?” Brian asked. The drone landed on his hand.

“The ones who fight Entities,” said Edmund.

“*Entities*? Bloody hell, there’s more of ‘em out there?”

Lena nodded. “There is. And let us pray they stay far, far away from Poland.”

Ozelki – Krakus House

January 27th, 2019

Sometime late that night, Edmund woke to a loud crash. He sat up and looked around, and judging by the strength of the fireplaces, it was a few hours past midnight. No one else was awake, making him wonder if the noise had been a dream. But when he found Marcus sitting up and peering around the room, he thought that maybe it hadn't been imagined after all. Marcus flopped back down, his snores returning almost immediately.

Edmund threw off the covers and stood, feeling the chill in the air creep into his bones. The train was idling outside the windows, the ghosts walking around inside the cars as if they were billiard balls winding down after the break. The engine was there, but he couldn't see Otto, only the other conductor, propped up like Norman Bates's mommy.

His instinct told him that the sound had come from outside. Without Otto there on the engine, he was probably on the prowl. Edmund thought for a moment, searching his own brain—was he being lured? He didn't think so, because he thought he could just as easily sit back down and go right back to sleep. Against his better judgement, he pulled the door open and stepped out onto the porch, shutting it behind him.

The night air was cold and rainy, and somewhere far off was the smell of fire. Even the train had a scent—like rust and oil. Edmund saw nothing outside that was unusual, unless he counted the ever-present unusual train. The ghosts inside were starting to stir as they caught movement at Krakus House.

Edmund walked the wraparound porch, first heading to the right, to where the train cars slumped, almost touching the house, and then backtracking around to the left—where he saw a body with rain pelting down on top of it.

Immediately he recognized the mess of blond hair. Her feet were bare and bent awkwardly at the knees, toes painted pink. Whether this was Margo or Gerta, he couldn't tell because she'd landed on the rocks to the east side of Krakus House. He was thankful she was facedown. Her body had simply exploded upon impact, yellowish bones poking through all along her back, arms and thighs.

And then, before he could even look up, to see from what point she'd jumped, another sound rocketed just next to him, startling him so badly that he fell and started to crawl backwards beneath the overhang of Krakus House's lowest roof.

And now both the girls were dead.

The second one to follow—had it been Gerta or Margo?—landed with similar force, hitting the edge of the first girl's target and then bouncing off. She rolled down the hill and into the weeds, but Edmund caught a half-second look at her face—and it was caved in so badly that it looked like a bowl.

"Bring them to me," said a voice behind Edmund. He whirled around to see the little girl who had addressed the group on the first night of internment. "I'll give them a good home." She was keeping her distance, at least twenty feet from the SUV parked by the front door.

"Go to hell," said Edmund, walking back around to the front door. "Did you make them do that?"

She shook her head, little pieces of her flesh flopping back and forth. "I could have, but I didn't. I'll have you all soon enough anyway."

"Then I suppose we'll see you then."

"The old woman is going to die soon, you know that right?" The little girl turned around and said, "Ezra, stand up, please."

Edmund followed the child's gaze to the third train car where an older man, his neck slashed horribly, held up a wobbly hand and waved.

"That's Matilda's oncologist. Seems the old lady has stage four lung cancer. He's surprised she's made it even this long. I bet this cold house isn't kind to her lungs. I imagine it'll be worse when the wood is gone."

"I'm leaving," said Edmund, feeling his blood boil, but also feeling the unease sweep beneath him. He didn't know if the Entity's words were true or not, but he reminded himself that deception was a tool it had used through the countless ages of its existence.

"Save them all the trouble. Kill her for me. You can do it humanely." The train moved a little, bringing one of the more distant cars to the forefront. A woman inside tossed something out, which struck the gravel near the SUV. It was a black case that, upon impact, sprang open, revealing an assortment of tiny syringes. "Just shoot her in the neck with that and she'll go right to sleep."

"I'm not doing anything of the sort."

"No? A more violent way then?"

Again, the train taxied, bringing another car to the front where a group of men and women stood by the windows, like bank tellers waiting the next customer. They began to reach into their cart and throw something out—many somethings that made them look like they were dumping buckets of water from their shoddy boat.

Edmund couldn't believe what he was seeing, but they were tossing out guns—more than he'd ever seen assembled at once. The firearms transcended all timelines—there were muskets, MP40s, Colt .45s, shotguns, rifles, bazookas, even a Gatling gun that looked like something straight from a war movie. When the ghosts were finished, there was a pile of guns, both new and old, almost four feet high. Edmund looked on with unimpressed eyes.

The little girl shrugged, and now Otto was walking up behind her. He couldn't address Edmund, apparently the Entity still needed a translator. But the look he gave was easy to interpret. Both ghosts turned around and walked off, the Entity fuming at the mortal's lack of reasoning. Edmund had no doubt that when the old woman drew her last breath, he would be the first to follow her to the grave.

***

He found a shovel in the basement and had every intention of burying the girls before the rest of the group woke up when the sun came back. But the only spot he could find was too far out, and he didn't want to venture so close to the train. Other than that, the ground was rocky and he couldn't turn the shovel enough to make a hole. So in the end, he settled for wrapping the first girl in a sheet. It was a grisly job because she was stuck against the rocks, but he managed to roll her up and place her on the east-facing porch. The other girl was gone, simply vanished, but Edmund knew she'd rolled far enough away from the house for the Ghost Train to collect her.

Addey was the first one awake that morning. Edmund hadn't gone to sleep after the unpleasantness of the night before, so he brewed a pot of coffee using the last of Matilda's propane-powered hotplate. He was sitting on the first step of Krakus House when his friend came down and sat next to him.

"Coffee?" asked Edmund, then handed Addey his own cup to drink.

"Did you sleep?" he asked.

Edmund shook his head. "No. It was a bad night." His friend just looked at him, eyes narrowing beneath his bushy eyebrows.

He told him the story of what had happened and then Addey surprised him by wanting to see the body.

"You don't know which one it is? Geez, Ed, we need to know at least that much."

Edmund couldn't watch as Addey rolled the girl onto her side, trying to determine identity. It's not like she jumped with her purse and her passport. But Addey lifted her wrist, and through the splatter of blood, showed Edmund the infinity symbol tattoo.

"I'm pretty sure this one is Margo."

Edmund just nodded. As if it even mattered.

"Woah," said Addey, rejoining his friend on the steps. He'd seen the pile of guns, so Edmund filled in all the blanks of what had happened.

"That old lady really has cancer, huh?" Addey said.

"I don't know. Maybe. But we have to protect her. The Entity is getting pushy. Maybe it's scared."

"Or just getting bored."

"Could be," said Edmund, nursing the black, tasteless coffee. "I think Brian is the one we have to worry about now."

"Brian? No way. He's a good guy."

"Yeah, he is, and I wouldn't put it past him to shoot the old lady if it meant getting Marcus to the hospital."

Addey didn't have much to stay about that, but Edmund could tell that he agreed with him.

They spent the morning tossing what guns they could over the train. The bigger ones, the bazookas and Gatling gun, they rolled down the hill where it crashed somewhere far below, sweeping the dew off the dead bushes. Half an hour later, the train made another circle, and when Edmund looked out the window, he saw them once again throwing the guns back onto the pile.

Ozelki – Krakus House

January 31st, 2019

On the last day of the month, the last day for a lot of things, Matilda came into the common room and announced that they had, at best, another two days' worth of food, four or five if they could ration it. This consisted only of cans of vegetables and one loaf of bread that had fallen behind the shelf and was so hard that it barely constituted food. When they became angry at such news, she assured them they would have already run out if not for the deaths of the two girls to make it last longer.

Sophie continued in a coma, for that was the word that Bill had been avoiding but knew it was true just the same. It had now passed the two-week mark and she showed no signs of waking up. Her face was gaunt, cheeks all sunken as Addey's had been after not eating solid food for so long. Her skin was always so dry and so cold, but that could be said for everyone's skin this deep into the holdout.

No one worried about Sophie, at least not like they did for Marcus. His health was so sporadic that it would have been just as expected for him to get up and walk around as to fall over and die. He'd found enough strength to sit up, once, but that expended all his energy and he was back down the day after. The violent cries and screams still bled from his lips, and everyone knew the infection and the fever were slowly eating away at his brain.

Brian even floated the idea that they put him out of his misery.

"We have those guns out there. Just put it on the base of the ole boy's neck and pop!" He said it with more exuberance than Edmund would have liked.

"And then what?" Bill asked. "Do my Sophie next?"

"No, mate, that's not what I'm saying."

"If we start killing each other now, where does it end?" Edmund said.

Brian threw his hands up in the air and walked off. "Forget I even bothered."

Edmund noticed a change in Lena, as the old woman seemed to grow stern with her in the last few days. He guessed she was giving her the same speech, that she was at the end of her life and that things would grow chaotic in the moments that followed. Lena didn't want to believe it anymore than he did. Had the girl known about her grandmother's health? Matilda was a strong woman, and he doubted anyone was privy to such information.

On the last day, Matilda looked stronger than ever.

***

They'd been sleeping in a line, straight across the common room with the invalids bookending the group. Marcus lay in front of the fireplace closest the door with Sophie in front of the one to the rear. Edmund was in the center of the whole group, sandwiched in between Addey and Matilda. This put him in the coldest spot of all, and it was probably why he woke so fast when he sensed someone was moving over top of him.

His eyes opened just before he heard the loud crack of gunfire. Even before he saw who was holding it, before his eyes went blank from the flash, his nose filled with the smell of cordite. The entire group jumped at once, a collective gasp that unsettled Edmund enough to crawl backwards.

He couldn't believe what he was seeing, and neither could the rest.

"Marcus?" Brian said from the front of the room. An invalid no more, Marcus had somehow found a gun and then moved to the center of the room, where he stood over Edmund. But the gun wasn't pointing at him—it was shaky, but clearly he'd drawn the barrel to hover on Matilda. Edmund looked down at her, just when the screams started.

She was gushing blood—he'd got her right in the chest, probably in the heart. Her lips were wet and a steady trail rolled down her left cheek. By the way she breathed, the bullet probably got her lung, as well.

Lena screamed, "Babcia!" and as she got to her feet to run over, Marcus aimed the gun and fired one off at her, as well. She hit the ground hard, clutching at her chest. By now people were screaming all over the room, backing away into corners. The gun was shaking so hard and Edmund couldn't tell if it was because he was scared or weak.

"Marcus, put the gun down," Brian said from the corner, holding his hands up nonthreateningly.

"I'm sorry, I'm sorry!" he said. "I didn't want this to happen, but I have to get out of here. I can't die in this place. My little girl needs me!"

"Put the gun down," Edmund said, standing up slowly. He moved in front of Matilda.

"Let me finish her, mate, and then I'll put the gun down."

"You're going to have to shoot me first. I can't let you kill an old woman in cold blood." But he was thinking the man already had.

Marcus's hand looked like it was working hard to raise, but he brought the gun up, tears in his eyes, and the next moment it fired, but the bullet went high, the concussive blast of it tousling Edmund's hair. He was so distracted by it that he failed to see the man twitching, and then fall to the ground where the gun skidded across the wood, landing at the bar.

Thrashing on the floor, Edmund saw the twin spiral of wires in his back, could hear the crackling of electricity, and he saw Sophie standing behind him, the yellow taser in her hand.

Bill came running, so transfixed on the grisly scene that he didn't see that his girlfriend had stood and retrieved the old woman's taser.

Edmund first went to Lena—he wasn't sure why—but when she saw him approach, she sat up and said, "He got my bloody arm, it's fine. Check *her*!" She pointed to the old woman who was currently gurgling blood. Addey moved to prop several pillows up behind her so she didn't choke to death before bleeding out.

"Babcia," said Lena, her voice trembling. She was bleeding profusely from the shoulder.

The old woman's shaky hand took her granddaughter's. Lena moved close and kissed a bloodless spot on her forehead. The room had grown silent now—Marcus was down and Sophie looked awestruck to see Addey.

"It's . . . it's okay," said the old woman. She was looking at Edmund more than Lena. "I have to. I have to die."

"Why?" Lena asked. "We need you. *I* need you!"

"I have to die," she continued, "so I can show them how to fight."

"Who?" Edmund asked, cradling her head. She'd begun to go limp. "Who, Matilda?"

Her good eye found him one last time, and she smiled. Her teeth were slicked with blood. "The buffalo."

And then, she was gone.

For a moment there was silence, and Edmund half expected something to happen, but it didn't. Her passing was as normal as if she'd been just any old woman dying in a hospital bed. Lena sobbed quietly, blood dripping off her fingers. That was the last person she had in her life.

No time to grieve, because the train's whistle bellowed out.

They stood up and saw light flooding into Krakus House. The engine was lined up, the pilot facing the front door. Otto was hanging out of the side of it, his nose turned up as if he were smelling the air. Perhaps he was tasting the old woman's death, as ludicrous as that sounded.

"He's dead," someone said behind Edmund. It was so alien, so unexpected that he didn't realize what Brian was saying when he turned around. The man had a finger to Marcus's neck. "That jolt right stopped his heart, I'm guessing. Damned thing was probably weak as a kitten anyway."

Sophie put her hands to her face. "Oh, God, I'm sorry! I'm so sorry!"

"Don't be," Brian said. "Had no choice."

Edmund looked back out the window, and now Otto had stepped off the train, the alligator wrench clutched tightly in his hand. Brian had scooped up the gun and was standing next to Edmund, but he thought it was all for nothing. What could a gun do to such evil?

Lena stood up beside him and took his hand. She looked at him with soft eyes, and why did he wait until now to notice just how pretty they were? Like little, sparkling emeralds. She smiled, but it melted from her face rather quickly.

"This is it," said Bill. Sophie was sobbing on his shoulder. "It's been a good run."

"Does this place have a back door?" asked Brian, looking the place over.

Lena said, "Yeah, and it's just as surrounded."

Otto took a step forward. Edmund moved to the doorway, refusing to retreat. The large man's boots sank in the mud, and seeing him now so close brought back the horrid images of when he'd first encountered him, what seemed like a lifetime ago. They were always going to die in this place, and Edmund was glad they at least made one last stand.

But then something unexpected happened.

Otto pitched forward because something had struck him in the back of the head. Edmund looked down, near the tire of the SUV. There was a boot—a shimmering, ethereal boot that no doubt belonged to a ghost. Otto regained his composure and slowly turned to where the assault had originated, only to be hit again by another flying boot. He staggered a little, then dodged just as another came hurtling.

That's when the train cars began to empty out.

Ghosts of men, women, and children flooded the little roundabout in front of Krakus House, each running up to Otto and striking him in the head with whatever they had. The bald man grew furious, let out a roar, and then the alligator wrench was flying madly. The living who stood inside Krakus House watched in amazement as he cut down ghosts, who flitted away on the wind as if made of ash. They came at him like antibodies attacking an infection. Otto mowed down each and every one of them, for the alligator wrench was deadly at such close proximity. It was the second time they'd tasted the sting of the metal. But the ghosts were staggering him, moving him back away from Krakus House little by little.

It was a constant give-and-take fight. The sheer number of ghosts flooding into the fray made it hard for him to do anything other than swat at flailing arms and legs. Some of them even came with weapons of their own, clubs and swords that they struck against his head with little effect.

"Look!" said Sophie, pointing out the left of the battle. Edmund wasn't sure what she saw, but as his eyes found one of the cars sitting several coiled rows back, he watched as it became as insubstantial as ash, and then floated away.

One by one, the cars disappeared. As Otto destroyed those riding, so to did he destroy the need for extra cars. Slowly, the train was shrinking. The Entity was no longer concerned with those at Krakus House and Edmund thought about what the old woman had said, during their last meaningful conversation.

If the Entity slips up at all and you can get away . . . head to Treblinka.

If this didn't constitute a slip-up, he didn't know what did.

Edmund pulled Addey and said, "You need to run upstairs, grab the vial and the flash drive. Go!" Addey nodded and was gone. Next he turned to Brian and said, "You have your car key?"

He nodded.

The train cars continued to disappear as Otto continued to be driven away and down the hill.

"What are you thinking, Ed?" asked Bill, just as Addey returned with the only things that kept Otto here.

"We have to get to Treblinka."

"What? Why?" Sophie asked.

"I don't know. We just do."

Brian said, "Mate, if we get out of here, we're heading to Belarus or Lithuania. Not going to a damned memorial!"

"Yes, we are!" said Edmund. "The old woman told me so and that's where we're going. If I have to walk there, I'm going to Treblinka."

"And I'll be walking with him," said Lena.

That admittance seemed to jar something in Brian and he dropped his head, then nodded.

The cars were disappearing faster now because Otto was in a frenzy. He'd started twirling the alligator wrench like some kind of samurai. Edmund couldn't tell for sure, but he thought the man had sweat on his brow, that his armband had ripped. Could the ghosts really be wearing down the Entity, could they really be *hurting* it? When the train car closest to the road disappeared, Edmund found that he didn't care.

"Go!" he screamed, then led the charge out the door. He slid a hand around the small of Lena's back and helped her into the SUV. There were three rows of seats, so Brian took driver's with Bill in shotgun. Lena and Edmund took the very back, just as he had the night Sophie almost succumbed to the train.

"Everyone hold on, the ghosts are still coming down the hill!" Brian threw it in reverse and almost backed them over the mountain because the wheels slid on the mud. Ghosts ran all around the car, not paying the fleeing mortals one ounce of attention. They'd been loosed, and now were after their eternal handler.

But now the supply was becoming exhausted. Where before they were a torrent, like a mighty fissure in a dam, they'd now dwindled to a drip. Even Edmund, from the rear of the SUV, could count the cars, and he knew it was smaller now than when the Ghost Train had first screamed out of that cave some eighty years ago.

Brian floored the gas, and Edmund looked up long enough to see Otto take notice of them and thump the grill with his wrench, knocking out the driver's side light. Still, the SUV barreled past him, hit the uneven road at the foot of the hill, and put Krakus House to the rearview.

The world was dark on the other side of the back window. Edmund didn't see anyone, no sign posts, no telephone poles, no trees. The Ghost Train had gutted the countryside.

"Christ, Edmund, you better be right about this!" said Brian. "I oughta drop you off and keep on me merry way."

"Fine," he said. "You know where it is? Keep straight. Another quarter mile."

"Yeah, yeah, I know."

"Are you okay?" Edmund asked Lena. Her fingers were bloody, but that was just as much from the old woman as her own. She just nodded, and he was glad he couldn't see her eyes in the darkness.

A flash of light filled the SUV and Edmund looked up, stricken with horror, and saw the engine's pilot nearly touching the hatchback. Fire was bellowing out from the wheels and the smokestack, and each time it lit the night sky, Edmund could see that the engine was alone—the trainset no more. Even the co-conductor was gone. It was only Otto now.

Brian sped up, but the train, as if grounded in natural physics, moved even faster. It pulled up alongside the SUV and with one, hard push, knocked it off the road.

"Everyone hold on!" Brian screamed at the last moment. The SUV careened, and then the train was back to give it another violent shove, this time turning the whole thing on its roof. No one was wearing a seatbelt, so the six meatbags inside bounced around, amid twisting metal and shattering glass. They rolled down a hill, and had a thin copse of trees not been at the bottom, they would have kept going.

Edmund kicked open the hatchback, seeing the fire spouting from the engine high up on the hill. It was just sitting there, watching them, perhaps curious as to why Brian had cut down the wooded path toward the camp, near where the Entity had first snatched the train.

Bill was limping as he moved around the side of the SUV so he could hold the door up and let Sophie slither out. She had a small cut on her forehead. Brian was wringing his hand, but looked fine. Addey was likewise unbothered after he gave the vial a check to make sure it hadn't ruptured. Lena simply shook the fog from her head and followed the group away from the SUV.

"There!" Edmund yelled. "It's there!"

They'd come in from the side of the camp, bypassing the place where they'd parked weeks ago. Now, somehow, the four eternal flames that marked the boundaries of the crematorium were lit, tiny pyres of dancing fire.

The group huddled around the giant memorial, the split rock that stood as a monument to all the smaller stones—villages, communities wiped out by the Nazis. Why would the old woman want Edmund to come here? What purpose did it serve to die in this place?

Their collective hearts sank when the engine's fire shined through the tiny, skeletal trees. Otto pulled it right up to the first symbolic stone railroad tie, the flames dying down as if he'd thrown a conventional engine into neutral. He stepped off, minced his fists, then reached back in and pulled out his alligator wrench. This was the end. He was no more than twenty yards away, and they were out of options.

***

For the first time since his existence, the Entity knew pain, or at least what equated to pain. He had no blood, no muscles, no nerve endings and no brain in which to carry that message. But when the ghosts started to attack him, emboldened by the old woman's death, it hurt his noncorporal body like nothing ever had.

And now, as he stared down the group of humans—children who hadn't even experienced the world and its cruel and twisted ways, he felt a bitter shame. He'd grown so strong over the years, and that strength had been his downfall because he'd been arrogant, quick to act. If only he'd let the scientists work without prowling for new souls, his lair would've never been discovered. What happened here tonight didn't matter. The work was finished. He was finished. More Opeikunites would show up and they'd form a ring around Poland so tight and so deadly that he would be immobile, forced to go mad while children gawked at him.

But tonight, he would satiate his soul with one last bit of revenge . . .

And on top of the Treblinka Memorial sat the old woman.

Only she wasn't so old now—not a child, per se, but vibrant looking with dark hair and a face that didn't droop. Both her eyes were staring at him. The little smirk on her face made him rage inside, because they both knew he couldn't touch her in life, and most certainly couldn't in death. There was a reason she had the children come here.

She'd been a light bearer, and now those who'd been searching for the light finally found her.

***

Edmund remembered Matilda's dying words:

I have to die so I can show them how to fight.

Only Matilda wasn't really talking about those on the train. She was talking about all the good people who'd been snatched away by evil. The Entity evolved when Matilda came too close. And now that she had passed, Matilda *herself* had evolved. She'd told Edmund she didn't believe that God would reroll the dice, that he would balance out good and evil—but she'd been wrong.

Thank God, she'd been wrong.

Treblinka II, the site of the former death camp, suddenly became so bright that it was as if the sun were coming up prematurely. The light was so intense that Otto, now only a few feet away, put a hand over his eyes, the alligator wrench gleaming.

Edmund looked around, and as far as he could see were the dead. Ghostly apparitions of a faded grey were standing shoulder to shoulder, like warriors about to do battle. A sea of faces, all staring intently on the man wearing a German SS armband. He didn't know how many ghosts stood around him, in front of him, behind him. But if history had been right, it was just short of a million.

The ghosts of Treblinka had assembled one last time.

They were deafening as they ran past, heading right for the Entity who'd begun to back away. The ghosts of Treblinka didn't bother the living at all, simply passing through them on their way to land at least one hit on the monster before becoming one with the world and disappearing on the wind.

Otto was overwhelmed far worse than he had been with the ghosts on the train. Edmund didn't know how badly they were hurting him until the ghosts created a sliver in their swings, and he saw that Otto had dropped the alligator wrench, and that his face had long, jagged scratches on it. But if they needed any evidence for how well he fought, they needed only to look at the train.

It was shimmering, little tendrils of smoke rising from its dingy metal. The ghosts continued to run past the group of humans, coming with such speed and ferocity that they hopped atop one another, making a mound that was growing out and up. The train blinked out of existence, the fires a tiny poof before they floated away.

And then, in a final push, the ball of flailing arms and legs exploded, sending ghosts through the air and knocking down the rest in a concussive blast. The ground was scorched where the Entity—where Otto—had stood, but now he was gone.

A small tendril of black swirled around, caught in the invisible wind, and then it too was gone. Edmund thought he saw little legs and wings in the mass, and remembered something Matilda had said not so long ago.

You can't kill evil, only change it.

The ghosts lingered for only a moment, as if they were trying to steal a final view of the mortal world, and then they too, began to melt away, becoming white feathers that danced on the air and became ash before hitting the ground.

Warsaw

February 9th, 2019

Edmund remembered how, after 9/11, the United States had become more unified than any other time in its long and lofty history. People put out flags, were a little nicer to their neighbors, and became overall more patriotic. Then, a year or two later, it was as if 9/11 never happened. People forgot about the tragedy, forgot how they'd been unified. As his little sister had said in school one day, in an attempt to be funny but actually being rather accurate: The world can often have an attention deficit disorder.

That had been the case for Poland and the world at large.

The train continued to be explained away as a terrorist job—one that had claimed over two-million lives and growing. Large parts of the country had been utterly destroyed.

Addey had been especially worried that the quarantine had been due to the typhus outbreak, but that wasn't the case. After reviewing the data on the flash drive, the Entity's best scientists had concluded that the typhus would have been contained had it been released in Poland. It needed to be set free in New Deli, India. That was the best nexus for air and land travel, and would cover the globe in only a month. Luckily, the Entity hadn't gained enough strength to get it there.

Brian, as it turned out, was ex-military, a sniper for British special forces, no less. His particular skillset was useless for ghosts, but he told his group of new friends that he had connections and would see that the vial of typhus go to the right people. With Polvec contained, there was no risk of it getting out. He said his goodbyes in Warsaw a week after the ghosts of Treblinka took care of the Entity, and flew out of Edmund's life forever.

When television services returned, it was nonstop coverage of the train—something which had no shortage. A team of investigators had traveled to Polvec and found the lab. That was what the world cared about. However, those who survived the ordeal noticed other details.

For one, the train was found inside the lair, dilapidated, rusted and covered in cobwebs. All of the dead men, women, and children were aboard, right where they'd been the moment before the Entity had merged with it. Even Otto was still slumped over inside the engine.

Curiouser still, bodies were found all across Poland. These included the victims who heard the call. Wherever a person died before boarding the Ghost Train, there is where they returned. Katherine Walker, Rebekah Mazur, and Josef Wozniak were identified, returned to family, and remembered.

The Americans had no money, no possessions by the time they'd finished answering all of law enforcement's questions. This wasn't the main problem, as they each were able to make calls back home and have money wired to them. The problem was their passports. They couldn't move about in most European countries, and certainly couldn't fly home to the U.S. without one. So once their parents were over the initial shock and relief that their children were okay, they wired them enough money to expedite replacements.

They stayed at another bed and breakfast, a far cry from the grandeur of Krakus House, but cozy nonetheless. Lena accompanied them for the whole journey, opting to pay for her own room with money she didn't even know she had stuffed into her jeans pocket. Addey also stayed with them, sleeping on the floor of Edmund's room. It bothered Edmund that, despite being only three miles from his mom and dad's, he chose to stay here. That relationship was taxed, and if something like this didn't bring them closer together, nothing would.

On the day the Americans were scheduled to fly back home, Addey and Lena joined them for breakfast in a bistro that was right across the street from the airport. They wanted to get there early to make sure there weren't any issues.

"What will you do?" Edmund asked Lena, surprised that the question hadn't come up until now. They had all been on autopilot since that night.

She shrugged. "I can run Krakus House on my own. I did it when Babcia was sick." Her eyes began to well with tears and she turned away to get herself under control.

"But is that what you want to do?" Edmund asked.

"I don't know. I don't know what else there is for me in this world."

Edmund smiled and put a hand on top of hers. "There's probably a lot more than you think."

Bill and Sophie looked at one another, all grins.

Addey was going to be starting college in the spring semester, and Edmund did all he could to convince him to come back to America. As much as he didn't get along with his parents, he still felt a loyalty.

"My dad is sick, mom is probably sicker, although she doesn't tell us those things. I think right now I'd better stick close to Warsaw."

A little while later, Edmund was coming out of the bathroom just as Bill was walking in. He pushed him back near the stalls and said, "I still have it, Ed. I still have it!"

"What? What are you talking about?"

Bill showed him his jeans pocket where a perfect cube pushed through the material. It was the ring box.

"What do you think, bud?"

"Do you still want to go to Romania?" Edmund asked.

"God, I don't know. Is this stupid? Should we just go home?"

"It's not stupid. Do you want to go to Romania, Bill?"

"Yes! God, yes! We've been through hell. Let's not go home with something so horrible as our final memory of Europe."

"Okay, let's do it then."

Back outside, the other three were talking quietly. There was a somberness in the air because in just an hour, they were due inside the airport, and Addey would float away until he decided to come visit and Lena . . . well, Lena would probably go away forever. What ties did he have with the girl, other than the mutual understanding and shared awfulness of the Ghost Train?

"Change of plans," said Bill. "Who wants to go to Romania?"

"I've never been," said Lena, sprouting up at the mention.

"Neither have I," said Addey.

"Then that settles it," Bill said.

"We have a plane to catch," said Sophie.

Bill just laughed and slapped Edmund across the chest. "Ed just told me he wants a little quality time with the girl, is all."

Edmund thought his heart would drop to the floor, but Lena was looking at the airport terminal, smiling and biting her bottom lip.

They started off, away from the airport and Bill pulled out his new cellphone to call a cab since they would never be allowed to rent another car in Europe. As they waited, Lena crept close to Edmund, put a hand across his back so she could whisper in his ear.

“Don’t you have a girlfriend back home?” It was playful, yet stern. Her true feelings on the subject were lost to her accent.

“Technically. . . yes,” he answered.

“Gonna be at least twenty minutes for the cab,” said Bill, pressing END CALL on his phone.

Lena giggled, then took Edmund’s hand. He first thought it was a sign of affection, but she was merely pulling it up so she could slap her own cell in his open palm.

“We have time. I guess you’d better tell her it’s over.”

Edmund Riley's fourth rule of travel: Always listen to Polish women.

Author's Note: Part 2

This book, like the Ghost Train, evolved several times over its life. In the beginning, it was much simpler because it was only meant to be a short-story. A group of teenage ghost hunters search for an elusive train filled with spirits. Nothing fancy. Then, it evolved into a novella—indeed, the front page carried the title: *Ghost Train of Treblinka: A Novella*, for many months. Finally, I knew I couldn't do this story justice without being a full-length novel. There was so much to tell, both about the characters and the setting.

I took many liberties while writing about the Polish. I have the upmost respect for them, and I never through I'd fall in love with Warsaw as much as I did while doing my research. I had plenty of help along the way, but if there are any inconsistences, they are completely my fault.

Most of what I wrote about Treblinka is true. I did not need to embellish how awful it was in '43 and '44. Many of the places such as Poniatowo and Wyszków are real. Places like Ozelki and Krakus House are not.

Finally, I leave you with this. As with all my books, I hope it spurs you to read more often. In this case, I would like for you to read something about the Treblinka death camp. I think it's important that we understand history, and learning about this particularly dreadful place is a good place to start. I recommend the books *Last Jew of Treblinka: A Memoir* by Chil Rajchman and *A Year in Treblinka* by Jankiel Wiernik.

Books are our last line of defense against history repeating itself. The storytellers have all gone away. As I said in my first author's note, as of 2016, all those associated with Treblinka and its horrors have died. It's up to us to remember their sacrifices.

Hubert L. Mullins

9/29/19

Made in United States
North Haven, CT
01 December 2022